Someone
to Call My Own
A Road to Blissville Novel

Own

AMAZON BESTSELLING AUTHOR

AIMEE NICOLE WALKER

Someone to Call My Own
(Road to Blissville, #2)
Copyright © 2017 Aimee Nicole Walker

ISBN: 978-0-9974225-9-7

aimeenicolewalker@blogspot.com

Cover photograph © Wander Aguiar – www.wanderaguiar.com
Cover art © Jay Aheer of Simply Defined Art – www.jayscoversbydesign.com
Editing provided by Pam Ebeler of Undivided Editing – www.undividedediting.com
Proofreading provided by Judy Zweifel of Judy's Proofreading – www.judysproofreading.com
Interior Design and Formatting provided by Stacey Ryan Blake of Champagne Book Design – www.champagnebookdesign.com

DEDICATION

To Michelle Slagan,
You make me laugh, you keep me sane, and you make the world a better place. I'm so proud to call you my friend! To the moon and back, beautiful lady!

PROLOGUE

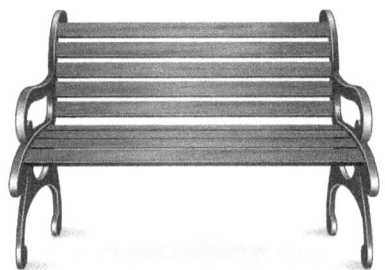

Emory Jackson

MY HEAD FELT LIKE VICIOUS ELVES TOOK A JACKHAMMER TO my brain, my throat was dry and raw, and I struggled to open eyelids that felt weighted down by something heavy. My first sense that sparked to life was smell when I inhaled harsh antiseptics through my nose, then I registered the sound of machines beeping near my head. My sluggish brain realized that I was in the hospital, but I couldn't remember why. The sudden memory of River's car careening out of control on the ice-covered bridge forced me to consciousness.

My eyes darted open, and reality slammed into me as hard as the impact of our car into the side of the bridge. One minute we were on a date for his birthday and the next our world literally spun out of control. I searched the semi-dark room for River and panicked when I didn't see him. We hadn't spent a day apart in over five years, and there was no way he'd leave me alone in the hospital. The pain in my skull increased as my blood pressure rose high enough to trigger a warning alarm on one of the machines I was hooked up to.

Several nurses and a doctor rushed into my room and their attempts to calm me only upset me more when they wouldn't answer my question. "Where's River?" It took me several attempts to get the words out of my dry, aching throat but they acted as if they hadn't heard me. I struggled to get free from their grasp so I could find my husband, but they easily controlled me in my weakened condition. Instead, the nurses and doctor just kept repeating the same thing.

"Calm down, Mr. Jackson. We're here to help you."

A heavy fog invaded the edges of my consciousness, and I realized they'd injected me with something to calm me. Ativan? Something stronger? The hospital staff eased off of me once my body started to relax.

"We need to get your blood pressure down, Mr. Jackson," a soft-spoken and kind-eyed nurse told me as I melted into the hospital bed. "You have a nasty brain injury, and high blood pressure is dangerous right now."

"River," I said weakly once more before my eyes drifted shut.

When I reopened them again, a different nurse was checking my vitals. "You're looking much better already," she said. I had no idea how good, or bad, I looked, and I didn't care. I only wanted to know one thing. "Let me finish checking your vitals, and I'll bring in your visitor."

My pulse kicked up a notch as hope filled my heart, but luckily not enough to set the alarms off again. I knew that River wouldn't have just left me alone. He must've gone home to get some clothes or got a bite to eat. The nurse's comment about my appearance momentarily worried me until I remembered that River didn't care if my hair was a mess or if I had cuts or scrapes on my face. He loved me unconditionally. *My God, he must've been worried out of his mind. How long have I been out of it?*

The nurse patted my shoulder and told me that she'd be right back. I tried to wiggle into a sitting position, but I was too weak. My face hurt to smile, but I plastered the biggest one I could muster when the door reopened. "He's been worried sick about you," the nurse said when she came through the door. The man who entered behind her wasn't the one I longed to see though.

My cousin Memphis, who felt more like a brother, looked at me with so much sadness in his eyes that my heart knew what he was going to say before the words left his mouth.

"No!" I refused to believe it. I childishly covered my face with my hands, so I didn't have to see the pity in his eyes. I willed my ears to block the sound of his voice when he told me that River was gone.

"I'm so sorry, Em," Memphis said softly.

The days that followed were the worst in my life. I learned that River's family claimed his body and buried him while I was in a coma. They refused to tell me where, so I had to spend what little energy I could muster on hiring a lawyer who would fight for my rights that the state laws didn't recognize at the time. The anger kept me from focusing on the agonizing reality that my husband, my lover, and my best friend was gone forever. Whenever the anger subsided, even if it was only a brief respite, depression moved in swift and hard. I couldn't get out of bed, and I tried to sleep as much as I could because at least I saw River in my dreams.

Those dreams of my husband soon morphed from fond memories and wishful hopes for an impossible reunion to odd predictions and pleas for my help that I didn't understand. The dreams were broken fragments of events, all terrifying and deadly. I saw names on mail, street signs, and a shadowy figure stalking an unsuspecting young lady. The fear, agony, and despair were so strong it would bring me out of sleep, gasping for air. I knew I had to be cracking up and worried that the brain injury was graver than the doctors first suspected.

River would always revisit in my dreams, and his presence would calm me. It took me a while to realize that the dreams were actually psychic visions of things that had happened or were future events. I didn't understand how something like that could just start happening to me. I'll never forget the first time I contacted a police department with information on a cold case. They thought I was a nut job, but looked into the lead that I gave them anyway. Once it panned out and they discovered the body of the missing woman, the cops treated me like a suspect until they cleared me. They gave me a wide berth when they realized that I was a psychic and not a psycho. In fact, I think they would've understood better had I been crazy.

The truth was, I *felt* crazy. The visions started coming closer together, and I began traveling around the country. My abilities became sharper and evolved over time. I was no longer just dreaming about incidents. I started having visions when I touched a garment or something that belonged to the victim or possible killer. Peaceful moments became frustratingly scarce as my visions came more frequently. Still, I had River to assure me in my dreams.

In one of them, River slid an envelope across our table to me. It had an address in Blissville, Ohio. I looked at River in confusion, and he gave me a smile that was equal parts sad and happy, if that was even possible.

"What's this?" I asked my husband.

"It's your new home. They need you there, and you need them," he said.

"Who's 'they'?"

River reached over and cupped my cheek like he had every day that we'd been together. "Just trust me, Em. Know that I'll always love you and I'll be looking out for you."

"You sound like you're going away," I tearfully said. "Don't leave me again, River."

"You're going to be just fine, Em. I promise you."

I had no intentions of moving from the home that River and I made together. It was a comfort to walk through the rooms that he had and sleep in the bedroom that had spawned so many beautiful memories. No, I wouldn't do it.

River didn't come to me in my sleep the next night or any of the nights that followed. It felt like I'd lost him all over again, and I couldn't function through the depression and despair. I had given up on life, and I knew it was only a matter of time until life gave up her grip on me, and I could be with my husband again. I was wrong. Life wasn't ready to give up on me, and the dreams of a quaint, white house in a lovely, small town kept recurring until I couldn't take it anymore. River might not have appeared in those dreams, but I was sure he was driving them.

I packed up my things and moved to the house in Blissville, Ohio, not knowing what River had in store for me.

PART 1

Denial

ONE

Emory

I T DIDN'T REQUIRE PSYCHIC ABILITIES TO KNOW THAT MY NEW neighbor didn't like me. The house in my dreams was available to rent, and I signed a contract without touring the place. River said it was where I needed to go, so that was where I went. I had hoped he would return to my dreams after I did what he asked. I felt my neighbor's intense regard the moment I stepped out of my vehicle on move-in day. I recalled a strong wind kicking up suddenly and wrapping around me like an embrace, but it didn't feel welcoming to me. I felt an intense focus aimed at me and looked up to see the silhouette of a man watching me from the second story window in the house across the alley from mine.

The first floor of the home was a salon called Curl Up and Dye, which I thought was witty and cute. The second story could've been used for salon services also, but I had a feeling it was the owner's personal residence. I was too far away to make eye contact with the guy, but it felt like I did anyway. I saw the man stiffen as if he felt it too, then he took a sudden step back and jerked the curtain closed. The last thing I wanted to do was alarm my new neighbor. I didn't know why, but I knew that he was an important reason why I moved to Blissville.

The minute I walked inside the rental property, I sensed the lingering traces of evil lurking in the kitchen. I knew without being told that something very bad had happened there and not much time had passed since then. Accepting that I had psychic abilities wasn't easy; in fact, I thought I had lost my mind. Once I realized my gifts were there to stay, I learned some basic psychic practices like cleansing a home by burning sage.

The following day, I walked to the salon and made an appointment to have my hair highlighted. I took a lot of flak from friends and family for my high-maintenance hair routine over the years, but River had always loved my long hair. He'd said the highlights made my green eyes stand out even more. It might've seemed silly to some, but I felt a connection to him when I continued doing the things that pleased him.

The interior of the salon was elegant without being fussy and chic without being feminine. I liked the mix of earth tones with old Hollywood style glam. Someone, I suspect the person I saw in the window the previous night, put a lot of love and attention into the design and decorations for the salon.

"Hi, can I help you?"

I turned my attention toward the guy behind the counter who offered me a friendly smile. "Hi, I'm Emory Jackson." I extended my hand to him, but he just stared at it oddly for a few seconds before he shook it and introduced himself as Chaz.

"You're new around here, aren't you?" he asked with a quirked brow. Perhaps they weren't as formal in Blissville as I was accustomed to with my upbringing.

"Just moved in yesterday," I confirmed. "I would like to book an appointment with a stylist, please."

Chaz narrowed his eyes and studied my hair. "Hmm, multi-dimensional coloring with a possible need for toning. Whoever did your hair was really good, but don't worry that you downgraded stylists when you moved to town. The staff at Curl Up and Dye is phenomenal. Let me see who is available first," he said, looking through the calendar on his computer. "You're in luck because Josh has a cancellation next week. You're going to love what he can do for your hair."

I had a name to go with the silhouette in the window. Like the night before, I could tell someone was watching me. When I turned to face the salon area, I expected to lock eyes with Josh, but everyone in the salon staring at me took me by surprise. I stood there motionless except for blinking as an awkward silence spread throughout the salon.

"I need a big cock!" a bird squawked from another room.

My eyes widened in shock because that was the last thing I expected to hear. A faint blush spread up Josh's cheeks, and I wasn't sure if it was from embarrassment or the nearly hostile vibe I picked up from him.

"Dirty Bird!" Josh said, and the salon erupted into laughter.

"Dirty Bird!" the bird repeated.

"I think I'm going to like living here," I announced.

"It's unforgettable," Chaz said, handing me an appointment card. "We'll see you next week."

I couldn't tear my eyes off the platinum-blond owner to respond right away. I couldn't explain the type of bond I felt toward him except that it wasn't sexual. "I'm looking forward to it," I told Chaz.

Josh turned his attention back to the client, and I could tell he'd dismissed me. I hadn't made a very good impression on the new neighbor, and for some reason, I kept thinking his opinion would matter to me some day. I gave Chaz a friendly smile and left the salon in search of lunch and groceries.

My height and long hair often made me stand out in a crowd, but it was never as obvious as when I walked into the diner. Everyone stared at me just like the salon clients had, and I realized that it would take me a while to get used to small-town living. The waitress was very friendly when she took my order.

"I'm Daniella," she replied. "Welcome to Blissville."

"Thank you, Daniella." At least she and Chaz seemed friendly. I couldn't say the residents of the town were hostile; it was more like they were cautious. Josh, who clearly wanted me to pack and leave town, was the only exception up to that point.

I'd spent plenty of time in small towns while helping investigators solve crimes, so I knew it was just a matter of time before I was able to squeeze some information out of the chatty waitress. I learned that Josh Roman was the owner of the salon. He wasn't married but was involved in a serious relationship with a hunky detective on the Blissville Police Department.

I asked Daniella for ideas on how I could get in the good graces of my new neighbor. She rattled off a brand of wine I'd never heard of and had to drive like twenty minutes to find. I went to his house later that evening with wine in my hand and a smile on my face. I rang the doorbell at the back of the house because I could tell they used it as their private entrance. *Great, I sounded like a creepy stalker.* Josh whipped open the door like he had been expecting someone. It was obvious by the frown on his face that I wasn't the person Josh wanted to see.

"Oh, it's you," he said flatly. Wow, my visit to his house wasn't going according to plan.

"Hello to you, too. I wanted to introduce myself formally," I said, pushing the bottle of wine toward Josh with a pleasant smile on my face.

"I don't drink," Josh said seriously. Had I misheard Daniella or was he deliberately lying? I wouldn't want to play poker with the guy because he wasn't giving anything away with his facial expression or tone of voice.

"Oh." My cheeks turned pink from either awkwardness or embarrassment. "Your boyfriend, perhaps?"

"He's not my boyfriend."

"Oh?" I was starting to sound like a broken record and question the credibility of my source.

"That's much too tame of a word for what Gabe is to me," Josh said. "He's more of a beer man, anyway. Thank you for thinking of us, though. Mrs. Hastings across the way loves that kind of wine. She's the beige house with burgundy shutters." Josh pointed to her house just in case his message wasn't clear.

"Uh, okay," I said slowly. I knew I should retreat, but for some unknown reason, I couldn't. "My name is Emory Jackson," I said, extending my hand toward him.

He scrutinized my hand like I had a contagious disease before he cautiously shook it. "Josh Roman," he finally replied. "My boyfriend is Gabriel Wyatt. He's a detective with the Blissville PD and has a big gun. Real big." Did he think I was going to give the man a reason to shoot me? Wow, I'd really botched my first impression with the new neighbor.

"Sunshine, are you touting my attributes to the pizza delivery guy again?" Detective Wyatt asked as he came down the stairs. Josh opened the door wider, and Gabe locked eyes on me. "Oh, hey, you're the new guy who moved in next door," Gabe said cheerfully. "Gabriel Wyatt." At least Gabe had no problem shaking my hand.

"Emory Jackson," Josh said in an annoyed voice as he introduced me.

"Look, Sunshine, he brought your favorite wine," Gabe said, unknowingly betraying his boyfriend.

I looked at Josh in confusion. Why would he lie to me about his wine preferences? It wasn't like I had a right to call him on it, and what good would it do if I did? "Sunshine, huh?"

"Yep," Gabe said, proud of the name he'd given his boyfriend.

"I just bet he's a ball of fire," I commented. My eyes widened when I realized how suggestive my statement sounded. "I-I didn't mean sexually."

"Why the hell not?" Josh demanded. "You don't think I can burn shit down?" I could tell Josh was working himself into a good fit. "I burn hotter than you could possibly handle."

"Take it easy there, Stud Muffin," Gabe said good-naturedly. "He wasn't insulting your sexual prowess. I think our new neighbor just meant you're a feisty guy."

Josh pinned me with a death glare and said, "I *am* feisty. All the time and everywhere."

"I think I made the wrong impression here," I told them. I pushed the bottle of wine toward Gabe, who graciously accepted my offering. "I'm hoping not to make an ass of myself the next time we run into each other."

"You're fine," Gabe assured me. "We're all good."

I looked at Josh for several awkward heartbeats. "No, but we will be in time," I told them before I turned and walked down the steps of the back porch. "Nice shirt, by the way." I don't know how I was able to remain serious with that large blow dryer on the front of his T-shirt that read: Want a blow job?

I laughed the entire way home, although I wasn't sure why. I had moved to a town where I knew no one, the residents watched me with cautious eyes, and the one guy I felt I needed to befriend didn't like me at all. I looked up to the sky and said, "I'm trying, River, but could you send me a sign?"

The next morning, I set out for a run. It had once been a passion of mine, and I hoped to fall in love with it again. As I approached the coffee shop called The Brew, I saw that Josh was standing outside having a heated argument with a sleazy-looking little man.

"Who do you think you are, you little fa…"

"Is there a problem here?" I bitingly asked, cutting the man off before he could finish. "Josh, are you okay?"

"We're fine," the sleazy jerk said, stepping back. "Thanks for clearing the air, Josh."

"Anytime you need me to straighten you out."

"Wow, that was intense," I said once we were alone. "I'm sorry that I interrupted you, but I feared for that man's safety if he let loose the word he was about to use."

"I wouldn't have hit him no matter how badly I might've wanted to," Josh told me.

"I was thinking more along the lines of what your boyfriend would do to him," I said, adding a rueful smile.

"Yeah, there's that," Josh agreed.

"Not that I don't think you can handle yourself," I amended quickly. "You were doing fine all on your own."

"I was, wasn't I?" Josh asked. Before I could answer, he spoke again. "Listen, Buddy and I were on our way to your house."

"You were?"

"Yes," Josh answered, reaching into the bag and pulling out a bakery box. He held the box out to me and said, "A peace offering from me for being a jerk last night."

"I'm allergic."

"Oh, I'm sorry," Josh said, pulling the box back then realized by the smile on my face that I was playing him. "You don't even know what's inside."

"I know things," I said jokingly, but the smile slid off my face when Josh stiffened. "Did you research my name, Josh?"

"Asks the psychic," he mumbled.

"You did!" I blew out a frustrated breath. "Is that why you were bringing me a… treat? You either felt bad about what happened to me, or you're afraid of what I might know. Which is it?" I didn't know what I hated more: the pity I saw in everyone's eyes when they learned about River or the fear when they discovered I was a psychic.

Josh grimaced and said, "A little of both perhaps."

"That's just great." I threw my hands in the air and paced back and forth in front of him. "I don't need your pity, Josh," I said vehemently, never breaking stride.

"What do you need, Emory? Why are you here?"

I stopped pacing and turned to face him. Damn, I wish I could say something that would alleviate the fear we both felt. "I wish I knew, Josh. I wish I knew." He had a confused look when I reached my hand toward him. "Can I have my treat now? I think I deserve it."

"Yeah, sure," Josh said, pushing the box in my hand. "Regardless of the reasons, I am sorry for my behavior last night. Your presence unsettled me, and I lashed out like an immature brat."

His words meant a lot to me. I smiled and said, "Thank you. I accept your apology"—I held up the bakery box—"and your peace offering."

"Great," Josh replied. "I guess we'll see you around the neighborhood."

"I'll see you next week at my hair appointment," I told him.

"That's right," Josh replied. An awkward silence descended on us again, but it didn't last for long. He cocked his head and raised a brow dramatically before he said, "I knew those weren't natural highlights."

I laughed at his snarky attitude and headed into the coffee shop to get a hot beverage to go with my tasty treat. I realized that Josh Roman made me laugh twice in less than twelve hours. I thought my ability to laugh and smile had died with River, but Josh was able to snap me out of my misery. Maybe it was only temporary moments in time, but maybe those moments could build up to a peaceful existence for me. I still had no idea what the hell my purpose in Blissville was, but I decided to make the best of it. I'd start by eating the delicious cookies.

TWO

Jonathon Silver

I STARED AT MY REFLECTION IN THE MIRROR AND HARDLY recognized the face that looked back at me. The tan skin, dark hair, and blue eyes were the same, but the stress lines at the corner of my eyes and frown lines around my mouth were recent additions. I found it ironic too since my entire adult life had been one stressful event after the other—wars, black ops missions, and learning that my mother had lied to me for my entire life. I lived and breathed stress for so long that I couldn't imagine living without it, yet it never took its toll on my face until recently.

"I'm going to head out now." Alexander stepped up beside me fully dressed. I looked down at his face still flushed from the pleasure I'd given him. He was too young for me, but I couldn't resist those pouty lips and the sensual promise I saw in his eyes. I discovered that Alexander's ass was as tight as he advertised in jeans that were more like a second skin, and his mouth had tighter suction than a vacuum cleaner. He was a temporary balm to my riotous mind, but I knew it was a mistake when I saw a hopeful gleam in his eye. I knew I was going to regret breaking my No Fraternizing With Club Employees rule.

"Listen, Alexander," I began…

"… I know," he said, interrupting me. "It was just a one-time thing. You don't do relationships, especially with club employees. I get it." His brown eyes darkened, and I knew he recalled the things we did together for the last few hours. "Technically, you fucked me more than once, but I understood what I was getting myself into with you. Thank you for a very memorable night—um, morning."

He was correct. I'd fucked him three times, and we both enjoyed every single second. I wasn't sure if his words were designed to seduce me again, but I felt my body reacting to the memory of bending him over my desk, him riding me reverse cowboy style on the leather couch, and sucking me off in the shower. Alexander was a vocal, eager, and flexible lover, but I could find that anywhere and not worry about a fucking lawsuit—pun intended. I walked a fine line with him and knew it. I didn't want to hurt his feelings, but I sure as hell didn't want to encourage him either. I had already given him my rules before I freed his cock from his underwear, and I would give him the benefit of the doubt until he gave me a reason to believe otherwise.

Therefore, I didn't beat a dead horse or reiterate the thought he had interrupted. "I'll see you tomorrow night."

Alexander's megawatt smile dimmed slightly but never faltered. I hoped it was a good sign that we could continue working together without awkwardness or attempts on his part to repeat our time together. "See you then."

I turned back and looked at my reflection again after he left. My face might've shown some wear and tear, but I had never had a problem getting some action. I just never imagined that there was a face identical to mine in the world. I couldn't look at myself any longer without remembering my mother's deathbed confession that I had a twin brother. At the time, I thought it was the morphine talking or her retelling a line from one of the many soap operas she had watched over the years. I even thought that perhaps all the alcohol and drugs she consumed over her lifetime had finally caught up to her until she told me about her box of secrets in the closet.

She raised her arm as best she could in her weakened condition and pointed to her closet. "Top shelf… on the right… behind the box of clothes that I'm donating." She struggled to catch her breath every few words and my heart pinched painfully in my chest because I knew the end of her life was near. I had always wanted a close relationship with my mother, and I knew it would never happen. Cancer would see to that.

Julia Black was not an ideal mother by any stretch of the imagination, but she was all I had in the world. We had our share of ups and downs over the years, but I loved her. I resented and hated her at times when I was growing up because of her alcohol and drug addictions. She would get clean and sober for a stretch, and things would start looking good for our lives, but she always stumbled back to her addictions. As a kid, I thought she loved cheap vodka and pills more than she loved me. After high school, I joined the military and got as far away from her as I could.

In between the ear-shattering explosions of war were moments of absolute stillness as you tried to anticipate your enemy's next step. No one moved, you were afraid to breathe, and the only sound you heard was your pulse pounding inside your ears. That's how I felt when I walked into her closet that day. I knew what I was about to find would change my life forever, and for a brief time, it was the absolute best thing that happened to me.

I can't look at myself anymore without recalling the way my brother's eyes widened when he opened the door and discovered me on his front porch. Nate Turner was as shocked to learn about me as I was when I'd found out about him. We didn't hit it off right away. Nate was justifiably skeptical about the wild story I wove for him, but DNA tests didn't lie. I finally had the bond I craved with another human being, and it was ripped away from me seven months later. All I saw when I looked at myself was sadness and loneliness that no amount of fucking a stranger could replace.

"Damn, I get all maudlin when I get tired," I said to my reflection with a sneering smile. Sleep beckoned me, so I started towel drying my head as I walked into my office where I'd left my clothes.

"Mr. Silver," a firm voice said.

I jerked to a stop and lowered the towel from my head but made no attempt to cover my naked body. Hell, he'd seen it already, or one that was identical to it anyway. The sexy police detective aiming his gun at me was the one I blamed for my brother's death.

"Well, this is a surprise, Detective Wyatt."

"You know who I am?"

"Of course, I know who you are. You're the man who rejected my brother when he turned to you for help," I said bitterly. "Do you mind putting your gun away?"

"Do you mind putting *yours* away?" Detective Wyatt's partner asked when he entered the room.

I chuckled as I wrapped the towel around my waist and knotted it while both men lowered their weapons. "Does my nudity offend your sensibilities, Detective Dorchester?" I asked him.

"How do you know my name?" Dorchester asked me. "Better yet, why don't you explain to us how we don't know about you? I find it odd that you've made no attempt to get involved and assist us with the investigation to find your brother's killer. Does that sound odd to you, Gabe?" Dorchester asked his partner.

"I'd move heaven and earth if it were my brother," Detective Wyatt replied. There was a reverent tone in his voice that had me wondering if this case touched a personal note for reasons I didn't yet know. That didn't mean I was going to let him railroad me for something I didn't do. I wasn't your everyday schmuck who didn't know better.

"And you think that makes me look guilty?" I asked. "Put yourself in my shoes and see how you'd feel. My brother, identical twin to be exact, is killed after reaching out to the good detective here," I gestured to Detective Wyatt, "two times and the Cincinnati Police Department once. Can you maybe see how I don't have any faith in you to catch whoever harassed and killed Nate?"

Detective Wyatt took a deep breath. "Put yourself in our shoes, Mr. Silver," he said, mimicking the words I had used. "We had a man who claimed he was threatened but wouldn't cooperate when we tried to help him through legal channels. What exactly could we have done differently?"

"More than what you did." I started to shake with anger. "I know all about the new task force, which is too little too late in my opinion, and those who are on it. I'm staying vigilant even when those who should are not."

I sounded like some sitcom vigilante, but I did have the means and know-how to track down and punish the man responsible for Nate's death. I was a heartbeat away from carrying out my threat. The only thing that stood in my way was my desire to be a better man, one that would make my brother proud.

"Mr. Silver, you weren't so vigilant when you left the back door unlocked," Detective Wyatt said accusingly.

"Ah, that's how you got in," I said. "I guess I need to have a longer chat with Alexander—well, perhaps an actual chat that includes words and not body language next time. Don't be too mad at him, Detectives, because I promise he wasn't capable of much thought when he left."

I whipped the towel off my waist and dropped it to the floor before reaching for my clothes on the desk chair. "If you want to talk to me, then you can do it in the presence of my attorney. It's the same one Nate used, so your task force should be familiar with him." I took my time pulling my underwear up my legs.

"Rick Spizer?" Detective Dorchester asked calmly. He either wasn't offended by a nude man or he liked them really well. I couldn't get a read on him.

"The one and only."

"That's great news," Detective Wyatt said. "We have an appointment with him at noon so why don't you join him at the precinct? This is your moment to step up and prove that you want to help catch the man who killed your brother, as you claim."

I didn't like his condescending attitude or the implication that I don't want to find Nate's killer. "You won't bait me, Detective. I don't owe you a fucking thing," I replied hotly, "but I will be there at noon."

"Thank you," he said.

"I'm not doing it for you; I'm doing it for Nate."

"We'll see you at noon," the detective said. "Be sure to bring your alibi information with you for the night that your brother died."

I didn't like him having the last word, so I waited until they were almost to the door before I asked, "Detective Wyatt, am I identical to my brother in *every* way?" The detective stiffened slightly but didn't stop or respond to my question. I was trained to read body language, pick up the most minute gestures, and see someone's unspoken emotions. I laughed long and hard at the discomfort he couldn't hide. *That's right, Detective. I know all about your past with my brother.*

"They don't have shit on you because you didn't kill your brother," Rick Spizer, my attorney, said when we stood outside the Cincinnati police precinct. "You have nothing to be worried about, Jonathon."

"I'm not worried, Rick." Even if I were, they'd never know it. Fuck, I could pass a polygraph if needed.

The attorney patted me on the back. "Let's get this over with then. I'm sure you didn't get much sleep."

He didn't know the half of it, but I didn't enlighten him. Once inside, Rick and I were separated. The detectives interviewed my attorney first, and I wasn't sure if they hoped to sweat me out or they hoped to glean info from Rick since he knew Nate longer than I did. That realization never failed to stab me in the heart. Rick's interview went faster than I anticipated, so it wasn't long before all three men entered the interview room where they'd stashed me.

"Thank you for coming in today," Detective Wyatt professionally said. "Can you please state your full name for the recording and relationship to the victim, Nathaniel Turner."

I flinched when I heard my brother's name in the same sentence with the word victim, which proved to me that training could be forgotten when a person reached their breaking point. "Jonathon David Silver and Nathaniel Turner is… *was* my brother." My words faltered and every ounce of bravado I felt that morning faded.

"Can you tell us who might've wanted to kill your brother?" Detective Wyatt asked.

"No," I replied softly. "Nate told me about the threats, of course, but said he didn't know why he was receiving them."

"Did you believe him?" Dorchester asked me.

I released a long frustrated sigh. "Honestly? No. Nate was a very private man and getting to know him had been hard. He was shocked to learn he had a twin brother and that he didn't really know the parents who raised him, so you can imagine that he had some serious trust issues."

"What do you mean that he didn't know his adoptive parents very well?"

"They never told Nate about me, so he began wondering what other secrets they hid from him," I replied. My mother refused to share the details of our conception or the reason she gave one of us up for adoption, but I had a feeling there were sinister reasons involved. I never shared my opinion with Nate because he loved his adoptive family. Still, he began questioning their character on his own.

"Are you implying that him digging into their background had something to do with the threats?" Dorchester asked.

I shrugged and said, "The timing works."

"As does your appearance in his life," Detective Wyatt said to me. "It's pretty easy to deflect guilt on the dealings of a deceased couple." He turned to Rick and asked, "Could there be any truth to what Silver said?"

"Not that I'm aware of, Detective. I wasn't Charles and Marie's attorney at the time of Nate's adoption. I found out about Jonathon from Nate," Rick replied. "I can attest that Nate was angry and bitter that he'd gone his entire life without knowing about Jonathon."

"How'd you find out about Nate?" Detective Wyatt asked me.

"Nate was given up for adoption, but I was not. Our birth mom raised me, and she told me about Nate just before she died." I swallowed hard because it was still difficult for me to discuss. "The details about the adoption are irrelevant to Nate's death, and I prefer not to speak about them." Of course, it was hard to talk about something I didn't yet know. My mother refused to discuss the past and spent all her remaining energy on getting me focused to find Nate. First, I was too excited to meet Nate to delve deeper into it, and then the devastation over Nate's death took up all my emotional energy. Learning the reasons why the Turners only adopted one of us no longer seemed to matter. It wouldn't bring either my mother or my brother back to me. Besides, who would I ask about the incident when all the main players were deceased?

As logical as all of that sounded, the largest part of me was afraid to learn the truth about my biological father and the reasons my mother seemed afraid to speak about him. Killing had come easy to me and maybe I came by it honestly. Perhaps my father was a really bad person, and I inherited all of his evil DNA. I decided that the old adage about letting sleeping dogs lie seemed like the best approach for me to take when it came to my lineage. Poking a stick around might unearth truths I could never accept.

"I take it that you are the beneficiary of your brother's estate," Detective Wyatt commented.

"Yes," I answered between gritted teeth. I knew where the detective was heading with his remark, and I didn't like it one bit.

He arrogantly smiled when he realized he'd struck a nerve. "Can you tell us where you were between the years of your birth and 2014 when you magically appeared in Louisiana?" Score another point for the detective. He was more thorough than I first thought.

"Don't answer that," Rick said, speaking up. "Detective, that's completely irrelevant and none of your business."

"I don't agree, counselor." Detective Wyatt leaned forward and pinned me with a damning glare. "Your client surfaces out of nowhere with no past to speak of, and his wealthy brother gets killed within months. Now he owns his brother's business, drives an identical car, and has access to his fortune. Do you live in his house too? Sleep in his bed?" he asked me.

"That's enough, Detective!" Spizer said firmly.

Not reacting to his taunt was the hardest thing I'd ever done. I found that place I went when I was called to do things no human being would voluntarily do. I breathed evenly through my nose as if my blood pressure hadn't soared to dangerous heights and I didn't want to reach across the table and punch that smug smirk off his fucking face. "You're barking up the wrong tree. I was ecstatic to find my brother, and I had no reason to hurt him."

"Nate's homicide was very personal," Detective Wyatt said. "Someone stalked him, threatened him, ran his car off the road, and put a bullet in his head. We're talking about a trained killer who leaves behind no evidence. Someone knows something, and they better start talking before whoever killed Nate decides to start eliminating risks."

"Is this an example of how you deal with bereaved family members after a loss, Detective?" Rick asked. "If so, I'm not at all impressed." Rick put his hand on my shoulder then said, "We're done here, Jonathon."

"Just one more thing," Detective Wyatt demanded. Rick and I halted from rising from the chairs and looked at him. "Where were you the night of January twenty-second?" he asked me.

"You don't have to answer that," Rick told me.

"It's okay, Rick," I said, patting my attorney's arm before I reached inside my suit jacket and pulled out a piece of paper. "These men can attest to my whereabouts that night and morning." I winked lecherously to let them know we hadn't been playing Monopoly all night long. I chuckled when I saw the scornful, yet curious, expression on Detective Wyatt's face. "What can I say? I have a very healthy appetite."

Rick and I rose to our feet and started to exit the room. "I'll let you know if I have any more questions," Detective Wyatt remarked. We didn't stop to acknowledge him.

Neither Rick nor I spoke until we stood in the parking lot near our cars. "You take care, Jonathon. Please call me if there's anything I can do for you."

"Thanks," I said before I got in my car. I sat there thinking things over long after Rick drove off.

I might not have liked Detective Wyatt's methods, and his questions might've ruffled my feathers, but two things were clear: the man was on a mission, and I'd greatly underestimated him. I wouldn't repeat my mistake again.

THREE

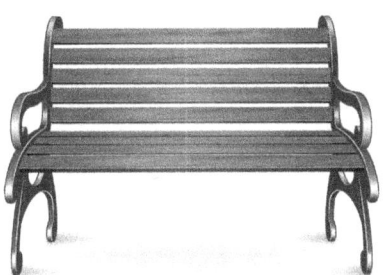

Emory

"How's life in Blisstown?" Memphis asked when I answered his call bright and early. He caught me just as I was about to head out for a jog.

"*Ville,*" I corrected. "I moved to Blissville."

"Excuuuuse me," he replied sassily. "So, how's it going?"

"Too soon to say," I answered honestly. "It started out on the wrong foot when I met my neighbor, although I'm not sure why, but I think I've righted the ship." Well, Josh's pity for my tragic past played a bigger part than anything I did or said. "Good thing too because he's also my hair stylist."

"Maybe he's only nice to lure you in so that he can take scissors to your mane of hair," Memphis teased. "Maybe I should plant a bug in the guy's ear. What's the name of the salon? Don't bother telling me, Em. I'll just google it because there can't be many salons in Blisstucky."

I knew he was trying to get a rise out of me and I didn't bother taking the bait. "How are things going on your end?"

"Same old thing, different day. Oh, I broke up with Caleb."

"Doesn't that fall into the category of same old thing, different day?"

"You're fucking hilarious, Em," Memphis replied, but there was no heat in his voice. "It just wasn't working between us. We wanted different things in life."

The problem with Memphis was that he had no clue what he wanted to do in life—professionally or personally. He had one passion: comic books. Unfortunately, that wasn't going to get him anywhere in life unless he started creating them himself or opened an online store and sold the rare comic books he found. He might've loved going to comic book conventions, but it didn't exactly pay the bills. He had multiple degrees from prestigious universities, including an MBA, and didn't use them because they were obtained out of obligation, not desire. I thought Memphis would be much happier if he at least found a job that paid enough so he could move out of Aunt Karen's basement and into an apartment.

I had the means to help him, but he refused me each and every time I made the offer. Smart men would've stopped offering, but either I wasn't smart, or I never wanted Memphis to forget how much he meant to me. He was the only person I could talk to about River and my psychic connections. I treasured his friendship and devotion to seeing me live even when it was the last thing I wanted for myself.

"I could always…"

"Nope." His response was the same as it always was before he changed the subject. "Has River returned to your dreams?"

His question hit me like a tornado and the effect to my heart was just as devastating. "No."

"I'm sorry for upsetting you, Em," he replied. "I won't bring him up again."

"I'm glad you did, Memphis. No one else is brave enough to speak his name to me and *not* talking about him is far more painful for me. It's just… I miss him." That line about time healing all wounds was utter shit. I shook my head to snap myself out of my melancholy. If I let it grab me, it would imprison me for the rest of the day. For River, I wanted to find some semblance of peace and happiness, but I felt like I was at a crossroads in my life and, no matter the direction I chose, none of them would lead me to him. "You can always come for a visit if you need a change of scenery. I have plenty of room."

"I might take you up on that, Em."

We talked for a few minutes about random things, and I could tell there was something he wanted to say but hesitated for some reason. It could mean only one thing. "My mother asked you to pass a message on to me, didn't she?"

"Yes, but I didn't make her any promises."

"Let's hear it, Memphis. What did Mommy dearest have to say?" I asked, bracing myself for a pithy, cold message about me shirking my duties. Perhaps she wanted to tell me to get my head out of my ass and come back to the company or maybe it was to ask me to see a psychiatrist for my "crazy episodes."

Memphis was quiet for a long time, and I worried that it must've been something really bad. "She said, and I quote, 'tell my son hello from me and that I miss him.' First, I nearly fell out of the chair, then I thought it was a trap. I replayed the words and the tone of voice she used to say them at least a hundred times before I called you."

"Huh," I replied. No other word came to mind on how best to describe how much Memphis stumped me that morning. "That's new."

"Tell me about it. And, Em, she sounded sincere."

"Thanks for telling me, Memphis. I'll think about calling her." I wouldn't make promises I couldn't keep. "You give my offer some thought too."

"I'll think about *visiting* you," he said, making sure I knew which offer he would consider.

"My door is always open to you," I said before we disconnected.

Hearing that my mother was looking for me was enough to make me want to build a blanket fort and hide like I did when I was a kid, but I wouldn't give her that kind of power over me. Instead, I went for the jog I planned before Memphis called me. The rhythmic sound of my feet slapping against the concrete and the steady rise and fall of my lungs centered me when my world felt chaotic. My mother and I had a turbulent relationship for as far back as I could remember. I wasn't foolish enough to believe that she had changed her ways. No, she wanted something from me. But what?

There was a cute little gazebo in the park that was the halfway mark of my jog. I hadn't lived there long, but I'd already developed a routine of stopping to stretch on one of the benches beneath the gazebo. I saw Josh running toward the gazebo from the opposite side of town. He looked surprised to see me but didn't say anything.

I propped my heel on the back of the bench so that my leg was extended out in front of me. I bent over my leg and reached for my toes, stretching my hamstrings. I felt Josh staring at me and looked up at him. His surprise had turned wary like I'd read his mind or something.

"I can't read your damn mind, Josh."

"You just did," he said suspiciously.

"It didn't take psychic ability to know what you were thinking," I said, switching legs. Josh's thoughts were plain to see in his expressions. "Did anyone ever tell you not to play poker?" It was a reversal of my original opinion about my neighbor.

"Yes, but then I took all his money and that of his parents too." Josh laughed maniacally.

"Good to know," I said with a nod of my head. I noticed that Josh's eyes kept straying to my man-bun and chuckled. "Not a fan, huh?"

"No, although I can appreciate the necessity to get it off your neck while working up a sweat. Not that I'm thinking about the ways you work up a sweat or anything." Josh's hazel eyes widened, and his cheeks turned pink with embarrassment.

"I didn't get the wrong idea," I told him. "I knew you meant jogging and not other, um… sweaty activities."

"You did it again." Josh took a leery step backward.

I was a passivist through and through and no threat to him, so his fear struck my funny bones. I threw my head back and laughed hard for several long seconds. I was shocked at how rusty my laughter sounded but realized I had very little to laugh about the past few years.

I expected Josh to retreat further, but he didn't. Instead, he tipped his head to the side and asked, "What are you doing on Sunday?" He shook his head slightly like he couldn't believe what he'd just asked.

"Sunday? Isn't that Easter?" I asked.

Regardless of his surprise, Josh rolled with his instincts. "Uh, yeah. Do you have plans?"

"I'll probably still be unpacking then." I started shifting my weight slightly between my right and left foot. I wasn't sure why, but Josh's question made me feel uncomfortable. Was this a pity invitation, or an offer of friendship? One left a sour taste in my mouth, and the other made me feel a glimmer of hope.

"Well, I'll be serving dinner around five if you'd like to come over," Josh said.

I nodded noncommittally then bit my bottom lip while I debated how I should respond. "I appreciate your invite, Josh. I'll think about it, okay?"

"Sure," Josh replied. "I don't mean to toot my own horn here, but I can pretty much guarantee that you've never had a glazed ham better than the one I'll serve you."

"Oh, I'm vegan," I said. I wasn't really, but I was still paying him back for lying about the wine.

Josh gasped and stood back from me like I announced I was a serial killer and he was a moment away from becoming my next victim. He was stunned by the possibility that I didn't want to come over and devour his ham. My twitching lips must've given me away because he said, "You're a complete shit, Emory!"

"Man, you're so easy," I told him between chuckles.

"Who told?" Josh demanded dryly. I loved his snarky sense of humor when he let his guard down.

I clutched my stomach and laughed even harder. "So sorry," I said, trying to catch my breath.

"If you think I'm funny then you should see my makeshift family. I can promise you a good time," Josh said, sounding like a bathroom stall promise.

"I'm not touching that one," I said, shaking my head. "No way."

"The offer is there if you want to accept it, but I won't take it out on your hair at your appointment next week should you not show up to dinner," Josh told me.

"Yeah, well, this style—or lack thereof—is from not giving a damn. I guess you could say my looks have lost their importance to me the last few years." I attempted a smile to soften the sadness behind my words. "Can I ask you for one favor if I do show up?"

"You can ask," Josh replied cautiously.

"Will you please not tell anyone about my… *gift*?"

"That I can guarantee," he said.

"Good," I said in relief. "I don't do parlor tricks. I take my abilities seriously, and I use them to help people, not hurt them." I wanted to take the opportunity to assure him that I wasn't there to cause trouble in his life.

"I understand. I doubt the rest of the group will whip out their phones and search your name as we did, but I do advise you make up a believable excuse as to why you moved to Blissville," Josh sagely replied. "It's a nice town and all, but rarely do people move here unless it's work-related."

I thought about it for a few seconds then asked, "What do you think they'd find acceptable? Honestly, I'm out of my league here. I don't know why I'm in Blissville beyond the fact that I knew I was needed."

Josh narrowed his eyes and looked me up and down. "How about a writer? Maybe you moved here to do research on small towns for a series you're writing. They may not drill you down as to exactly how or why you picked Blissville, but have an answer ready if they do. My friends have an attention to detail like you won't believe."

"Oh, I believe it," I remarked. "Thanks for the advice. You know," I said after a brief pause, "it's not far off the mark. Right now, I'm just jotting things down in a journal, but I have tossed around the idea of publishing a book about my experiences."

"Can I ask you something, Emory? You can say no, but I need complete honesty if you're willing to answer my question."

"Ask away." I had an idea of what he wanted to ask, and I had no problem answering it.

"Will you share with me exactly what you saw to make you move here in the house behind mine?"

"Honestly, Josh, it was a vision of a piece of mail with my name and the Blissville address on it. Nothing else. It was the oddest thing to ever occur to me. I ignored it for a few weeks until I started to see the vision daily. I knew it was time to pack up and move here to find out what was waiting for me."

"Do your visions ever help you prevent crimes or do you only help solve them after they're committed?" Josh asked me.

"That's two questions," I replied jokingly.

"You're right. I apologize."

"Don't apologize, Josh. I was only teasing you." I blew out a long breath then said, "I've worked in both situations, but the majority have been the latter scenario you described." I had hoped my answer would ease his concern a little, but it was obvious by his tense posture that he was still worried about my appearance in Blissville. I hated that I'd upset him so much, but leaving town wasn't an option until I figured out why River sent me here.

"Well," Josh said, ready to end the conversation and move on with his day, "you know where I live if you feel like having company."

"Will there be an Easter egg hunt?"

"No," Josh answered with a laugh. "Deal breaker?"

"Nah," I replied good-naturedly. "I'll see you around. Perhaps on Sunday."

"See you, Emory."

Josh and I continued on our original paths, which took us in opposite directions. We must have had similar strides because we reached our driveways at the same time. I had returned Josh's wave before I headed inside. I went straight upstairs to shower off the sweat and tried to come up with something to do with my time while I waited for cosmic answers to appear, but my mind kept straying to the conversation I had with Memphis. My mother said hello, and she missed me. Did I dare hope that was the case? Did I even care?

I shut the water off a little more forcefully than it required and was glad I didn't snap the faucet with my hand. I gritted my teeth in frustration as I dried off and got dressed. I knew it was a mistake to call my mother, but I would drive myself crazy if I didn't.

I was surprised when she answered the phone on the second ring instead of letting it go to voicemail. Then I heard the voice on the other end and knew why. "Hello," Tamara, my mother's longtime personal assistant said. "It's good to hear your voice. Let me get Audrey on the line for you." Instead of muting the phone, Tamara covered it with her hand when she informed my mother that I was calling her. Unfortunately, she must've forgotten that the speaker was at the bottom of the phone. I heard my mother's voice loud and clear.

"He always calls at the worst possible times." I imagined she was dramatically rolling her eyes like she was prone to do. "Tamara, please tell him that I'll call him later." There wasn't an ounce of excitement or affection in her voice. *Missed me?* No, something else was going on. Too bad for her that I wasn't giving her a chance to tell me. I hung up before Tamara came back on the phone.

My mother's behavior wasn't anything new; she'd acted that way my entire life. She never wanted anything to do with me, preferring to let nannies oversee my day-to-day activities. Audrey McIntire-Whelan was perfectly happy with a quick goodnight at bedtime, if I got that, until she saw that I had developed a close relationship with a nanny. My mother didn't want me, but she wanted all of my affection aimed at her at the moments she chose to enter my life. When that didn't happen immediately, the nanny was fired and a new one took over. My mom would insert herself into my life, giving me hope that she finally wanted to spend time with me and that I was worthy of her love until she either got bored or figured she had solidified her position in my life. The pattern repeated itself through several nannies until I was wise enough to catch on to the game.

River was the one person my mother couldn't run off, and I had refused to allow her to ruin the beautiful love I'd found with him. I don't know why I'd held false hope that my mother had changed her ways after all this time. I shook my head in disgust. I had thought that moving to Blissville would bring meaningful changes to my life, but I learned that the more things changed, the more they stayed the same.

FOUR

Jon

A FEW DAYS LATER, I LEARNED THAT MY SUSPICION ABOUT
Detective Wyatt was correct. He was like a bulldog with a
bone in his mouth and wasn't going to give up until he solved
my brother's case. I wasn't involved in Nate's death and didn't fear
anything the detective had to say to me, but I was still surprised when
he contacted me directly rather than go through my attorney like I'd
instructed him.

It was ironic that a shower was also involved the second time
Detective Wyatt reached out to me. Except, the shower was in my
dreams, and he had joined me. My ringing cell phone woke me before I got to the good parts. I was irritated about missing out on that
delectable fantasy of running soapy hands all over that body and

pissed at myself for not silencing my phone.

I debated whether I should listen to the message or just call Rick to let him know the detective was harassing me. A surprising thought tickled the back of my brain. The sexy detective didn't have to be my enemy. In fact, we both had the same goal, so why not find out what he wanted?

I played back the voicemail message without further hesitation. "Mr. Silver, this is Detective Wyatt with the Greater Cincinnati Task Force." I wasn't aware that the task force had a name, but that wasn't what struck me. It was the deep timbre of the detective's voice, and it momentarily distracted me from the reason for his call. "It's very important that I speak to you about your brother's case." The detective rattled off his cell phone number and asked me to call him at my earliest convenience.

His firm, urgent tone caused my heart to flare with hope. Could there be a crack in the case? *There would never be a more convenient time like the present to find justice for my brother.* The only inconvenient thing was the semi-erection the detective gave me. I'd learned long ago to ignore those types of urges.

"You rang, Detective," I said into the phone once he answered. I sounded equal parts sleepy and horny.

"I'm sorry that I woke you, Mr. Silver. There's been a development in your brother's case, and I need your help."

"Are you serious?" I asked, suddenly feeling alert. "Um, give me an hour to wake up and get my crap together. Where do you want to meet me?"

"You name the place and time, and we'll meet you," he said.

"We?"

"Yes, you met my partner," Detective Wyatt reminded me. His partner was a wisecracker at my office but said very little at the precinct so I'd temporarily forgotten about him.

"Oh." I sounded disappointed. Perhaps I was confusing reality with my dreams, or maybe I wanted to push the sexy man to see how far he'd go. "I was hoping you were coming alone." I wouldn't classify my tone as seductive, but I was positive it got my point across.

"Not going to happen," Detective Wyatt said firmly. "Dorchester and I will meet you. When and where?" he asked me.

I let out a dissatisfied sigh and said, "Four o'clock in my office. I'll even wear clothes this time."

"We'll be there."

I tried to go back to sleep, but it didn't happen. *Why didn't Detective Wyatt call Rick? Should I call Rick and ask him to be present? Was the detective as good in bed as the vibes he emitted?* Yeah, sex is never far from a guy's mind. My thoughts spun in a hundred different directions and made me feel like someone had scrambled my brains. That thought reminded me of the way Nate loved ketchup on his scrambled eggs and my grossed-out response that it looked like brains.

The pain in my chest, whenever I thought about my brother, hadn't lessened since the day Rick notified me of his death. Nate and I had tried to cram the forty years we missed with one another into the seven months we'd had together. It wasn't enough time, and I didn't get to know all the things I wanted to know about him. It was a hard blow that was a hundred times more painful than any injury I received in battle or on a mission. I learned that scars on hearts remained open long after the ones on our bodies healed.

Instead of moping around in bed, I got dressed and worked out in Nate's—*my*—gym. The detective's crack about me living in my brother's house was spot-on because Nate had left his estate to me, but I did not take over his bedroom. I did buy out his silent partner in the club as soon as I could because Marlon Bandowe was a coward undeserving of my brother's affections and I wouldn't waste a second of my time looking at him.

Running Nate's business was never one of my goals, but my brother loved his club. Selling it didn't seem right to me either. It no longer mattered what I wanted, because it was mine, and I would keep it running successfully to honor my brother. I knew nothing about the kind of club my brother operated because my preferred haunts offered more debauchery, but Corbin Bouchard, my best friend, black ops brother, and owner of Voodoo in New Orleans assured me that a club is a club and offered his assistance.

"Good accounting, reliable employees, and sticking to your club rules are critical whether your patrons just like to dance to the latest hip hop single or they like to get tied down and fucked in the center of the room for everyone to see," Corbin had said.

God, how I missed the freedom I had found in those private rooms at Voodoo. I wasn't a man who needed to pay expensive club memberships to find sex, but I wanted it that way. Everyone there knew to follow the rules, or they were not-so-kindly escorted to the door. "Rule number one is to *never* have sex with an employee," he'd warned me. Well, I fucked that all to hell—literally and figuratively. Luckily, Alexander wasn't behaving weirdly around me or in front of the other employees. I might've caught a wistful gleam in his eyes a few times, but he never acted on it. I hoped it stayed that way.

I felt almost human after I completed my daily ritual of work out, shower, and jerk off. I had several hours left before I had to meet the detectives at the club, so I made a hearty breakfast and worked in my home office. The biggest piece of advice Corbin gave me was to install software that allowed me to keep track of my inventory and money instead of relying on my employees or accountant. "They smell fresh blood in the water and think it would be easy to skim a little off the top or take a bottle of hooch without you knowing it. No, sir, that's not how you run a business."

I'd diligently tracked every aspect of the business using the software that Corbin suggested, and I'd never had a single incident raise a red flag, but something about the inventory didn't add up. I went back through the trends and flow from the previous week, and my suspicion rose even more.

"It'll start with a few bottles of inexpensive liquor because they think that'll fly under the radar. Next thing you know, the top shelf liquor is going out quicker, and the incoming money doesn't match. That's why I use a system where my bartenders enter the booze used for each drink, and it generates what the sales should be that night. If it doesn't match up, I start knocking heads together until I either get them to quit being lazy and enter shit correctly, or I find the thief." I had a feeling that anyone who stole from Corbin didn't forget the lesson he gave them. The story went that Corbin's family had ties to a French Quarter mafia; it was a rumor that he'd neither confirm nor deny.

Someone was either incompetently entering sales and liquor use, or one of my employees was stealing cash or liquor, possibly both. It was not a trend I would allow to continue. It appeared that I would need to have a mandatory staff meeting after I met with Detectives Wyatt and Dorchester. I sent an email to my club manager, Michelle, and told her that all hands needed to be on deck no later than five o'clock for an important meeting. If an employee couldn't make the meeting on short notice, then they were required to check in with me personally later that evening. I might not have had mafia blood running through my veins, but I wasn't a person anyone would want to fuck over.

"Come in," I said after someone knocked on my office door.

Alexander opened the door and popped his head inside. "Detectives Wyatt and Dorchester are here to see you, Mr. Silver. They said they have an appointment." He sounded and looked nervous. Why? Was it because the police were there or was he hiding something else? The discrepancy between the liquor and cash flow didn't show up until after I fucked him. Was he trying to fuck me over or did he think his sexy, tight ass could save him if I discovered what he'd done?

I didn't give away any of my thoughts when I looked at Alexander. I simply nodded and said, "Thank you, Alexander. I am expecting them."

"You got it, boss."

The detectives nodded cordially at Alexander before he shut the door then focused on me. I couldn't get a read on their moods, and I wasn't sure if they were going to tell me good news or bad.

"Thank you for seeing us on such short notice," Detective Wyatt said, extending his hand toward me. Detective Wyatt had made it clear that he was not available, so I didn't attempt any coy tricks when I shook his hand.

"It sounded urgent, and I must say that I was pleased that you turned to me for help instead of accusing me of killing my brother." I held up my hand when Detective Wyatt started to speak. "I know that you're just doing your job, Detective. I'm trained in interviewing… suspects." My time in black ops was completely classified, but the man wasn't stupid. He'd already realized that my sudden appearance in New Orleans was fishy. Funny how the government didn't mind me sticking my body out for them, but when it came to retiring, they barely gave me sufficient credentials to rent an apartment. Jonathon Black became Jonathon Silver—new name, new life. Too bad it wasn't as easy as it sounded. "Tell me how I can help you catch my brother's killer."

"What can you tell us about Nate's involvement in the planning of a casino?"

"Nate said that he'd attended a few meetings and was definitely interested in pursuing the idea. Do you think that had something to do with my brother's death?" I asked.

"It's very likely," Detective Wyatt replied then told me about the previous attempt to build the casino in Carter County where Nate had died and what little he knew about Lawrence Robertson's death and how similar it was to Nate's and someone named Owen Smithson.

Owen Smithson? The name didn't ring a bell, and it was the first time someone mentioned the name in connection with Nate. Instead of interrupting the sexy detective, I let him continue.

"In Mr. Robertson's belongings, we found notes from the meetings he attended, and he used initials to identify the others involved. This morning, we met with his attorney who represented him at all the meetings, and he identified the names of the people who represented the casino developer," Detective Wyatt said.

"And?"

"There's one person we can connect to both Nate and Lawrence Robertson," Detective Dorchester said.

"Who?"

"Rick Spizer," the detectives said at once.

I flinched in my chair like one of them reached across my desk and slapped me. I would've been less surprised if they had. There was no one in the world that Nate trusted more than Rick Spizer. There had to be a mistake. "*Rick?* You think *Rick* was involved in killing Nate, Smithson, and this Robertson guy?" I asked in disbelief. If they were right, Rick was the connection between Nate and Robertson at least.

"He at least knows more than he's letting on," Detective Wyatt told me. "I don't believe it's a coincidence."

"I don't either," I replied absently while my mind tried to find ways to exonerate Rick because it was too much for me to believe that he harmed Nate. "Put a wire on me."

"Excuse me?" Detective Wyatt asked.

"Put a wire on me and send me in to talk to him," I repeated. "I can get him to talk."

"He's your attorney," Detective Dorchester said. "There's a close line we're straddling if he does say something incriminating."

"Not if we have a warrant," Detective Wyatt said to his partner. "We'd need to find a judge we can trust, preferably one with a clerk that doesn't have a big mouth."

"Weston and Harris will know," Dorchester replied. "This is our best bet."

"I'll fire him as my attorney," I volunteered. I hated to set Rick up, but I couldn't think of another way. I just hoped that he was cleared of wrongdoing and would listen to my explanation once it was all over.

"Then he might get suspicious and refuse to speak to you," Dorchester replied. "Let us go through the official channels and make sure our i's are dotted, and t's crossed. The last thing we want to do is let someone off on a technicality."

"Okay," I said in frustration. "I don't know how I'm supposed to act like nothing is wrong when I meet with him to go over business tomorrow."

"Oh, I think you can dig deep and rely on your training for that," Detective Wyatt told me. I decided not to remark on his comment.

"Is there anything else?" I asked them.

"Not at the moment," Dorchester said. "We'll be in touch soon." They rose from their chairs and headed to the door.

I called Detective Wyatt's name before they could leave. "I think I was wrong about you, Detective."

"You wouldn't be the first person, Silver," he tossed over his shoulder as he walked out the door.

I sat in shock in my office for several minutes after they left. I knew there was a high probability that Nate knew his killer, but I wasn't prepared for Rick Spizer to be that person. There had to be another explanation, and I was tempted to demand it from Rick, but I wouldn't betray the detectives like that. I could tell that they didn't trust me completely, but they had enough confidence to ask for my help. No matter how hard, I would follow through with the agreement I made with them.

I pulled myself together and entered the bar area to have our impromptu meeting before the club opened. I was honestly surprised to see that the entire staff had shown up. Honestly, they'd been great to me since day one, which made the theft that much harder to swallow. The club looked like a completely different place with the bright overhead lights on instead of colored lights and disco balls. It was so quiet without all the loud music thumping that I could hear the slapping of the soles of my dress shoes against the floor.

"Thank you all for coming," I told them. I made eye contact with each of them to gauge their reaction. I saw respect, lust, and even annoyance, but I didn't see guilt or fear. On the one hand, it was a good thing because I didn't want any of them to be guilty of stealing. I wanted it to be a trainable incident that could be avoided in the future. On the other hand, I knew better than to hold my breath. If there were a thief amidst my staff, I would find them. Laying out all my cards on the table wasn't the way to go about it. I was better off to act like it was an honest mistake and watch to see what happened. "I want to go through the process of properly entering the liquor sales into the system. I understand that it's still a new process for you, so I'm not here to beat anyone up. I just want to make sure that everyone is following the same procedure."

I spent half an hour going through the process with the bartenders, wait staff, and managers. "No one is exempt from using this method," I reminded them. "Is that understood?"

"Yes, sir," they all said in unison.

"Let's all have a good night," I told them then returned to my office.

I watched their body language through the monitors as they finished getting the club ready to open. It was obvious from our meeting that each of them knew the system well, which meant that I either had a lazy employee or a thief. I would tolerate neither in my club. I released a sigh of frustration and wished for a millionth time that there was some type of establishment like Voodoo in the Queen City so I could blow off steam and lose myself, if only for a short time.

FIVE

Emory

AFTER RUNNING INTO JOSH FOR THE SECOND TIME, I REALIZED two things. I missed laughter almost as much as I missed my husband, and I liked the idea of writing a book about my psychic experiences more than I originally thought. I also realized that I missed the human interaction with people outside of solving a cold case. I had Memphis, of course, but he was a few thousand miles away, and I realized that I wanted to share a meal with someone while we chatted. Josh offered me the opportunity, but I wasn't sure I should accept. I didn't want him to offer his friendship out of pity; I wanted to be... wanted.

I needed to have a purpose in life again—one that I could grasp. I just didn't believe that I was meant to travel around the country and help solve missing person and cold cases for the rest of my life. I'd lived a purpose-driven life up until the moment my world ended when River died. I knew exactly what I was supposed to do, where I was supposed to go, and who was supposed to be with me until that fateful day in February. After I lost River, the life I knew no longer felt right to me. I tried going through the motions of the corporate America I'd lived and breathed, but I was miserable. My expensive silk tie felt more like a noose, and the fine material of my custom-tailored shirts and suits made my skin itch like I was allergic to them.

My family thought I'd lost my mind when I walked away from the whiskey empire my family started more than two hundred years ago in Ireland. In fact, my mother warned me that I had to see a psychiatrist or she'd block my access to my trust fund. And she would've rather seen me homeless than compromise, but my grandfather—her father-in-law—overruled her decision. Connor Whelan might've been knocking on eighty years old, but his mind was as sharp as ever, and I was still his favorite person in the world. It also helped that he disliked my mother from the moment they'd met. I was the only reason my granddad tolerated her presence after my father died in a small engine plane crash with his mistress. I knew that Granddad wanted me to resume my rightful spot in his company, but I knew in my heart that I never would.

I needed to forge my own path and put down roots where I wanted them. I wasn't sure that writing books and living in Blissville were the long-term answers, but it felt right to me for that moment in time. Acknowledging that much at least gave me a sense of peace and a jolt of determination that had been sorely lacking in my life. If I was going to make a nest in Blissville, then I needed to make the rental house feel more like home. I needed vibrant colors, decorations, and wall art. I could've hired someone to ship the things I bought with River, but I could almost hear him whispering, "New life equals new stuff, my love." I decided to liven up the space with a more vibrant paint scheme, and I was lucky that my landlord didn't care. He even suggested the name of a painter who could do the work for me, but I'd always liked working with my hands. Once the new color scheme settled, I could pick out art and decorations that suited my new life.

I underestimated how much paint supplies to buy and had to make a quick dash to Harry's Hardware in the middle of a project one afternoon. I was in a hurry to get back home and didn't pay attention when I exited the aisle with the items I needed. I nearly plowed into Gabe from next door. I clutched my chest with my free hand and smiled sheepishly at him.

"I'm sorry, Gabe. I wasn't paying attention to where I was going." A husband and wife walked by us and gave me the once-over. Oh, the downside of being the new guy in town.

"No problem, Emory. How's it going?" Gabe asked me. "Are you getting settled in okay?"

"It's going to be an adjustment," I admitted, "but Josh's cookies and thoughtful invitation made me feel welcome."

"Josh? *My Josh*?" Gabe asked in surprise. "An invitation to what?"

"Um, dinner," I replied uneasily. "On Sunday."

"Sunday dinner? This Sunday, as in Easter?" Gabe raised his eyebrows.

"Is that a problem, Gabe? I don't want to cause any trouble," I said, backing up slowly. The last thing I wanted to do was create a problem between the happy couple. Gabe snapped out of his surprise and offered me a friendly smile.

"No, there's no problem," he said. "It's just that Josh's Sunday dinners are very sacred. They're very important to him, which means that you've made a good impression on him." I figured it was closer to that adage that said you should keep your friends close and enemies closer. Josh had thawed a bit toward me, but he was still wary. Gabe wasn't though, and it made me curious. Usually, law enforcement officers typically didn't trust me as far as they could throw me.

"I think it's more like pity, Gabe, but I appreciate what you said. If you're sure it won't be a problem…"

"You're more than welcome to join us for dinner, Emory. I mean that." Before Gabe could say anything else, a short, older lady, who introduced herself as Mrs. Miller from two doors down, stopped by to welcome me to town. It was obvious she wanted to chat, so Gabe excused himself. "I'll see you Sunday," Gabe tossed over his shoulder as he walked away like my attendance was a given.

My quick trip to the hardware store turned out to be the exact opposite because Mrs. Miller thought the best way to welcome me to the neighborhood was to tell me all about her family. I wondered what possessed her to think a stranger would want to know the names of all her children, their spouses, and her grandchildren, where they went to school, and where they worked. Was that how small town USA worked? I quickly realized she had a master plan all along when she mentioned her youngest granddaughter, Sabrina, who happened to be single.

"Tell me, dear," Mrs. Miller said, leaning toward me, "are you single?"

I fought the urge to blow out a frustrated sigh. Technically, I was a single man, but River took my heart with him to his watery grave. I never wanted to get it back because I never planned to love again. That was information I only told the people closest to me, not a complete stranger. "I'm a widower," I said. I saw the hopeful gleam in her eyes, and it seemed that widower equaled a yes. I knew I had to act fast, so I told her as much of the truth as I was willing to share. "I'm nowhere close to being ready to date again, Mrs. Miller."

"Oh, dear, I'm truly sorry for your loss," she said kindly. "I'll pray for you."

"Thank you," I said, not sure how else to respond. It wasn't that no one said that to me before, but again, it was someone who knew me well—or at least longer than five minutes. I held up my basket with paint supplies. "I hate to run, but I need to get back to my project. I have just a quarter of the living room left to finish."

"Oh, don't you apologize to me." Mrs. Miller waved the idea

away. "Thank you for entertaining a silly old woman."

I looked around the hardware store then back at her. "What old woman?" I playfully winked at Mrs. Miller before I headed to the register, and she giggled. *Ah, I still had a little charm left in me.*

"What did you do today?" Memphis asked when he phoned later that evening. For once I did something besides read a book.

"Painted the living room," I answered.

"You did?" Memphis asked in surprise. "Does that mean you're staying there?" I couldn't tell if he was happy or sad, but I thought I detected a hint of both. Was he happy that I seemed to be moving forward with my life, but sad that it was far away from him? That was honestly how I felt about the situation.

"For now," I replied because that was the only truth I knew. "I looked up some paint ideas on Pinterest, and I like the finished look." I designated one wall as the accent wall and painted it a charcoal-gray color, which looked fabulous behind my white leather couch. I painted the remaining three walls a smoky blue-gray color that I thought was serene and peaceful. "Tomorrow, I'll shop for artwork."

"I'm happy for you, Em." Memphis got quiet, and I knew what he was going to ask next, so I saved him the hassle.

"I called her, but she was too busy to talk to her only son," I told him. "She didn't attempt to call me back either so she either tested me to see if I would call or whatever she'd wanted to say to me was no longer relevant. Either way, I've called Audrey McIntire-Whelan for the last time." I released a frustrated breath. "Besides, your mom was more of a mother to me than my own. I don't know where I'd be in life without those summers spent at your house, Memphis."

Our mothers were sisters, but you'd never know it by looking at them or talking to them. They looked nothing alike, and their personalities were as different as night and day. My aunt Karen married her high school sweetheart and lived a happy middle-class life filled with love and laughter. Middle of the road had never sat well with Audrey McIntire, so she used her looks to enter beauty pageants and earn college scholarship money that put her in the vicinity of some of the wealthiest men in America. She snagged one of them when she met my father, but I knew for a fact her life didn't turn out close to what she'd planned. The summers I spent with Aunt Karen, Uncle Scott, Memphis, and his little sister, Marcy, were the best times in my life.

When I sent a Mother's Day card or flowers, it was to my aunt Karen, not my incubator. Just thinking about my mother soured my mood. I needed to dispell the gloom that settled over me, so I changed the subject. "Well, it's been a few days since you and Caleb broke up, so can I assume you've met someone else by now?"

"Hardy har har," Memphis replied sarcastically. I could practically hear his eyes rolling through our phone connection. But I could also tell I was right.

"What's his name?" I asked, pressing for more information.

"It's not what you think," Memphis replied.

"It never is," I remarked. "So, what's the deal? Let me live vicariously through you."

"Em, you have a mirror. You know damn well that you're a good-looking guy," Memphis countered. "Don't even act like you're some ugly codger who couldn't get a date."

I knew that people found me attractive, but that never mattered to me. I never wanted to fuck around or pick up strange men; I wanted someone to call my own. For nine months out of every year, I was the loneliest person in the world. I was nothing more than a pawn used in a power play between parents who hated each other. In fact, the only thing they could agree on was their disappointment in me. I wanted someone to love me for *me*, and I found that with River.

I chose to ignore Memphis's remark and said, "Tell me about your night."

"I don't kiss and tell," he replied.

"Ha! I knew it," I said gleefully. "Since when don't you kiss and tell?" I countered. He loved to brag about his conquests. "This guy must be special to you."

"It was one date," Memphis said dryly. "I'm hardly ready to send out wedding invitations." I knew that I wanted to marry River on our first date, so I didn't think it was that far out of the realm of possibility. "But yeah, it felt special to me."

"I hope everything works out for you," I told my cousin. He was an amazing person with a kind heart and whimsical spirit, who often fell for the bad boys. He wanted to help them, but they didn't always want his help.

"Thanks, Em. I'd ask you for hints about my future, but you don't do parlor tricks," Memphis said.

The truth was, I had no clue how to tap into my ability to see what else I could do and had no desire to change that. "Would you want to know?" I asked.

"No," Memphis replied. "Well, unless he was a serial killer and you could prevent my painful, torturous death."

"That's a given," I replied. "Nothing else though? You wouldn't want me to spare you the pain of heartbreak?"

"Would you have wanted that with River?" Memphis asked. "Would you have walked away from River to avoid heartache or would you have loved him anyway?"

"Walking away from River was never an option," I softly said into the phone. I wouldn't trade a single second of the time I had with my husband for the promise of a pain-free future. Not knowing River's love, not hearing his laughter, and not seeing his eyes light up when I walked into a room would've been the bigger tragedy.

"I wouldn't want the knowledge of the future to rob me of my present either," Memphis said. "Besides, I think we both know how this is going to end."

"Someday the right guy is going to come along," I told him.

"Yeah, but I'll ignore him for a tall, dark, and dickhead." Memphis's sardonic laughter brought a smile to my face.

"Oh, I think you're going to be pleasantly surprised," I said, trying to sound mysterious and intriguing.

"Do you know something?" Memphis asked, taking the bait.

"You just told me that you never wanted to know your future events unless it involved saving you from a serial killer," I reminded him. "I'm pretty sure 'pleasantly surprised' isn't a phrase I would use if you got nabbed by a serial killer."

"You're an asshole, Emory. Did anyone ever tell you that?"

"Goodbye, Memphis," I said into the phone before hanging up.

I smiled up at my bedroom ceiling because I loved riling him up. I reached for the remote and unmuted the sound of the college basketball tournament game I was watching before Memphis called me. The lead had shifted to the underdog at some point during our conversation, and I suddenly found the game a lot more exciting. I rarely watched television in bed anymore, but the living room walls were still wet.

I fell asleep before the game was over, but it was hard to be upset about not knowing who won the game because River finally returned to me in my sleep. I was lying on my right side in the center of my bed, and he spooned up behind me like old times. I released a long sigh of relief because I never thought I'd feel the heat of his body again. River raised his right arm up and gripped my hand where it rested on the pillow while he moved my long hair off my neck with his left.

"You've been gone for so long," I whispered into the night.

River didn't say anything; he used his lips to communicate by kissing the back of my neck, and it had my dick hard as a spike instantly. River slid his left hand down to cup the back of my thigh on my left leg and pushed forward so that it angled up, giving him access to my cock, balls, and ass. As thrilling as it felt to have his hands on my body again, the tiny hairs on the back of my neck stood up for a reason other than excitement, but my brain was too fogged with lust to figure out the cause for my unease.

River continued to kiss the back of my neck while he gently worked my ass open for him. I loved when he took me in that position because it meant he would love me long and slow until my eyes rolled back into my head, and I came hard all over the sheets. I shamefully moaned and pushed my ass against his slick fingers, needing more friction and deeper penetration. It had been so long—too long—since we'd last made love, and I was ready to come just from his fingers.

Again, River didn't say anything; he just kept kissing my neck. "Please, baby. I need to feel you inside me." I felt tears of frustration burning behind my closed eyes and heard them in my voice.

River removed his fingers from my ass and pressed the tip of his erection against my puckered opening. I cried out when he pushed inside me slow. Damn, it felt like I was giving my virginity to him all over again. River waited for me to adjust to his penetration and continued loving on my neck and shoulder. When I was ready, I pushed my ass against him eagerly. River didn't need further instruction and slowly eased his way inside me.

"Fuck!" I cried out when he grazed my prostate. "So good, baby." I felt my balls pull tight and firm against my body as my orgasm neared. River felt wider and longer than I remembered, but I was too lost in the pleasure to give it much thought. "More!"

He placed his left hand on my hip and started thrusting harder and faster, nothing like we used to do in that position. I didn't care; I needed to come, and I was almost there. When my orgasm hit me, it was so powerful that my breath got stuck in my throat and no words or sound escaped me as I silently came all over my stomach and sheets.

River's grip on my hand and hip became almost bruising as he chased his orgasm too. I smiled when moans of ecstasy escaped him when he came inside me, but my euphoria didn't last long. My body, which had been warm with pleasure, turned to ice with fear. That moan didn't belong to River. I noticed the distinct feel of a ring on my lover's left hand. River and I never exchanged rings; we said it was too heterosexual. I hated that decision once I lost him. I stiffened in horror when I raised my left hand and saw a wedding band on my ring finger. *It couldn't be right, so why did it feel that way? Why wasn't I struggling to get away? Why did I nestle into him instead of tearing myself away?*

"I love you, Em," my lover said into my ear.

"I love you too." *No! I promised that I'd never give my heart to someone else.*

I jerked out of my sleep gasping for air. Hot tears poured down my face, and cum cooled on my stomach and chest. My sex-deprived body enjoyed the fuck out of that dream, but my heart felt bruised and shattered. It didn't matter that it wasn't real; I felt like I was unfaithful to River.

I sobbed in the shower as I scrubbed my skin repeatedly to wash away the evidence of my body trying to move on when my heart still said no. The words of love exchanged between my dream lover and me echoed through my brain and nothing I did silenced them. After I turned off the shower and toweled off, I wrapped myself in the ratty robe he loved so much and curled into a fetal position in the middle of the bed.

"I'm sorry, River. Please come back to me."

SIX

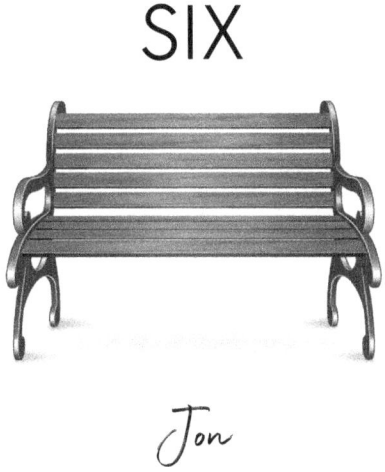

Jon

LIVED MOST OF MY ADULT LIFE ON THE EDGE AND HAD STOPPED getting nervous decades ago. My hands always remained steady, and my focus never wavered in any situation. I didn't second guess my decisions, and I never looked back once I took that step forward. I learned to control adrenaline when it coursed through my veins and used it to my advantage. Nerves, doubt, and second-guessing would've led to one thing—my death.

It seemed like all my old habits returned to me the night I was supposed to meet Rick while wearing a wiretap. A million ants crawled beneath my skin as nerves invaded my body, I had a hard time focusing on the mission—for lack of a better word—when the tech guys wired me for sound and video, and I questioned my decision every other minute. What the hell had I agreed to do? There was no way Rick Spizer had anything to do with killing Nate. I knew it to my core. Then it occurred to me that I could use my time to prove his innocence rather than trap him. And just like that, my nerves and doubt disappeared.

"Detective Wyatt, relax." I stood up from the bed across the one Detective Wyatt sat on in the hotel room. I looked at Dorchester, Weston, and Harris. "Is he always like this?"

"Mostly," Dorchester replied, "but he knows his shit, so maybe you should stop busting his balls and listen to him for a damn minute."

"Too bad you weren't this dedicated when my brother turned to you for help," I snarled. "Maybe he'd still be alive."

"Clear the room," Detective Wyatt commanded. His team obeyed the order immediately. He slowly rose to his feet and squared off against me. "You have every right to be angry over the loss of your brother, but blaming me for his death isn't going to bring him back. Instead, focus your damn energy on catching his killer by listening to what I'm telling you." The detective pointed his finger at me and said, "If you go in there half-cocked you could destroy *everything*. Are you listening to me?"

I turned and paced away from him, running my fingers through my hair in agitation. I turned to face Detective Wyatt and released my pent-up frustration in one, long breath. I was ready to listen.

"I didn't *refuse* to help Nate; he refused to help *himself*. He should've been up front about everything because it was highly unlikely he didn't know why he was targeted. He might not have known who, but he might've had an idea of why. His asking me to sneak around outside of the law to find his harasser was wrong. He wasn't forthright with the CPD when he finally turned to them. We can't help someone who doesn't want it, Silver."

"I know," I said softly. "I was out of line. I'm sorry." I didn't truly know a damn thing about the detective, but I was certain that he was an honorable man. He didn't give me the impression that he would try to railroad Rick into an arrest and conviction just to close his case.

"Trust me when I tell you I know how powerless you feel right now. My brother was killed in a robbery when I was fifteen. He was my hero, and I was devastated," he told me. "His killer was never arrested, so please believe me when I tell you that I will do everything *legally* within my power to solve Nate's case. I need your help to do that, which means you have to listen to what I say."

Detective Wyatt was right; I couldn't start acting like a vigilante if I wanted to bring Nate's killer to justice. A year ago, I would've wanted to hunt the fucker down myself and slit his throat, but I promised my mother that I would find my brother and try to live a normal life. Finding Nate had been easy, but keeping my other promise was harder than I anticipated. That moment in the hotel room with the CPD was my chance to prove that I could change and have a better life than the path I'd been on since I was sixteen years old. Christ, it was a miracle I had reached my fortieth birthday.

"Call the team back in. I'm ready to cooperate," I said.

The second time around, I listened to Detective Wyatt's instructions. I committed to memory what he wanted me to say so that I avoided any legal traps. In my last line of business, we didn't follow too many rules. We saw an opportunity to set things right and did it.

I headed to the restaurant a little early so that Rick didn't catch me exiting the elevators. It was my favorite place to eat, and the staff knew me well, but that night a young guy I didn't recognize greeted me as I entered. He was young, blond, and had lips made to suck my dick. Had it been any other night, I would've encouraged the arousal I saw blooming across his cheeks and sparkle in his eyes.

"Good evening, sir. My name is Stephan. What can I do for you?" Damn, he said that in a voice that made me want to bend him over my knee and... *Focus on the mission, Jon!*

"My name is Jonathon Silver, and I have a reservation for two," I replied coolly.

"Your wife or girlfriend?" he asked, fishing for information.

"Lawyer," I replied, not taking the bait. I had too much on the line and couldn't afford the distraction.

"Okay, follow me," he said in dramatic resignation that made my lips tilt up into a half-smile. He perked up a little when he saw that he got a reaction out of me, even a subtle one, and made sure he swayed his even perkier ass in a way that had me questioning my sanity for denying myself the pleasure. "I hope you have a most pleasant meal tonight, sir. Might I suggest you save room for dessert? I hear the blondie here is exceptional." Stephan playfully winked before he left me alone at my usual table. I knew damn well he wasn't referring to the blond brownie dessert on the menu.

An hour later, Rick still hadn't arrived, and I was getting aggravated. Had he somehow figured out that something was going on and decided not to show? I pulled out my cell phone from my jacket pocket and dialed his number. "Rick, I've been sitting here at the restaurant for thirty minutes waiting for you. Did I get the time wrong? Give me a call, buddy."

I drank another glass of water and ate another piece of bread before my phone rang. I pulled it out of my pocket, expecting to see Rick's name on the caller ID, but it read as unknown. A sick feeling washed over me as I stared at it while it rang a few more times.

"Jonathon Silver," I said into the phone.

"Mr. Silver, this is Detective Dorchester. Can you come back to the room please?" he asked. I could tell by his voice that something bad had happened.

"I'll be right there," I told him then signaled for the waiter. "Archie, my dinner guest won't be able to meet me tonight, and I received a call that there's an urgent matter I need to attend to at the club. Can you just add the charge for the bread to my tab?"

"There'll be no charge for the bread, sir." He shook his head like he couldn't believe I'd suggest such a thing. "Good luck, Mr. Silver."

"Thank you, Archie."

I didn't make eye contact with anyone else, especially that tempting morsel at the reservation desk, as I made my way back to the hotel room. "What's going on?" I asked when I entered the room. I could tell by Detective Wyatt's face that Rick was dead. Why else would he have stood me up?

"Spizer was found dead in his home," the detective told me. "We're going to head over to his house right now. I'll call you when we know more, either tonight or tomorrow."

Even though he confirmed what I suspected, I was overwhelmed by shock and grief. "I don't believe it," I said. "Honestly, I thought there was another explanation for Rick's involvement instead of him killing them or hiring it done, but this can't be a coincidence. He was good to me when everyone else was skeptical of my appearance in Nate's life, including my brother."

Detective Wyatt crossed the room and patted my shoulder. "I'll be in touch."

The rest of the team followed him out, of course, and I stood alone in the center of the posh hotel room. God, whoever killed those other men must've killed Rick also. Damn it, had he been involved all along or did he know too much? My brain spun with the possibilities or was it the room spinning? Fuck! How long had it been since I ate a meal? The stress of the situation and low blood sugar was a dangerous combo. I sank down on the edge of the bed and rested my head in my hands and willed my brain, or room, to quit spinning.

I debated leaving and going through a drive-thru of a fast food restaurant but didn't trust myself to drive. How the fuck could I even be thinking about food when Rick was lying dead in his home? I had truly become the animal my mother had feared. Hunger and disgust warred inside me while my heart ached over the loss of a man I considered a friend. Hunger eventually won out, and I ordered my favorite foods from room service. The hotel wasn't the kind of place you rented by the hour, which meant the CPD kept a room there or they rented it for the night. Either way, I was physically and emotionally wrecked and wasn't going anywhere until I got some food in my system.

I removed my jacket and tie then loosened the top few buttons of my dress shirt before I lay on the bed and waited for my food delivery. I turned on the television, but I didn't have a clue which two college basketball teams played one another, nor did I care. I was relieved when room service knocked on the door.

I dug into my perfectly seared steak and mushroom risotto like I hadn't eaten in a month. I didn't start to feel human again until I nearly finished my food. Exhaustion moved in swift and hard; I could barely keep my eyes open and decided, why should I? Who would it hurt if I took a little nap before I went home?

I don't know how long I was out before someone knocking at the hotel door woke me up. I was briefly disoriented when I woke, but it didn't take long for reality to penetrate the daze. Rick was gone, and we were no closer to finding Nate's killer. Whoever was at the door was a persistent fuck and never let up knocking.

I flung open the door expecting to find the CPD or hotel management on the other side with a request to vacate the premises immediately. Instead, I found one blond host whose smile told me he was certain he offered the most in several areas.

"What are you doing here?" I asked. "I thought it was an urgent matter with the way you kept knocking on the door."

"It is an urgent matter," Stephan said, brazenly pushing past me and entering the room. "I want you to fuck me."

"I didn't invite you in."

"Well, I'm not a vampire, so I don't really need one," he replied sassily.

"I think you misinterpreted my words," I said slowly. "I didn't say that because you wouldn't be physically able to enter my room without an invitation; I said it because I don't *want* you here."

"Yes, you do," he replied, just as slowly. I had to give the guy credit because I'd never met anyone as bold as him, and I'd worked with cold-blooded killers for two decades. Stephan had made quick work of the buttons on his dress shirt before he untucked and removed it. "One blondie for dessert coming right up." He opened his pants to reveal that he wasn't wearing anything beneath his slacks besides a hard-on and that he was natural blond.

I shouldn't have even entertained the idea of fucking the guy, but what better way was there to celebrate the fact that my heart still beat in my chest and blood still pumped through my veins, especially in my hardening cock. Stephan wickedly grinned when he saw that he'd won. He pulled out a condom and packet of lube from his back pocket and tossed them on the bed before he shoved his pants to his ankles and stepped out of his shoes and socks.

"Not so fast," I said when he moved to get on the bed. I stroked my erection through my slacks and smiled at the way his eyes burned with lust. "Bring those pretty lips over here?"

Sex with Stephan was a welcome distraction that helped ease the loneliness and disillusionment, but it was only a temporary fix. The misery I'd felt earlier returned as soon as he redressed and left my hotel room. I took a shower to wash away the smell of a guy I didn't even like and hoped the hot water would cleanse the guilt that permeated my soul. What kind of man was I? I had just learned that my friend died and instead of grieving, I banged a twenty-something kid with more confidence than sense.

I turned the water as hot as I could take it and stood beneath the spray while I tried to add up everything that had happened in the past three months. I had no answers, no clue where to go next, and no one to talk to about my problems. Hell, I already pestered Corbin a lot for club advice and my other best friend, Beau, was a deputy sheriff in Big Timber, Montana. They didn't have time for my whining. Hell, they probably would want to know when the body snatchers took the real Jonathon Silver and left the cry baby in his place.

I didn't hear my phone ringing when I was in the shower, but there was a voicemail from Detective Wyatt for me. I called him straight back without listening to his message.

"Detective," I said when he answered the call.

"I just wanted to let you know what I've discovered so far tonight," he told me. I listened as he explained that Rick died from a single gunshot wound to the head. "On his desk was a note that said he was responsible for the deaths, but didn't say that he killed them. I'm not sure what it means right now, and I'll continue to vigorously investigate this case, as well as your brother's and the other victims."

I was nearly at a loss for words. What did Rick mean when he said he was responsible? Something didn't add up, and it sounded like Detective Wyatt felt the same way. I believed that he would investigate until he had answers. "I appreciate the information, Detective." I started to hang up, but he said my name.

"What are you doing on Sunday?" Detective Wyatt asked, catching me off guard.

"Sunday? Isn't that Easter?" He had me scratching my head.

"Yes, do you have plans for dinner?"

"Are you asking me…"

"My boyfriend is an amazing cook and is making enough food for three armies. You've had a rough time lately, and I thought you could use a home-cooked meal and some good company. No pressure," he added. "I'll text you our address in case you want to come."

"Okay," I replied. It shocked me that Detective Wyatt would invite me to his house. Did he think I was so pathetic that I didn't have someplace to go? Fuck, if it wasn't true though. I knew I wasn't going to be very good company, but on the bright side, I could meet the man who clearly had a tight grip on the sexy detective's heart. "I'll give it some thought."

"Goodnight, Silver," the detective said before he hung up.

A little voice in the back of my head said, *what the hell do you have to lose by going to dinner?* I shrugged and said out loud, "Not a damn thing."

SEVEN

Emory

"**J**UST WALK UP TO THE DOOR AND RING THE DOORBELL. YOU can do this, Em." It wasn't my inner voice cheering me on as I stood at the end of my driveway, it was Memphis. "Don't be afraid to make friends and live again, cuz."

Live again? Like in my dream? I inhaled and exhaled a few times, trying not to sound like a heavy breathing perv on the phone. I'd been a mess ever since I had that dream of having sex with another man. I was too afraid to fall asleep and see him again, but afraid I'd miss River if I didn't sleep. I was starting to believe my mother was right and I needed to seek psychiatric help.

"You're just trying to get a break from my drama," I said into the phone. I used humor to mask the fear I felt inside when I watched

Josh's best friends and employees enter the back of the house. They seemed nice, but I tried not to let myself become too attached to people. Memphis was the only one who seemed to stick.

"Nice try, Emory," Memphis replied patiently. "Stop stalling and get to living."

"Okay. I'll call you later and let you know how it goes."

"I *always* look forward to hearing from you, Em."

I disconnected the call and slipped my phone in my pocket. What was the worst that could happen if I joined Josh, Gabe, and their friends for dinner? I could have a bad time and have to leave early, or have a good time and stay longer. I knew which of the two concerned me the most. I stood taller and inhaled a calming breath deep into my lungs then released it slowly. I decided I would go to dinner even if it were just to make Memphis proud of me.

I rang the doorbell and plastered a smile on my face when Gabe answered the door. "So glad you could make it." I didn't see any pity in Gabe's smile, just warmth, and welcome.

"Thanks."

I followed Gabe up the steps to the private residence above the salon. The aroma of delicious food permeated the air, and every step I took brought me closer to the food that smelled good enough to make me drool. "How do you not weigh three hundred pounds?" I asked Gabe.

"I work out a lot. I cranked up my cardio once I started dating Josh." *I just bet he did.* Those two put out some serious sparks when they were in the same room. You just knew they burned hotter than the sun when they were together. *Okay, Emory, back away from creepy thoughts about your new friends.* "That didn't come out the way I meant it to," Gabe said humorously. "His cooking skills require that I exercise more to maintain the weight I want."

I laughed because he sounded like an infomercial at best or one of those pre-recorded messages at worst. "I'll go on an extra-long jog tomorrow."

Josh's bright smile was so blinding that I almost missed the relief I saw in his eyes. *Was he worried that I wouldn't come? Why did he care so much?* I could hear Memphis urging me to stop questioning their kindness and embrace it.

"It's good to see you again, Emory," Chaz said. It had been so long since I had to exchange pleasantries in polite company, but I surprisingly slipped back into the groove.

"You too." I turned to the beautiful African American woman who smiled warmly at me. "I don't think we've formally met. I'm Emory Jackson." I extended my hand to her which she used to pull me into a hug.

"I'm Meredith Richmond," she told me, pulling out of the embrace. "I'm happy you're joining us today."

The doorbell rang again, and Gabe went back downstairs to answer the door. I noticed the various expressions on the faces around me. Chaz looked nervous and rubbed his hands against the thighs of his jeans while Josh and Meredith looked hopeful. Just who the hell were they expecting? It was obvious by everyone's reaction that he wasn't the person they anticipated. Well, Josh's huge smile and laughing eyes told me he knew it was a possibility and enjoyed watching Chaz and Meredith's surprise. I wasn't that curious about the newcomer until I saw their reactions.

My eyes widened slightly in surprise when I saw the dark-haired man with piercing blue eyes standing awkwardly next to Gabe with a bottle of wine in his hand. The guy wore dark jeans and an impeccably pressed, white dress shirt that was open enough to get a glimpse of dark chest hair. What stuck out to me the most wasn't the clothes he wore, but the expression on his face. He looked wary, cynical, and a little lost—all things that I understood well. I felt a tiny little sliver of recognition and chalked it up to the fact that it appeared we both were going through a tough time in our lives.

"Guys, this is Jonathon Silver," Gabe said. "He's Nate's twin brother. Jonathon Silver, this is Meredith, Chaz, and Emory." *Who the hell was Nate?*

Chaz was the first to snap out of his surprise to cross the room and shake Jonathon's hand. Meredith hugged him and told him she was sorry for his loss, which Jonathon seemed to appreciate. I realized the sadness I saw in his eyes was from losing his brother, which drew me to him even more. I slowly stepped forward and tilted my head slightly as I studied Jonathon because it felt as if I knew him somehow. There was something so familiar about him, but I'd never seen the man before; I was certain of it. I could tell I was making the other man feel uncomfortable but felt powerless to stop myself from wondering about him.

Aware that every eye in the room was trained on us and gauging our reactions, we cautiously extended our hands toward one another. "Emory Jackson," I said. When our hands touched, I felt an electrical current zap throughout my body. I finally understood what it felt like to grab a live wire. I narrowed my eyes suspiciously at the stranger as if he were solely responsible for the fire burning inside me. I wasn't the only one unhappy about the development because Jonathon returned my glare.

I closed my eyes for a few seconds to escape his penetrative blue eyes. When I did, I was transported back to my dream, which confused the fuck out of me. My lover held me tightly against him and nuzzled the back of my neck with his nose. "*I love you, Em.*" That voice! It was Jonathon Silver's. That was why he seemed so familiar to me, but that couldn't be possible. I never… we never… and we never would. I slowly opened my eyes and blinked as the dream—I refused to call it a vision—faded from my mind.

Jonathon's face was completely devoid of expression as he looked back at me. Did he feel the zing between us too? Did he think I was some fucking weirdo who didn't let go of his hand? I dropped it and took a sudden step back.

Josh stepped between us like he sensed the rising tension. I welcomed his intrusion and took another step back. "Welcome to our home," Josh said to Jonathon. "It's nice to meet you."

"It's nice to meet you too." He looked over at Gabe and smiled wryly. "No wonder you turned me down. Twice. Your man is adorable."

"Wait until you eat his food," Gabe proudly said to Jonathon.

Well, that was just fucking awkward! What kind of asshole came into someone's house and said something like that? Josh stiffened and looked toward Gabe. *Uh oh.* It looked like the hunky detective left that part out about their dinner guest. Jonathon shook his head slightly like he couldn't believe what he'd just said. Josh spun around and headed into the kitchen with his man fast on his heels.

The living area wasn't small, but it wasn't big enough to disguise the fact that Gabe was in there doing some quick groveling. I couldn't quite make out the hushed words he spoke, but his tone was conciliatory and regretful. Or maybe, not. Gabe cornered Josh and it looked like the tone of their conversation was heating up quick. I was right; they burned hotter than the sun. It was no wonder Gabe called Josh Sunshine.

"Should we leave?" Meredith asked them good-naturedly.

"Speak for yourself. I'm not leaving here until I get some of that ham."

I turned to see who had joined us while the little showdown in the kitchen happened. I recognized the tall, muscular man from around town, but we hadn't formally met. People in the diner referred to him as Dr. Vaughn, and I overheard someone else refer to him as the town vet.

"You made it after all," Josh said happily.

"You sound a little too eager, Sunshine." Gabe looked at Josh through narrowed eyes.

"I hope you wore pants with an elastic waistband on them," Josh told the newest arrival. "I bought a second ham just for you."

"Yeah?" the man asked hopefully. "These jeans might be a little too tight." Chaz was standing behind the hunky town vet and doing his best not to stare at his ass, but failing miserably. *Ah, this guy was the reason for Chaz's nervousness.* "I should've worn maternity pants like Chandler on *Friends* in the Christmas episode."

"It was Joey and Thanksgiving," Chaz said suddenly, then turned bright red.

Dr. Vaughn turned to face Chaz, who luckily had shifted his eyes upward in time so he didn't get caught ogling his ass. "Yeah, it *was* Joey at Thanksgiving."

"Let me help you get the food on the table while it's still hot," Meredith suggested. She grabbed Josh's arm and tugged him toward the stove while shooing Gabe into the dining area with the rest of us. Chaz joined his two best friends, and the rest of us stood looking at each other while the three of them whispered to one another. Some might've found it rude, but I thought it was cute. It appeared that the three of them sometimes shared the same brain because they looked to be finishing one another's sentences during their heated debate. Which one of us caused the stir though? I was pretty certain it wasn't me, which left the vet or the twin. It was also possible that both of those men created a stir for different reasons.

"Hi, I'm Kyle Vaughn."

I jerked my head away from the scene in the kitchen and smiled at the veterinarian. I didn't hesitate to shake his hand when he offered it to me nor did I feel a damn thing when my skin touched his. I didn't look to see if Jonathon was watching us because I didn't need to; I could feel it. I was tempted to go back home, but I didn't want to hurt Josh's feelings. My rumbling stomach reminded me that I hadn't eaten much that day, so I decided to tough it out. I could ignore Jonathon Silver for a few hours then I'd never have to see him again.

The three friends in the kitchen burst into raucous laughter over something Chaz said. They laughed so long and hard that they leaned on him while they caught their breaths. Then they collectively gathered themselves and started carrying food out to the dining area. One table was set up to hold the food so we could feed ourselves buffet style and the other was beautifully set with china and sterling silver utensils that rivaled my late grandmother's.

Chaz rattled a few lines from *Friends* and Kyle joined him. Chaz smiled brightly at the doctor, and they kept repeating lines until all the food was on the table. We each grabbed a dinner plate and made a pass around the table to fill them. Chaz was in front of me, and Meredith stepped up behind me. Both of them seemed eager to make me feel welcome with small talk.

"How do you like living in Blissville?" Meredith asked.

"It's different from my hometown, but I truly like it here. It's quaint and friendly." I left off how it differed from my previous life because I had no desire to expand on it.

"What do you do for a living?" Chaz asked. Josh had warned me it might come up. I had practiced my answer a few times earlier in the day, but it wasted my energy because I couldn't remember a damn thing I rehearsed.

"I'm a writer," I said. *Oh shit.* I made that sound as if I had actually published a fucking book instead of just thinking about it.

"Really?" Chaz asked, perking up. Then he began asking me a bunch of questions that I could only vaguely answer. I was hoping for a mysterious writer vibe instead of clueless dumbfuck, but I couldn't tell by his expression what he thought.

I wasn't sure where the hell to sit once I loaded up my plate with food, so I sat beside Meredith. She smiled up at me then turned her eyes on Kyle and Chaz who sat across from us. It seemed that the two men were making a connection in front of our very eyes. I was stunned when Jonathon Silver chose to sit down beside me instead of taking the empty seat next to Kyle.

I bowed my head as Meredith said grace, although I hadn't given God or faith much consideration after I cursed him for leaving me behind to live a life devoid of love and happiness instead of taking me too. Neither time nor distance from the life I shared with River had changed my mind. I didn't think the people gathered for dinner wanted to hear my sad tale, so I closed my eyes and pretended to pray too.

We dug into that delicious meal before the last echo of "Amen" left the room. Josh must've made every side dish known to mankind, and I vowed to sample it all. I glanced across the table and noticed that Kyle's plate looked a little empty for as hungry as he claimed to be when he arrived. He had a huge portion of ham, but the rest was mostly vegetable side dishes and deviled eggs. I didn't see so much as a bite of mashed potatoes, stuffing, or macaroni and cheese. How did a man live without biting into a buttery roll? I mentally shrugged and tucked into my food.

Halfway into my plate, I recovered my manners. "So, how did the two of you meet?" I asked, looking at Josh and Gabe so they knew I was addressing them.

I expected the typical story of meeting at a club or mutual friends introducing them. Nope! I listened as Josh theatrically wove a tale about a tall, dark, and dickish detective who showed up at his door to interview him as a potential witness to a murder. *Murder!* He just continued chatting after that little bombshell, and everyone around me seemed to accept it as nothing out of the ordinary. What the hell kind of town had I moved to? I glanced at Gabe, and he's leaned back in his chair with his arms across his chest and a sly smile on his face as if he was enjoying Josh painting him with an unpleasant stroke at their first meeting.

Gabe didn't interrupt the tale until Josh claimed he shot the mirror in his bedroom to distract a madman who was trying to stab him with a knife. *What the ever-loving fuck?* I glanced around the dinner table, and everyone was smiling as the two of them argued about Gabe shooting the mirror. Had I landed in *The Twilight Zone*?

"Stop and think about how many gunshots you heard. The responding officers took my gun from me, and only one bullet was missing from the clip," Gabe said.

Josh tipped his head to the side and appeared to think about what Gabe said for a few seconds. "There *was* only one shot fired. The mirror shattering was very loud, but it wasn't anything close to the noise the gun made when it went off. How the hell did the mirror just shatter?"

"I can't answer that. I just know I didn't shoot it."

"Huh," Josh said.

I couldn't take it any longer. "One of your neighbors was killed?"

"She lived in the house you're renting," Chaz said automatically then froze when he realized what he'd said.

I nodded somberly. "I knew something bad had happened there because I could feel the residual negative energy in the house." I felt my cheeks flush when everyone looked at me. "I'm just sensitive to stuff like that." I hoped they would accept my statement without asking a bunch of questions.

"Tell us about yourself," Josh said to Jonathon, diverting attention away from me. I was so grateful to him for his help. Everyone looked at Jonathon, but he was too busy looking at me to answer right away.

Finally, he looked at Josh and said, "Well, that's not an easy story to tell." I could tell he was searching for something that he could share. Something about Jonathon Silver felt dark and mysterious, possibly deadly. For some reason, it compelled me and made me curious instead of scaring the daylights out of me.

"Another time perhaps," Josh said, saving him too. "How are things going at the club?" *Club?* I once again felt clueless.

I could see the tension fade from Silver's frame, and he began to talk about the club. "I'm more excited about my revitalization plans for Cincinnati. I bought the club because it meant a lot to Nate, but I thought a better way to memorialize him was through improving the city he loved so much."

"Wow," I said softly. "That's a wonderful thing to do." I had done a few of those types of things to honor River as well, but they never brought me the peace I sought. I hoped that it worked better for him.

Jonathon looked at me and winked. "I have my moments," he said. His tone of voice and expression was friendlier than I wanted it to be and I wasn't sure how to react.

Somehow, most of us decided we had enough room for coffee and dessert. The small talk continued as everyone except Kyle ate scrumptious sweets. Talk turned to travel and various places that Jonathon and I lived. My list of places wasn't quite as exotic as his, and I found myself drawn to the deep timbre of his voice.

"What brought you here after living at all those fabulous places?" Chaz asked the both of us.

"I'm researching for a book that I'm planning to write," I said, hoping to clarify the blunder I made earlier. "I like it here, although I'm a little worried about the number of homicides in a small town." The room got quiet, and I realized I said something wrong. "What did I say?"

"My brother was one of the guys killed here," Silver told me.

"Oh damn," I said. "I'm so sorry, Jon."

Jon? I didn't know the man well enough to touch him or use a nickname, but it felt inexplicably right. I placed my hand over Silver's. There it was again, that burn and sizzle that I'd never felt before, not even... No! I would not go there. It was wrong to think like that. Yet, touching him felt... familiar. I wanted to jerk my hand back but couldn't.

"It's okay, Emory." Silver smiled softly and turned his hands over to squeeze mine before he pulled them back. He rose from his chair and said, "I should be heading back to the city. Gabe. Thank you for inviting me to dinner." He then turned to Josh and said, "Dinner was magnificent. Thank you so much." His words of gratitude couldn't disguise the sadness I heard in his voice.

"Anytime," Josh told him. "Have a safe trip home."

The room grew quiet as everyone seemed to get lost in their own thoughts after Gabe walked Jonathon downstairs to say goodbye. I felt terrible for upsetting the guy so much that he practically ran out the door. I felt like I ruined everyone's evening and the best thing I could do was head home.

"I'm going to head home too," I said. "I have an early day tomorrow." I didn't have a fucking clue what I was going to do, but it sounded as good as any other excuse I could make up on the fly.

"Oh, I hate that you're leaving so soon," Josh said. He rose to his feet and offered me a friendly hug. "Thanks for coming tonight, Emory."

"Thanks for the invite. You've all been wonderful company. I'll see you at my appointment in a few days."

"I'll be sure to sharpen my scissors," Josh replied then laughed evilly.

"Goodnight," I said with a wave.

"Goodnight, Emory," they all said collectively.

When I got downstairs, Jon was still talking to Gabe at the door. "I am sorry that I disrespected your relationship with my flirting. It won't happen again."

"Thanks," Gabe told him. "I'll be in touch if I learn anything else." Jon nodded his head and walked out the back door.

Gabe turned when he saw that I'd come downstairs too.

"Man, I feel terrible that I ran your friend off, Gabe."

"You didn't run him off," he replied. "His loss was recent, and he's still coming to terms with things."

"Still, I didn't help matters any."

"You can't be blamed for what you didn't know, Emory." Gabe tipped his head to the side, and I could tell he was deliberating if he should ask me a question.

"Go ahead and ask me," I told him.

"Did you have a vision or something when you shook Silver's hand?"

"Yeah, you could say that," I replied dryly. "He wasn't in danger in my vision, if that was what you were concerned about." Gabe looked relieved. "Thank you for a lovely evening," I said. "I'll see you around the neighborhood."

"Take care, Emory."

I held my shit together until I got home then I did two things I hadn't done in quite some time. I got rip-roaring drunk and prayed for a night without dreams. I didn't want to see Jon Silver again in my sleep, and I sure as hell couldn't face my husband.

EIGHT

Jon

DIDN'T LEAVE GABE AND JOSH'S HOUSE BECAUSE I WAS UPSET; I
left because the evening stirred feelings inside me that I didn't want
or need in my life. I still felt out of place in the sit-down dinners
with fancy china, real silverware, and crystal drinking glasses,
because until I met Nate, I was a takeout food and paper plate kind of
guy. I was slowly becoming acclimated to the finer things in life, even
though I tried not to get too dependent on them. I didn't want to
become too soft, in case I needed to uproot my life and start all over
again someplace. It wasn't the dishes or silver that had me on edge; it
was the people—or their close relationship to be specific.

I had two best friends that I would lay my life down for at any
given moment. We forged that bond while under fire in the heat of

battle. I knew that Beau Rossi and Corbin Bouchard would do the same for me too. Still, what we shared was nothing like Josh and Gabe had with their friends. I couldn't complete Beau's sentences or anticipate Corbin's next move outside a mission. I wouldn't be able to jump in and start quoting lines from their favorite television shows or movies. Hell, we never had time to watch movies or television. Our life was one mission after the other. What little downtime we had was spent fucking, although never with each other. Nothing would screw up a camaraderie quicker than fucking, sucking, or jerking each other off. Were we tempted? Hell yeah, but we made a pact to let nothing come between our brotherhood, and we stuck to it.

I was flattered by Gabe's invitation and appreciated his kindness, even if he extended it out of pity, but I felt like a fish out of water. I wouldn't say that all of them were on the same page because Emory seemed a little out of place also. *Emory.* Damn that long, beautiful brown hair that hung to his shoulders, luminous green eyes that showed his every emotion, and lips made for kissing revved me up. I wondered if his fair skin felt as soft as it looked. *Kissing? Since when did I look at a man's mouth and think about kissing?*

I was ready to fist his long strands of hair and kiss him until we were breathless. Hell, I didn't even like long hair on a man, so what the fuck was it about Emory? The sadness I saw in his eyes called to me. I wanted to ease his pain and maybe find a way to lessen mine in the process. What would it be like to wake up one day and not feel the burn of heartache and sting of disappointment? It wasn't something I ever entertained until I looked into his green eyes.

Hell, I was randy and ready to fuck before he even introduced himself. When our skin touched during the handshake, it felt like I'd stuck my dick in an electrical outlet. I knew that Emory felt it too because his eyes widened before he closed them for a few seconds. When he reopened them, I saw so much grief and pain that I wanted to do anything to make him feel better. I'd never reacted to anyone as I did him. I never wanted to pull someone into my arms just so

I could tuck their head beneath my chin and hold them. I had this intense feeling that Emory needed me and that I needed him just as much, but he shut down right before my eyes. A cool distance replaced the sadness and awareness I saw moments earlier. I felt his silent rejection like a slap in the face.

My gut instinct told me not to back down, so I sat beside him to eat dinner. Josh served some of the best dishes that I'd ever had, but even that wasn't enough to diminish my awareness of Emory. When the conversation turned to getting to know both Emory and me, we both seemed a little reluctant to divulge information. Hell, most of my locations and activities were top secret, and I couldn't share with the group, but what was Emory's deal? He seemed more mysterious than any spy I'd ever come into contact with during my years in covert ops.

I chastised myself the entire meal for even thinking about chasing a guy who clearly didn't want my attention. He sat ramrod straight next to me throughout the dinner until he learned that my brother was one of the murders in Carter County. Then he turned his luminous eyes on me, covered my hand with his, and sincerely apologized. It was that moment that I was certain of two things: I hadn't seen the last of Emory Jackson, and I would one day know if his lips were as soft as they looked.

Maybe that knowledge was what pushed me to my feet and out the door so quick. Perhaps it was the culprit for my restlessness and the feeling that something important like a vital organ was missing in my life. I resented the images of Emory that popped up in my head like fucking screenshots on a cell phone. Oh look, here's Emory smiling across the table at something Chaz said. Oh, wouldn't I like him to run his middle finger along my dick like he did the water goblet? How the fuck did I even know it was called a goblet? For fuck's sake, I was losing my ever-loving mind pining over a man I didn't even know.

Get to know him, Jon! I ignored that damn thought the first million times it crossed my mind, but finally gave in a few days after the dinner. I didn't have a lot of expectations, but I sure as hell didn't expect what I found. *A psychic?* He didn't advertise his abilities or have his own business. He spent his time traveling around the country helping state and local law enforcement agencies solve crimes. He even appeared on a few psychic detective shows, but he didn't seem to profit off his work. His story about writing a book was the shittiest cover story I'd ever heard. I didn't know jack about writing a book, and it was obvious Emory didn't either. How did he pay his rent or buy groceries? His clothes were casual, but they looked expensive to me.

I scrolled further down and clicked on an article that discussed when and how his abilities began. Then the reason for his sadness became crystal clear to me. Emory was still devastated by the loss of his husband, River. Was he living off his husband's life insurance money? Wrongful death lawsuit? I wasn't sure why it was important for me to know; it just was.

I kept scrolling through the pages until I finally found an article that included his surname, Emory Connor Whelan. The psychic articles shocked me, but the ones that came up when I googled his surname knocked me for a loop. Emory was the son of Donovan Whelan and Audrey McIntire-Whelan, which didn't ring any bells, but I sure as hell recognized his grandfather's name. Emory was the only grandson of Connor Morgan Whelan, CEO of Whelan Whiskey. Fuck, that was my absolute favorite and some seriously expensive stuff.

I saw an article where Whelan Whiskey welcomed Emory on board as Director of Research and Development. They included a picture with the article and Emory couldn't have been more than twenty-one or twenty-two at the time. His smile was broad and confident, and there were no signs of the sadness and disillusionment I saw a few days prior. Of course, who wouldn't look confident in a suit that easily cost nine thousand dollars? I couldn't take my eyes off his smile though. That was Emory before life kicked him in the balls.

That was the Emory I wanted to kiss awake after a long night of loving so I could do it all over again.

Wait! What? Oh, hell no. I didn't do sleepovers and slowly kissing a lover awake. *You will with Emory*, my mind whispered. I wanted no part of the protective feelings that surged through me every time I thought of how much he hurt or the desire that hummed through my body when I pictured his face and remembered the way he made me feel alive for the first time in… ever. Emory Jackson was a broken man who would require a lot more than I had to offer him. Besides, most days I felt just as shattered as he did. What kind of help was half of a man to another who was also missing huge pieces of himself? *Two halves make a whole.*

"Shut the fuck up!" I said out loud. Fuck, what I feared had come true. I had gone soft.

Quick! I needed a diversion! I looked at my watch and saw that it was only ten o'clock. I could get dressed and head to the club to pick up some action. Maybe fucking someone else would wipe out Emory's face every time I closed my eyes. Maybe I could sink my dick in a tight, welcoming hole and not picture fisting that glorious mane of hair while I rocked in and out of Emory. I rose to my feet and headed to my bedroom to give it a try when my ringing cell phone stopped me.

I walked over to the hallway table where I laid it and saw that Beau was calling me. I smiled because I was certain that talking to my best friend would pull me out of my funk.

"Howdy, Deputy," I said into the phone. In a surprising move, Beau had retired from our unit first and moved to Big Timber, Montana, to pursue a career in law enforcement. He'd taken a lot of ribbing from us about his decision, but he held firm. He had said that it just felt right. I always suspected there was a bigger reason, but I decided to wait until he came clean on his own.

"That's Sweet Grass County Sheriff to you, asshole," Beau said into the phone. I heard the smile and pride in his voice.

"Sheriff? Hell, you've only been there a year. Who'd you have to fuck or kill to get the job?" I pondered out loud.

"I didn't fuck or kill anyone, but the old sheriff went boots up a few months back, and they held a special election. Yours truly won in a landslide," Beau replied.

"Again, who'd you fuck or kill?"

"You just jumped to the top of my shit list," Beau replied sarcastically. "I haven't had a moment to catch my breath since the election, and I've missed talking to you. How're things going?"

"Nothing as exciting as winning an election."

"Let me be the judge of that," Beau told me.

"Okay, but I'll probably bore you to death," I warned. I told my friend about the suspected theft in the club and the latest development in my brother's case. "I just can't believe that Rick was involved."

"Then he probably wasn't. I've never known anyone as intuitive as you are when it comes to reading people." *You should meet Emory.* I tried to stop the snort that left my mouth but couldn't. "What's that snort supposed to mean?" Beau asked. "You know damn well that you're a human lie detector." He got quiet suddenly then added, "I could use a guy like you on my team."

"Not gonna happen, my friend."

"It's fucking beautiful here, Jon. The clear blue skies, lush grass, breathtaking mountain views, and the people are as friendly as can be."

"If it's so peachy then why would you need a human lie detector?" I inquired.

"There's this cold case that I'm working in my free time. A ranch hand went missing ten years ago, and no one seems to know what happened to him."

"Do you suspect foul play locally?" I asked.

"Man, I don't know. Big Timber was his last known whereabouts. The rancher who hired him admitted that there had been a big fight amongst his ranch hands and this guy quit. He demanded his last paycheck and another ranch hand drove him to the bus station north of Big Timber. The rancher said he could've gone anywhere."

"Well, he had to cash his check," I replied. "Did the rancher provide a copy of the canceled check? I mean, it's been ten years, but he could still get a copy."

"He doesn't use checks for payroll; he hands them cash each week," Beau replied.

"Well, that right there sounds suspicious."

Beau let out a frustrated sigh. "Yeah, I thought so too. The family hasn't given up after all this time, and I'd love to be able to give them some closure."

"I know how they feel and my brother has only been dead a few months. Nate's murder was a horrible shock, but not knowing what happened to someone you love has to be the worst kind of torture." I knew all too well that emotional torture was far more harmful and painful than the physical kind.

"Man, I'm sorry," Beau said. "I didn't mean to be so damn thoughtless."

"Nah, I don't want you tiptoeing around me or treating me like fragile glass. Neither applies to this battle-hardened bastard."

"I know what a badass you are, Jon, but that doesn't mean I just run roughshod all over your feelings," Beau replied.

"I don't have feelings."

"I remember you singing about them in a bar in Albuquerque."

"I lost a bet and was forced to sing karaoke," I fired back.

"Mmmm hmmm. That's what I'd say too." Then he started humming the tune to Barbara Streisand's "Feelings."

"Shut up, man."

Beau's laughter cheered me up, and I felt better than I had in months. "You seemed to know the words pretty well, buddy. You didn't stumble and stutter while you read the words on the screen like everyone else. In fact, I seemed to recall you not needing to read the words at all."

"You were too drunk and fixated on that little blond bit of a waiter to even notice what I was doing up on stage."

"I'm a multitasker, and I wasn't even close to drunk. You knew the words and sang from the heart."

"It was one of my mom's favorite songs, okay?" I groused.

"Finally, the truth comes out."

"Five minutes ago I would've said that I missed you, but now I'm hoping a coyote eats your sorry ass," I said. Beau heard the laughter in my voice, and he only chuckled more.

"Not a chance, my man. You take care of yourself and don't be a stranger. Seriously, come see me in Montana if you need a break or some fresh air. There's nothing more beautiful in the world than drinking a cup of coffee while watching the eagles soar over the mountain ridge."

Emory's image rose up swift in my mind, and I knew that Beau was wrong. I could think of something—or someone—more beautiful, but I kept my mouth shut. I wasn't ready to acknowledge the emotions Emory stirred inside me, let alone speak them out loud to my friend. "I'll keep that in mind," I said instead.

I felt marginally more settled after I got off the phone with Beau, but I still thought about going into the club. No sooner had the thought left my mind, Michelle called me. "Everything okay?" I asked her.

"I don't think so," she replied nervously. "I hate to bother you at home, but we're having a staffing issue."

"Don't apologize, Michelle. I'll be right there." She was a very capable woman so it must've been a pretty big deal. It looked like I was destined to go to the club after all. At least I wouldn't be sitting around my house thinking about a guy that wasn't meant to be mine.

NINE

Emory

F I WERE WRITING AN AUTOBIOGRAPHY ABOUT MY EARLY DAYS IN
my new town, I would title it Blissless in Blissville. Yeah, there
were some high points like meeting Josh, Gabe, Chaz, Kyle, and
Meredith, but the rest wasn't nearly as pleasant. Restless on Elm St or
maybe Crushing Heartache in Carter County would also be suitable
titles. I hadn't eaten or slept much in the days that followed, and I was
in a downward spiral ever since the first night I dreamed about Jon…
Jonathon Silver. Shortening his name to Jon was a familiarity that I
didn't want or need.

*Your vision indicated you get pretty damn familiar with all of Jon
Silver.* I wanted to deny what I saw was a snapshot of a future event.
I needed it to be nothing more than my deprived sex drive conjuring

up dreams of faceless men followed by my tricked-out psyche filling in the blanks. I knew for a fact that I wanted absolutely nothing to do with Jonathon Silver and there was zero chance of us developing the kind of relationship where he would whisper love words in my ear. No fucking way. My heart rejected the idea outright even though the rest of my body, especially my brain, said he was the key to… something.

I tried not to sleep, but the body could only be deprived for so long before it started making the decision for you. One minute I was watching television and the next I was sound asleep experiencing a new dream with my unwanted lover. In reality, he was unwanted, but in my dream world, I was all over him like a bear on honey. The more dreams I had, the sicker I got inside until I worried that I would fall into a pit of depression so deep I wouldn't be able to climb out of again.

I lost track of time and even the day of the week while I wallowed around in self-pity. Life—like it always did—reminded me that I wasn't the one steering the boat. I sat at my kitchen table staring into my cup of coffee trying not to recall my most recent dream of piercing blue eyes that seemed to look into my soul and touch me in ways that I didn't know I wanted when someone knocked sharply on my back door. *Oh my God! It's him! So much for not thinking about it.* I froze in place, afraid to move or even breathe. He'd leave if I didn't answer the door. Instead of leaving, the knocking became more persistent.

"I know damn well you're inside, Emory," Josh said angrily. "I see your black Mini in the driveway with its showy, look-at-me stripes. Answer this damn door before I call the cops and tell them I smell an odd odor coming from your house. They'll think you're dead because that's our new normal and come busting through the door." He banged some more and added, "You better have clothes on unless you want them to see you in your skivvies or buck-ass naked."

Fuck! I remembered that I had an appointment to have Josh color and trim my hair. I was slow to move even though I was relieved that it was only my new friend and not my future lover. I made my way to the rear door and parted my curtains so Josh could see that I was alive and there was no need for him to call 911. I had avoided looking in the mirrors so that I didn't have to see my traitorous reflection. I worried that he would look satiated and happy when I felt dead inside. I must've looked horrible because Josh audibly gasped when our eyes met through the glass.

He'd been furious when he came over; I heard it in his voice and could tell by the way he pounded on my door. He took one look at me, and the starch faded immediately from him.

"Please let me in, Emory."

I unbolted the door and opened it a crack. I had no intention of letting Josh inside. "Hey," I said softly. "I'm sorry I didn't call and cancel my appointment."

Josh plastered a stubborn look on his face and shoved past me. He was much stronger than I expected. He stood in the middle of my kitchen looking at me expectantly. What did he want? I already apologized to him. I felt frustration rising to the surface, and I was happy to embrace another emotion besides sorrow.

"Josh, now isn't a good time."

"Now's the perfect time because I happen to have an empty salon chair for the next one hundred and eighty minutes. So," Josh pulled out a chair and sat down at my kitchen table, "why don't you tell me what's going on. Every time I turned around, you were in my face, and today I had to force myself on you. That's a big turn of events. I'm starting to get my feelings hurt that you didn't like my cooking or something."

"You know that's not the case," I said in a grim voice. "I just had a setback and needed time and space to deal with it." I just wanted to be left alone so that I could sort things out. Hell, I hadn't returned Memphis's phone calls, and he was closer to me than any living person. *Not for long.* I fisted and unfisted my hands, unsure of what to do with them. I wanted to press them to my ears, but it wouldn't do any good. The disturbing dialogue was internal. I glanced at Josh to see how he was taking my nervous breakdown, certain that he was ready to bolt from my house. He was too busy looking around my kitchen speculatively to notice my fidgeting and twitching.

I couldn't tell what he was thinking, which I thought was odd until I remembered he claimed to be a hellacious poker player. His impassive mask slipped the second he locked eyes on me again. "Talk to me, Emory. You can tell me anything; I promise you that I won't gossip."

I looked away from Josh's earnest eyes and watched my finger draw the infinity symbol on the shiny wood surface of my kitchen table. River and I had planned to get matching infinity tattoos, but he died before we got them. *So what's stopping you from getting one now?* That was the first thought I'd had in days that didn't make me sick to my stomach.

"I'm not sure talking about it will help me, Josh, but I appreciate your willingness to listen," I said after several quiet moments.

Josh covered my hand to stop the motion. "I have to be honest with you, Emory. It looks like not talking is killing you. Is this about a vision?"

I snorted and said, "You could say that."

"It's about Jonathon Silver, isn't it?" I snapped my gaze up to Josh in surprise. "I saw the way you reacted to him when your hands touched. Is he in trouble?"

"I don't know about that, Josh. It wasn't *that* kind of vision," I somberly said.

Josh looked confused for a long moment then said, "Oh," when he realized why my vision shook me.

"Yeah," I replied. "I, um… *we* appeared to be very happy in the vision." My tone of voice was so grave that you would've thought I just announced the end of the world was near. To be honest, that was exactly how I felt.

"You don't want to be happy, Emory?"

"I don't deserve to be happy, Josh, and that's my problem. I just can't. Not after what happened…" My words broke off before I could finish. Josh seemed to know what I almost said, but how could he? Josh couldn't possibly begin to understand the depths of my despair unless he had experienced a similar type of loss. I prayed that he didn't know how it felt because I wouldn't wish that on anyone, especially not someone I was starting to think of as my friend.

"You don't think River would want you to be happy?" Josh asked me.

"River wouldn't want you to be lonely." "River would want you to move on with your life and be happy." "River would want you to rejoin your rightful place in the company." Everyone was suddenly an expert on what my husband would and wouldn't have wanted for me. Odd, when some of them didn't bother to know him while he was alive. I'd heard every variation of what people thought River would want for me, but I couldn't be sure. Besides, moving on and finding happiness isn't something River could choose for me. My heart had to choose, but it had died with River. I mean, I still had a beating organ in my chest that pumped blood and oxygen throughout my body, but the part that knew how to love and accept love was gone.

"Josh, if not for me, he wouldn't be dead. I don't have the right to go out and be happy after what I did."

I could tell Josh wanted to know what happened, but I also saw that he'd never ask me. Instead, he reached across the table and covered both my hands with his. "Whenever you want to talk, I promise to be here—well, unless your visions tell you differently," he added wryly. "Until then, why don't you tell me what you had planned to do with your hair today. I'll get my stuff and do it here instead."

"You don't have to do that, Josh. I can reschedule."

"Honey, your roots will be grown out hideously by the time you get in again. It was a miracle you got in when you did. My skills are in high demand," Josh said confidently, but not arrogantly. "I've got the time and skill; you have the peace and quiet."

My lips quirked up in the first hint of a smile in days. "Okay," I finally said after a long pause. "Thank you."

Josh rose to his feet and headed for the door but stopped suddenly. He turned and looked at me suspiciously. *Did he think I would ignore him when he returned?* Instead of leaving, Josh called Chaz and asked him to bring the things he needed to my house.

When the knock came on the back door, Josh was careful to block me from Chaz's view. "Do you need me to reschedule your next appointment?" Chaz asked Josh in concern.

"No, I'll be back in time. Thank you, though." Josh faced me again once he shut the door. He smiled then asked, "Color and trim?"

I was ready to say yes automatically, but an irrational thought occurred to me. In all my visions, Jonathon Silver was fascinated by my long hair. He fisted it, ran his fingers through it, and pushed it back off my face. My life had seemed out of control, as if I was nothing more than a puppet on an invisible string, once I started having visions. I did everything they revealed to me because it at least felt right, but not Jonathon. That was too much. "I want a haircut, not a trim." I felt an insane rush of power flow through me once the words left my mouth.

"Like a few inches or…"

"Short," I replied. "I want something new." It was such a drastic change; I could tell Josh was uncertain. "I'm positive," I told him before he could voice his concern.

"I told you to quit reading my mind, Emory. It's just fucking rude." Josh's prim tone was at odds with his crude language, and it made me laugh for the first time since… the last time he made me laugh. Maybe Josh was the reason I moved to Blissville.

"You search for hairstyles you like on your phone while I whip up magic potions in my bowls," Josh said while he unpacked the bag Chaz brought him. "It'll help me know where best to place your highlights."

"I want something chunkier this time," I told him while searching on my phone. "It doesn't need to look natural. In fact, I want it to be more obvious."

"Damn, you sound like one of the dramatic before and after advertisements," Josh teased. "If that's what you want, Emory, then that's what I'm going to do."

"It's what I want," I said with more conviction than the last time.

"Then that's what you shall have, Emory."

Josh wrapped a cape around my shoulders and got to work. I closed my eyes and enjoyed the feel of his fingers through my hair, which was nothing like I felt with River or... When Josh touched my hair or scalp, it felt relaxing, not sensual. I relaxed for the first time in days as stress seemed to melt away beneath his talented touch.

A little over an hour later, Josh looked at me like he was seeing me for the first time. "Damn, I'm good," he said. "Let's go find a mirror so you can see your new look."

I stood up and went to the guest bathroom off the living room. I flipped on the light and couldn't believe my reflection. A wide smile slowly spread across my face. "Holy fuck! I look so different with short hair."

"Do you like it?" Josh asked.

Like was too tame of a word. "I love it, Josh. It's just the change I needed too." I ran my fingers through the long bangs that cut across my forehead. I'd picked an asymmetrical cut that made my bone structure look more prominent. My eyes looked bigger, and my mouth seemed wider with the new style. "There won't be any hair for him to fist," I muttered under my breath. My eyes widened when I realized what I spoke out loud. "Um..."

"You don't have to say anything else," Josh told me. "I'll pretend I didn't hear it." He left me alone in the small bathroom, and I stared at my reflection for a long time.

I returned to the kitchen and headed into the pantry. I walked back into the kitchen with the broom and dustpan in my hands. I hadn't planned to talk to Josh about my sorrows. They just rolled off my tongue when I opened my mouth. "I saw something that I am not prepared for now, probably never if I'm honest. I just thought maybe this," I gestured to my hair, "might change the course of things."

Josh looked skeptical but didn't reply.

I began sweeping my hair into piles. "River didn't want to go out that night," I said softly. "He wanted to stay in, order pizza, and watch his favorite movies. I insisted we go out on the town for his thirtieth birthday. If I had just listened to him..." My words broke off, and I began to cry.

"Emory." Josh dropped what he'd had in his hands and hugged me tightly while my body shook with the force of my sobs. "I'm so sorry."

"He was my whole world, and I didn't listen to him. I put myself first and lost everything that had any meaning to me. I don't want to feel or love again. That part of me died with him in that icy water." I ran my fingers through my bangs again and said, "River loved my long hair; I just can't stand the thought of anyone touching it as he did."

"I wish I could make this better for you, Emory." Josh sounded tearful, and I hated that I upset him.

"Nothing and no one can help me," I told him. Why couldn't I just shut up and let Josh get on with his day? Why did I feel the need to pull everyone into my quagmire of misery? I groaned and covered my face with my hands.

"I hate to leave you here like this, Emory. I will cancel the rest of my appointments and..."

"No! Don't do that for me. I promise you that I'm okay. The whole thing with Jonathon hit me hard and has left me reeling since. I feel better now, Josh. Thank you." I wasn't lying just to get him to leave either. The new haircut felt like a fresh start and would help me move forward.

I could tell that Josh didn't want to go, but he didn't argue. He threw his arms around me once more and hugged me. "I'm just a short walk or a phone call away," Josh said. "Anytime you need a friend."

"Thank you." It amazed me that a person's kindness could move me to tears as quickly as something hurtful. "I'll talk to you soon."

Josh gave me a small wave and walked out the back door. I dried my eyes and went into the living room to retrieve the notebook where I'd recorded my book ideas. I made a few notes while they were fresh on my mind then picked up my cell phone when I finished. I clicked on the camera icon and chose the selfie feature. I was happy to see that my eyes were no longer red and puffy. I snapped the picture before I could talk myself out of it and sent it to Memphis with a message that read: *Guess what I did?*

His response was swift. *I will show up on your doorstep in Blisstucky if you ever ignore my motherfucking calls and texts for three days again. Do you hear me, Em? You scared me to death.*

Knowing I upset him so much caused fresh tears to form in my eyes. *I'm sorry, Memphis. I just had a really bad setback. I won't do it again. I promise. Love you.*

Love the new haircut. And the rest of you isn't so bad either.

At least that part was right again in my world. I would be thankful for small favors.

TEN

Jon

I WASN'T CUT OUT TO MANAGE PEOPLE. I EASILY KILLED ENEMIES of the United States of America without blinking, but settling a dispute between two pissy bartenders, who were fighting each other over a club patron, was not my area of expertise. It would've been easier to take them out and make it look like an accident, but that wasn't my life anymore. Besides, they weren't an enemy to me or my country, and I drew the line at killing people just because they got on my nerves. I wasn't a psychopath for fuck's sake!

Two fucking days later, I could still hear those two dumbasses bickering in my office like two little kids while Michelle and I looked on.

"You're just jealous because he gave *me* his phone number and not *you*," Tyler had said to Jamar.

Jamar looked down at his nails as if the entire conversation was boring him. "I've had his phone number for a few weeks, jackass." Jamar rolled his eyes dramatically. "You know what? You can have him because I don't want a guy who has such pitiful taste in men."

Tyler put his hands on his hips and cocked his head to the side. "Oh yeah, Jamar? I seem to recall that you liked how I tasted just fine. What happened to, 'Oh, baby, you're the best I've ever had'? I believe those words slid out of your mouth right after my cock did."

"That was last week," Jamar said with a casual shrug.

"Then why don't you want me calling Brandon? Are you jealous?" Tyler demanded.

"Of you?" Jamar sounded like it was the most ridiculous thing he'd ever heard, but I wondered if Tyler might be right. Then I questioned why the fuck I even cared.

"That's enough!" I yelled before Tyler could answer. Both men jumped a little and stiffened at the harsh tone I used. "I can't believe I got called in here for some *Knots Landing* bullshit." I could tell by their confused expression that they'd never heard of the show. I only knew because it had been my mother's favorite. "Never mind," I groused. "You two work out your problems *after* your shift is over. I don't want to see you bring your personal shit in here again? Do you hear me?"

The two men glared at one another briefly before they responded to my question. "Yes, sir," they said at the same time.

"For what it's worth, I'm not sure how any of you had time to notice the patrons when you're so busy eye fucking one another. Sort. It. Out. Fuck. It. Out. Just do it *away* from the club."

Their faces flushed pink with embarrassment, but I noticed they dropped their pretenses when they looked at one another again.

"Do you want to come over after work?" Jamar asked Tyler.

"I'd love that, J."

"There you go," I said encouragingly. "Now get the fuck out of my office."

They left without another word. I saw Tyler pull Jamar to him for a quick kiss in the hallway before the door shut. I returned home after the argument was solved. *Home?* It was Nate's home, but it never felt like mine. It was too modern and wasn't a good fit for me, but selling the house seemed wrong.

Nagging thoughts of Emory didn't do anything to alleviate my discontent with my surroundings and new career as a club owner. I couldn't get his haunted green eyes out of my mind. I felt like I was losing my freaking mind in the days that followed Easter Sunday. I kept as busy as I could by staying on top of things at the club and monitoring the sales and income data. So far, the thief hadn't struck again. I had a feeling that he or she would wait until they thought I'd lost interest before they started siphoning money and liquor from my club again. If so, they didn't know jack about me.

By mid-week, I was ready to climb the ceiling. I was minutes away from making arrangements for a long weekend in New Orleans to see if I could find my center again, but that didn't feel right to me either. I hated the hold that Emory unknowingly had on me. It felt like he had my cock in a cage and had the only key. I wasn't used to being on anyone's leash, and I hated it with a fucking passion.

"Fuck it," I snarled after running five miles on the treadmill. I headed into the home office to retrieve my phone to make the arrangements and saw that I missed a call from Gabe. He left a brief message and asked me to call him at my earliest convenience. There was a lightness to his tone that I'd only heard when he spoke to, or about, his boyfriend. He sounded happy. Did that mean he had a break in Nate's case?

"What's up, Gabe?" I asked when he answered the phone. I figured we were on a first name basis after our little holiday dinner together.

"I made an arrest in your brother's case, Silver." Okay, maybe he wasn't quite ready to be best buds, but I was willing to overlook it in light of his announcement. "I can't give you any details right now, but I'm certain I've got the right man. I'll share more with you when I can."

I dropped in the nearest chair as all the air whooshed out of my lungs in relief. Damn, I worried that the day might never come when I heard those words. "Thank you, Gabe. This means so much to me."

"You're welcome, Silver." I expected him to hang up right away, but he surprised me. "We host a dinner every Sunday for our friends. There's always more than enough food, and you're welcome to join us anytime."

"I don't know how to respond to that," I said honestly. Was I the kind of man who gathered with friends every Sunday for dinner and chatting about the things going on in our lives? I didn't use to be that kind of man, but could I be?

"You don't have to respond," Gabe said casually. "Just know that our door is always open."

"Thank you."

"Take care, Silver."

I sat there for several long moments after we hung up. I didn't care that I was getting my sweat all over the leather sofa in my home office. I cared about the fact that Nate was going to get his justice after all. I was curious as hell to know who was arrested and the kind of evidence the cops had, but I knew Gabe would tell me as soon as he could. I hoped like hell that Rick's name would get cleared in the process.

It took a few more days for the information to cycle around. Attorney Rylan Broadman from Goodville, which was a neighboring community to Blissville, was arrested for the murders of Nate, Owen Smithson, Lawrence Robertson, and Rick Spizer. Broadman had been Robertson's attorney at the time the casino consortium tried to buy the farmer's land to build a casino. The local county commissioners shot the casino down, so the wealthy consortium CEO pulled strings to get the issue on a statewide ballot. The initiative failed, the casino was never built, and that appeared to be the last of it until Rick pitched the idea to my brother.

That one conversation most likely led to all of the deaths. Was that why Rick said he was responsible? He didn't physically kill anyone, but did he feel those deaths on his conscience just the same? The police released frustratingly few details in the early days, but I knew they didn't want to risk fucking up a trial. That, or they still only had pieces of the puzzle—enough to arrest him, but maybe not enough to get a conviction. As much as it pained me, I knew I'd have to wait it out.

"You've waited this long, what's another few weeks?"

Those few weeks turned into months. The next thing I knew it was June and I was still stuck in a fucking rut. I tried to avoid restlessness by going to the club more and getting involved in the Queen City initiatives I started to honor my brother. I did things like attend weekly Rotary meetings and clean parks at the ass crack of dawn on Saturday mornings. I attended ribbon-cutting ceremonies at new outdoor sports complexes for kids. Oddly, the more I was around people, the more isolated I felt.

Every Sunday, I remembered Gabe's invitation to their weekly dinners. Every Sunday, I was tempted to get in my car and drive to his house, but I stopped just short of doing it. I didn't want to see Emory. I couldn't get him out of my mind, and he chased me in my sleep. Of course, it didn't help matters when I continuously searched for more articles about him or watched the episodes of the psychic detective show that featured him. I had it bad, but I wasn't quite sure what *it* was. Lust? Obsession?

Toward the end of June, I couldn't take it any longer. I had to see him again to know if the pull I felt toward him was real or imagined. Was he as gorgeous as I remembered? Were his eyes the lightest shade of green I'd ever seen before or was that me just being fanciful? Did he still wear that sadness around him like a cloak? Were his lips as full and plump as I recalled, and why did I want to kiss them until he smiled? Since when the fuck did I start thinking like some sappy-ass, bodice-ripping, romance hero from a Harlequin novel? Yeah, okay, maybe I read of few of my mom's books when I was a teenager, but I treated it as a How Not to Act guide. Yet, there I was taking a page from one of those books.

I tried losing myself in someone else's ass once, and I was miserable afterward but couldn't understand why. I owed Emory Jackson nothing. He was no one to me. *But he could be everything to me.* I hated that voice in my head that was always right. It had never led me astray in any situation or on a mission. That voice told me to get in the fucking car, drive down the fucking interstate to some town named Fucksville, and spend time with Emory. I noticed that my little voice didn't say spend time fucking Emory. Spend time with him. Like how? Gaze into his eyes across the table? Hang on to every word that left his lips? I wasn't that guy! That same little voice that told me to go to Emory also informed me that Emory required more than I could give. *Wanted to give.*

I got in my fucking car and drove down the interstate toward Fucksville to see Emory. I had talked myself in and out of going so many times that there was no way in hell that I would make it to Gabe's house in time to eat. I'd settle for Josh's cold leftovers in place of most people's hot cooked meals any day. I questioned my actions every mile that I drove because Emory and I had nothing in common besides heartache. We both survived losing people that meant the world to us. I wasn't sure that was the best kind of foundation to build a relationship on and I...

That thought almost shocked me enough to pull off at the next exit and turn around. I didn't do relationships. That wasn't what I wanted. I didn't need to sleep with the same person each night and wake up next to them the next morning. I didn't need someone to anticipate my desires or finish my sentences for me. That was the last damn thing I wanted. *Liar,* that little voice said.

I pushed on and arrived at Gabe and Josh's well after the party started. They were playing some backyard game where they threw bags at a board with a hole in it. They were so into it that they didn't notice my arrival, so I just stood there for a few seconds. I couldn't deny the disappointment I felt when I didn't see Emory, but it was brief because I knew where he lived from one of the conversations at Easter dinner. There were several more people there than the last time, and I felt guilty for just popping in unannounced.

My stomach started growling when my nose picked up the scent of delectable grilled meats in savory sauces. Gabe told me I was welcome anytime and I was there to collect. "Hey, everybody. Sorry I'm late," I said, waving awkwardly. I was so fucking clueless how to behave properly in social gatherings. Everyone stopped what they were doing to look at me. "Maybe I shouldn't have dropped in on you guys," I said, sounding as embarrassed and uncomfortable as I felt.

I looked around the crowd hoping to see a welcoming face. All I saw was curiosity from the guests who hadn't met me on prior occasions and surprise from the ones who had. Then my gaze locked on a pair of particularly green eyes that looked irate that I had showed up. My first thought was, *why the hell does Emory look so angry?* Unfortunately, I blurted out my next thought. "What the hell did you do to your beautiful hair?" And what was with the designer beard he'd grown? No wonder I didn't recognize him until his eyes met mine. I wanted the old Emory back. I needed—not wanted—to run my fingers through his hair, tangle my fists in it while he sucked my dick.

Emory narrowed his eyes, sat straighter in his chair, and lifted his chin proudly. "Josh cut it for me." He ran his hand over the shorn locks and smiled smugly. *Well, he'll just have to grow it back out.*

I pinned the hair stylist with my meanest look. How dare he? Was he getting back at me for flirting with Gabe? *Don't be ridiculous, dumbass.*

Josh didn't look one bit intimidated by me. "Hey, I do what my clients ask. Emory wanted the Bieber special, and that's what he got," he announced. I had no idea what the fuck a Bieber special was, but I didn't like it.

"Not that it's your business," Emory said icily.

I made a beeline for Emory, ignoring his standoffish tone and demeanor. I sat in the vacant seat beside the man and kept staring at him until he couldn't ignore me any longer. "What?"

"It makes your eyes look even bigger and greener," I told him.

"I don't have to sit here and listen to this," Emory replied as if I'd just insulted him. He jumped to his feet and practically stomped across the yard in the direction of his house. Although I couldn't say why I did it, I jumped up and followed him.

"What's your problem?" I demanded to know. I had never done anything to him to deserve such blatant animosity from him. Sure, my question about his hair was rude, but then I followed it up with a nice compliment. Emory didn't reply; he walked faster, and so did I.

He turned around when we reached the steps at his back door. "Leave me alone, Jonathon," Emory whispered in a voice thickened by tears.

I wanted to walk away from him and just forget I had ever met him, but I knew that wasn't going to happen. "I don't think I can, Emory."

ELEVEN

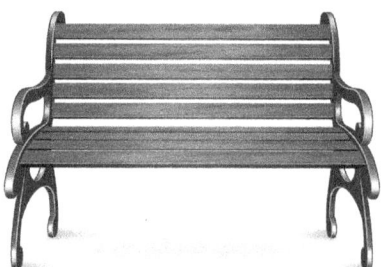

Emory

SWALLOWED HARD TO DISLODGE THE LUMP OF PANIC THAT formed when I laid eyes on Jonathon. I hadn't seen him in two months and had convinced myself that the magnetic pull I'd felt toward him was born out of loneliness, not reality. Damn it; I felt the air crackle around me when he walked into Josh's yard. I didn't even have to look to confirm he had arrived because I felt it. My dreams about him didn't stop completely during his absence, but they were fewer and less intense. I expected them to stop completely over time, but then he showed up, and I knew they'd start all over again.

I worried that I would start craving the sound of his voice and the feel of his arms around me while he slid in and out of me. I couldn't allow that to happen and needed to shut him down before I did something I knew I'd regret for the rest of my life.

"Well, try harder," I said then turned to open the door. I expected Jon to back off, but he didn't. I felt the heat of him as he stepped up behind me.

"If only it were that simple. Do you ever get the feeling that something is destined to happen, even if you don't think it's the best thing for you? That's how I feel right now, Emory."

"I can't give you what you want."

"How do you know that when I don't even know what I want?"

I snorted then said, "Keep telling yourself that and maybe you'll believe it." I remained standing with my back to Jonathon, hoping I would be stronger if I didn't look into his eyes. "I want you to leave. That's what's best for me and if you care for me at all, even the tiniest amount, you'll leave here and never look back."

"I can't do that, Em." I closed my eyes but not before hot tears slid down my face. "I'm going to come inside, and we're going to talk. I promise that I will not touch you." He sounded like he was coaxing a wounded animal out of a corner, but damned if it didn't work for me too.

Even though I knew it was a mistake, I nodded my head. Jon followed me into the kitchen. I watched him as he looked around the room. What did he see? What did my belongings say about me?

"How long have you lived here?" he asked me.

"I moved in right before Easter."

"I moved to Cincinnati a year ago, and I'm still not as settled as you." He finally looked back at me and gave me a tight smile that showed how tense he felt. Why was he nervous? He wasn't on the brink of betraying his husband. Or was he? I knew nothing about the man.

"I'm particular about my space," I lamely answered.

The truth was that setting up my house gave me something to do. As much as I resented the visions at times, they gave my life a purpose. Without them, I was flailing about, untethered to anything or anyone. It wasn't a feeling I liked or wanted, but I didn't know how to change it. I didn't want to move on from River; I wasn't ready to find another man to fill my bed and life, but I couldn't deny how lonely I'd become. I might not have known what the answer was, but I knew what—or who—it wasn't. Jonathon Silver was nothing but trouble for me.

He stood in my kitchen with his legs slightly apart and squared shoulders like he was bracing himself for a fight. He wasn't wrong either; I would fight with everything in me to prevent my premonitions from coming true. His expression wasn't as easy to read. His face was a mask of indifference, but his light-blue irises burned hot. Lust? Anger? Regardless, I would not be the moth to his flame.

"I think we need to clear the air," Jonathon said in a calm, rational voice.

"There's nothing to clear," I countered. "I'm nothing to you; you're nothing to me."

"You think it's that simple?" Jonathon took two steps toward me. I took three steps back. Jon jerked to a stop when he saw my reaction. "Emory…" He broke off and ran both his hands through his hair. "I know you felt *it* the night we met. I saw your eyes widen in surprise when the electricity shot through our bodies."

"So." Denying it existed wasn't working. It was time to change tactics. "That doesn't mean I want or will act on *it*." I ran my hand over the infinity tattoo I had inked over my heart. It felt like River's name was burning my skin like he knew the truth and was calling me a liar. Or, maybe it was anxiety that gripped my heart in its tight fist. Whatever the reason, I felt lightheaded and dizzy. Suddenly, my body felt cold and hot at the same time, and tiny little needles pricked my skin from head to toe. I licked my lips that had suddenly gone dry and numb.

"Emory?" I heard Jonathon's voice, but it sounded like he was calling to me at the end of a very long tunnel instead of five feet away. He walked toward me, but I kept backing away. I hoped he would stop, but I saw the determination in his eyes. "Emory, I just want to help you."

"Then leave," I wheezed between gasps.

"I'd never leave anyone alone in this condition," Jonathon said angrily. "Now be quiet and let me help you." He gripped my bicep firmly, but not painfully, and guided me to a kitchen chair. He gently set me in the chair then placed his hand on my stomach beneath the center of my ribs and the other on my chest. I burned beneath his touch. I wrapped my hands around his thick wrists and tried to push his hands off of me. "Stop it, Emory," he said firmly. "You're hyperventilating, and I can help you. I. Will. Not. Hurt. You."

Hot tears of humiliation flowed freely down my face. No one had ever seen me in the midst of a panic attack and I'd always been able to pull myself out of them on my own. That one was different, and I knew I needed help.

"Ignore my hands on your body, but look into my eyes and listen to me." His demanding, deep voice was nearly hypnotic. "Inhale deeply through your nose, Emory. Hold it for a count of three and release it slowly. When you do, you'll feel my hands moving up and down with your lungs, and your brain will recognize you're breathing even before the fresh oxygen pushes the carbon dioxide out of your body. Do it with me, Emory."

I breathed in slowly, held it for three seconds, and released it. I focused on the way his hands moved up and down with my breathing and pretended that I expelled all the bad energy with every exhale. I repeated the process ten or twelve times before I was completely calm again.

Jonathon pulled his hands off of me and balled them into fists. He didn't look angry or like he wanted to hit me. It looked like he needed to do something with his hands but wasn't sure what. He lowered himself into a chair beside me.

"What caused your panic attack?"

"You," I replied sullenly.

"Emory, I haven't done anything to you so why would the sight of me cause you to panic?" Jonathon sounded truly baffled and a little insulted.

I knew it would take drastic measures to push him away, so I let him have it with both barrels. "I had a psychic vision about you—well. Us."

I expected him to look wary or alarmed, but he squinted his eyes and asked. "What kind of vision?"

"I tell you that I'm a psychic and you don't question it?" My voice had risen by the time I finished my question. I'd never had someone blindly accept my confession. The announcement was always met with a variety of emotions, but acceptance wasn't one of them. "You've searched my name on the internet." Somehow, Jonathon knowing my story felt more personal. I didn't want him to know anything about me, but I was powerless to prevent him from reading about my history.

"I did," he admitted. "I would've believed you if I hadn't."

That comment piqued my curiosity. "You would?"

"I'll share a little bit about my history so that we're on a level playing field." I shook my head because I didn't want to know a single thing about him. *Liar.* Jonathon ignored me and continued talking. "I was a soldier in one capacity or another from the ages of eighteen to thirty-eight. There were too many times on a mission that one of us had a strong feeling that we needed to veer from our plan. We were never wrong when we listened to our instincts."

"And when you didn't?"

Sadness washed over his face. "Lives were lost."

"I'm not sure it's the same thing," I replied.

"Perhaps not, but I'm willing to concede that the brain is capable of things beyond my grasp and that life isn't all black and white. There are many shades of gray."

"And silver," I added. I could tell by the crooked smile that he thought I was doing a word play on his last name, but I wasn't. "Your aura is many shades of silver."

"What does that mean?" he asked uncertainly.

"Silver signifies a person's physical or spiritual awareness. The brighter the silver, the more abundantly the person is in tune with those things. Pure silver usually signals a spiritual awakening." Jonathon snorted skeptically. He could doubt all he wanted, but my eyes clearly detected bright shades of silver mixed in with the darker, murkier tones. "The darker tones result from a person blocking energy. It means they're skeptical, guarded, and not open to new ideas."

"I'm surprised you don't see pure black," he responded.

"Do you know what a black aura means?"

"No, but it sounds ominous."

"It can be," I replied, thinking of the grief and repressed anger the color represented, "and you do have some black mixed in with the bright and murkier shades of silver."

"You're saying that I have a spiritual or physical awakening inside me, Emory?" I noticed that he didn't deny or doubt the other parts.

"It's a small part, but it's there."

"Back to us," Jonathon said, clearly uncomfortable with the thoughts of spiritual and physical awakenings.

"There is no us," I corrected.

"Emory," Jonathon said with a sigh, "you said you had a vision about us. Care to tell me what it was about?"

"No."

"Oh, I think I can guess." He smiled wolfishly at me, and my body reacted on its own accord. "Emory, I don't have the advantage of psychic premonitions, but I don't need them when it comes to you and me." I opened my mouth to argue, but he held up his hand. "Let me say what I need to then I'll go." I nodded my head for him to continue. "I felt the way your body reacted to my touch, and I have never felt that in the twenty-four years that I've been sexually active. I know that you felt it too. I'm also aware that the thought of us together terrifies you and I understand why."

Jonathon inhaled a shaky breath and released it slowly like he was trying to calm a racing heart too. "It scares me too, Emory. You see, I've never had someone to call my own and my soul tells me that you're the one it's waited for all these years." I had to fight the urge to cover my ears. I just told myself to listen to what he had to say so he would go home. Listening didn't mean I had to take it to heart. "I don't know when or how, but someday I will call you mine, and you will turn to me instead of away. You're the answer to everything that's been missing in my life. I'm not psychic, but I know it's true."

I tore my gaze away from his because I saw the truth in his eyes. No matter how much I wanted to deny it, our lives were put on a path to intersect.

Jonathon rose slowly to his feet and made his way to the door. "Emory, do you want me to stop coming around Josh and Gabe's house? They were your friends first."

As much as I wanted to say yes, I couldn't. Loneliness clung to Jonathon like a cheap cologne, and I would never deprive him of friendship. Yet, I couldn't form the words to answer his question, so I just shook my head.

"I gave you an out, but you didn't take it. I think part of you wants what I can give you, but you're still too far in denial to accept it." I couldn't look away from Jon's face as his blue eyes darkened with desire that burned hot enough to singe me where I sat. "One day, I'm going to learn every part of your body with my hands, mouth, and my cock. There will be no parts of yourself that you keep from me, Emory. Until then, take care of yourself."

I slumped over the kitchen table when I heard the door click softly behind him. I willed my heart not to listen to his words, even if my body was jonesing for a chance to take him up on his sexy offer. I was physically and emotionally exhausted and knew there was no way in hell I could return to the barbecue across the alley. I groaned when I remembered the childish way I acted. I bet their tongues would be wagging for days. Josh and Gabe would probably ban me from attending their dinners for making an ass of myself in front of Gabe's colleagues and friends.

I didn't think the day could get any worse, so I didn't even bother checking the caller ID on my phone when it rang. I kept my forehead pressed to the table while I pulled the phone out of my pocket and blindly slid my thumb across the phone as I brought it up to my ear.

"Hello?"

"Are you ready to stop this nonsense now, Emory?"

I was wrong. My day definitely took a turn for the worse when I heard my mother's voice. You know, the same mother who wanted to reconcile but couldn't take my call and waited over two months to return it. I responded by hanging up on her without uttering a single word.

One of the perks of being the heir to the Whelan Whiskey empire was that I never ran out of liquor. I rose to my feet and grabbed a bottle from the cabinet. I didn't bother getting a glass or ice. The kind of day I had was enough to drive anyone to drink, but the biggest reason was the unshakeable belief that Jonathon Silver was right.

PART 2

Acceptance

TWELVE

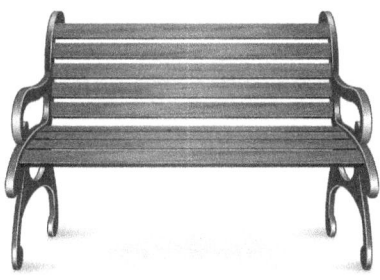

Jon

I SAID I WOULD LEAVE HIM ALONE, YET I STOOD ON EMORY'S FRONT porch not even three months later. I had a legitimate reason for being there, but I wasn't sure he would believe me. We'd seen each other a few times since the chat in his kitchen, and we were always cautiously civil to one another. I was always aware of where he was in a room or even a crowd, but I knew he didn't want to hear that from me.

I had never been much for dancing, but on the night of Josh and Gabe's bachelor party, I wanted nothing more in my life than to hold Emory in my arms while we moved to music. I didn't care if it was fast or slow; I just wanted to feel his body close to mine. Emory never got on the dance floor even with his friends, and I didn't have the nerve to ask him. He went back to his hotel room early, and I retreated to my office because I wasn't sure what else to do with myself anymore.

The phone conversation I had with Beau the morning after the bachelor party prompted me to drive to Emory's house and ask him for a favor he had every right to refuse. Hell, I didn't even expect him to answer the door, but he surprised me.

"Jonathon," he said flatly. He sounded like some stuffy schoolmaster or something, not that I had fancy schools in my background. It was obvious that he wasn't going to make this easy on me, but that was okay because nothing had ever come easily to me in life. "What are you doing here?"

Okay, maybe I was hoping for a little friendlier reception. Damn, Emory's attitude annoyed me. I'd given him space and left him alone when all I wanted to do was hold him close. Did he think this was easy for me? I had never wanted to hold on to a man long enough to let the sweat dry on our bodies after a bout of hot, rough sex. Not Emory; I wanted to hold on tight and not let go. It really pissed me off too.

"Forget it." I turned away headed for the porch steps.

"Jon, wait!" The way he shortened my name stopped me more than his words he chose or the resigned tone of voice he used. "If you drove an hour to my house then it must be important."

I turned slowly to look at him once more. Emory smiled hesitantly and opened the door for me. "I didn't come for myself; I came for a friend."

"Is it Gabe or Josh?" he asked.

"No, Emory. I didn't mean to worry you." I took a seat on his couch, and he sat in the chair on the opposite end, which was as far away from me as he could get without standing across the room. He acted like a prim spinster too afraid to sit next to the big bad wolf for fear of losing his virtue. It rankled my nerves, but I needed his help. "My friend is a sheriff in Big Timber, Montana, and he's working a cold case that doesn't look too promising." I knew there was more at play, but Beau wasn't ready to talk about it. I didn't pressure him because I knew he'd talk when he was ready. "I think he could use your help if you were willing."

"You're asking for a friend, huh?" Emory asked. Was that a little bit of humor I detected? Was Emory letting his guard down enough to make a joke? I felt like I walked on eggshells around Emory all the time and wasn't sure how to answer him. "How good of a friend are we talking?"

"I don't think I follow where you're going with this line of questioning, Emory."

Emory shrugged his shoulders casually then diverted his eyes away from mine. "He must be special if you're showing up at my door asking for favors. That was all that I meant." Was he jealous?

Over the years, I'd had my fair share of run-ins with percussion grenades that left my ears ringing, my head spinning, and severe disorientation, but none of them compared to the upheaval that Emory caused in me. I wanted to tell him it was none of his fucking business what kind of friend Beau was, but I would be lying to both of us. I didn't have the luxury of living in a state of denial because one of us needed to accept the inevitable. When put like that, it sounded like I was comparing our eventual *something* to death, but that wasn't what I meant.

A part of me said to get up and walk out of there and never look back, while the rest said to stand my ground. I wanted to yell that I didn't owe Emory an explanation, but I did if I wanted his help. Were his questions that unreasonable? I was about to ask him to get on a plane and fly to Montana to help a man who was a stranger to him. When the silence between us stretched to an uncomfortable length, Emory raised his head and looked at me.

"I've known Beau for twenty years. He's the best kind of friend," I said in the way of explanation. I could tell that my answer only made Emory more curious, but I also knew that he wasn't going to ask me additional personal questions.

"What can you tell me about the case?" Emory asked.

"Ten years ago, a guy named Kent Jessup disappeared from a ranch in his jurisdiction. Beau told me that one of Kent's family members was pressuring him to look into the disappearance."

"Why now?" Emory asked. "Ten years is like a hundred years in the life of a missing persons investigation—or any for that matter. Why are they suddenly putting pressure on your *friend?*"

I couldn't say he was jealous, but he was definitely curious about Beau. I hoped that curiosity led him to help my friend. "Beau was recently elected sheriff after his predecessor died suddenly."

"So the family hopes the new guy will take a look at the case with fresh eyes or at least an open mind." Emory's eyes had taken on a far-away look, and his reply had come across as him thinking out loud rather than responding to me directly. Then he nibbled on his bottom lip while he processed things internally. I saw the shift in clarity in his beautiful green gaze the second he returned from wherever he'd gone. Emory's cheeks flushed pink beneath my stare like he was embarrassed that he zoned out in front of me. He cleared his throat and said, "What's changed in the case that your sheriff would want to use a psychic?"

"He's not *my* sheriff," I clarified. "What do you mean by what's changed?"

"Well, I've worked with law enforcement officials enough to know that they only call in a psychic on a cold case for two reasons: they're desperate, or they have a new lead and need some guidance. Which category does your *friend* fall into?"

"Why don't you ask me what you want to know?"

"I believe I just did." Emory looked confused about the turn our conversation made. "What has changed for your—"

"—*friend.*"

"I didn't say it like that," Emory argued.

"You did, and more than once. You even referred to Beau as my sheriff. He's not my private sheriff."

"That isn't what I… I meant your sheriff *friend*." He blushed when I quirked a brow at his tone. "I'm not implying anything."

"Maybe not intentionally, but you're giving away your subconscious feelings."

"Are you going to psychoanalyze me now, Jon?" He used my nickname again, and I loved the natural way it rolled off his tongue, like we'd known each other longer than a few months. Hell, we didn't know each other at all.

"Not at all, Em."

"Let's get back to the conversation about your… friend's missing persons case." Emory continued like he hadn't heard me use a nickname for him too, but his eyes had widened slightly, and he had swallowed hard before he spoke again. "You might not have liked my tone, but my question was serious. What has changed?"

"Honestly, I'm not sure. Beau called me this morning to catch up, and he sounded stressed beyond normal. I asked if his new position was creating problems for him in the department since he was the newest member of the group but the one elected to the office of sheriff. Beau denied that there was anything wrong at first, but then he finally admitted it was the Kent Jessup case that had him down."

"Why? If nothing has changed, then why the sense of urgency or despondency?"

"The case might be ten years old, but it isn't to him. He's only lived there for a little over a year," I explained. "Maybe he thought he could approach it with new eyes and make a difference only to come up short like everyone else."

"Or there's more to it," Emory said absently.

I sat quietly while he mentally checked out of our conversation again. I used the time to catalog everything about him and store it in my memory because I wasn't sure how long it would be before I saw him again. I loved the vibrancy of his eyes and the way his bottom lip was slightly fuller than his top one. I found myself staring at the tiny little indentations his teeth left behind in the plump flesh from biting it a moment earlier. I wanted to lick that bottom lip and feel the grooves with my tongue.

Emory cleared his throat to get my attention, and I realized he caught me staring at his mouth. Did he know what I was thinking or did he suspect my thoughts were far dirtier than tracing his lips with my tongue? Fantasizing about those lips wrapped around my cock would've been next. I noticed the familiar way he pressed his hand over his heart. He'd done the same thing the last time I was in his house, and I recognized it as either a sign of distress or comfort. His expression gave nothing away.

"Do your friends always call you early on Sunday morning?" That was the absolute last thing I expected him to say.

I let out a frustrated sigh. "As a matter of fact, Sunday mornings are a great day for me to catch up with Beau and Corbin. And before you ask, Corbin is my other best friend. The three of us make one hell of a trio, but it's never been sexual between us, Emory. I love these men like family, and I'd lay down my life for them. Hell, I'd nearly done that many times in battle just as they had for me. They're my brothers in arms and two of the finest men I've ever had the privilege to know." I paused to breathe. I needed to stop the temper I felt boiling beneath the surface from rising to the top and spilling over. It would ruin whatever tenuous truce we'd made in the past. I realized that the only way to accomplish that goal was to leave. Too bad it wasn't working.

"Maybe you don't care that they had my back and pulled my ass out of the fire, but it means a hell of a lot to me, Emory. You probably wish they weren't so damn good at their jobs a few years back when we were outmanned and outgunned. It would make things a lot easier for you, wouldn't it?"

Emory loudly sucked in a stunned breath. "How can you say that to me?"

"You know what? Forget I ever came here, Emory. While you're at it, try and forget I exist because I'm going to do my damnedest to forget about you." I rose from the couch and headed to the door.

"Jon, wait!"

I ignored his request and walked away without looking back. I couldn't remember a time when I'd been so fucking furious at someone. I was halfway home before I realized that I wasn't angry at Emory; I was mad at myself. Emory told me that he couldn't give me what I wanted. And instead of moving on with my life, I hovered in a holding pattern like a plane circling an airport waiting for permission from the flight tower to land. Emory was never going to give me the go-ahead so it was time to find a new airport that would welcome my approach. *Damn, what the fuck was with my lame-ass analogies?*

It had been a while since I'd had sex with a real person and not just a fantasy version of Emory while I jerked off. I ignored the subtle hints Alexander had thrown my way at the bar and ignored every bit of flirtation from hot, horny men who obviously wanted me. Why? Emory was honest with me from the very start. He. Did. Not. Want. Me. Maybe his visions weren't of things to come but things his body felt deprived of and filled in the blanks. Yes, that was what I needed to keep telling myself, so I could stop jerking off to what could be and start fucking men who were both physically and emotionally willing.

I went home and worked out my frustrations on the elliptical machine and free weights. I thought I had my shit together until I got to the bar. Alexander sauntered into my office wearing painted-on jeans, and I lost my shit. I knew it was a mistake when I rose swiftly from my desk and went to him. He backed up in alarm at first but then wickedly smiled when he realized it was lust, not anger, etched on my face. He continued to back up, but only to lock the door so we wouldn't be disturbed.

It was a fast, furious fuck that left my body satiated but tore my heart to shreds. The combined feeling of guilt for betraying Emory and shame for taking advantage of my employee sent me home without a word to anyone. I didn't even stick around to shower because I wanted to get away from the scene of my disgrace as fast as I could.

Even if Emory wanted me, I didn't deserve a guy like him. Sleep eluded me most of the night, and when I did crash, dreams of a heartbroken Emory invaded my sleep like unwelcomed insurgents. At first, I tried to comfort him over the loss of his husband then I realized that *I* was the one who made him cry. That was an unforgivable crime.

The best description for my mood the next morning was somber. My heart was as heavy as the morning of Nate's funeral, and I realized that I buried my dreams the night before when I buried my dick inside another man. Crude? Yes, but true. I let my pride ruin something great before it even started because I had known that something special would happen between Emory and me.

My dark mood only got heavier when Beau texted me and let me know that Emory had contacted him to say that he was heading to Big Timber to see if he could help him.

"Fuck! What have I done?"

THIRTEEN

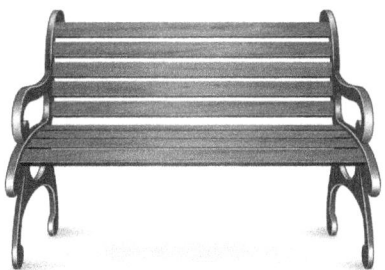

Emory

T HE DAY AFTER JON LEFT MY HOUSE, I WALKED ACROSS THE street to say goodbye to Josh and promise that I would be back in time for his wedding on Saturday. Josh, Mere, and Chaz screamed when I knocked on the back door of the salon.

"Josh, you guys okay in there?" I yelled through the door. Josh immediately opened it and let me in. Meredith was giving Chaz an ass chewing when I walked inside the kitchenette. "Is this a bad time?" I asked, looking over at my friends.

"Meredith is ripping into Chaz for misbehaving; same speech, different ear," Josh told me. "What's going on? You sound upset."

"I have some bad news, I'm afraid," I said.

"Oh my God! What is it? Did you have a vision? Is Gabe in

danger?" He fired one question after the other at me. I felt terrible about causing him a moment's panic. The news that Gabe's ex-part-ner was on the run from the police to avoid a murder indictment had to be stressful for him. It didn't help that the Marshals Service suspected that Jimmy De Soto was heading to Ohio to take out Gabe in the act of vengeance for what he perceived as Gabe destroying his life. No wonder Josh and the gang were jumpy.

I placed my hands firmly on Josh's shoulders, hoping the weight of my hands would calm him like Jon had done for me in my kitchen when I had a panic attack. "No, Josh. My visit has nothing to do with Gabe or the vision. I came over to tell you that I'll be leaving town for a few days, but I'll be back in time for your wedding."

Josh's eyes searched my face for signs, and I knew exactly what he saw. The dark circles from lack of sleep stood out against my un-naturally pale face. "Is everything okay?" Josh asked me.

"No, not really," I admitted, "but I'm going to see if I can change that. I plan on returning Friday in case you need my help before your big day." I pulled Josh to me for a hug and whispered, "You've been a great friend to me, Josh. You can't possibly know how much that means to me."

My words sounded like a goodbye. I could see how concerned Josh was for me, and I was once again grateful to River for sending me to his neighborhood. I wasn't crazy about all the things that had happened since my arrival or *all* the people I'd met, but it was an ex-perience I wouldn't change. An image of Jon Silver storming out of my house in hurt or anger, I couldn't be sure, popped up in my mind to mock me. I just shoved it aside before I lost my nerve.

It had taken courage for him to show up at my house and ask me for help. I'd given him no reason to believe I'd lend him air if he were stuck in a jar. Still, he drove an hour to my house in an effort to help his friend. I couldn't get past the jealousy that unfurled in my gut every time he said the other man's name. Why? I. Did. Not. Want. Jon! Regardless, I behaved out of character for me and pushed Jon to his snapping point. I refused to think about how badly it hurt when Jon said he was going to do his damnedest to forget about me, or the reasons why. I couldn't allow Jon to mean anything to me, not even as a means to scratch the itch that had burrowed beneath my skin.

"Running won't change anything, Emory. Sometimes we must accept that fate—or a higher power—knows what's best for us when we aren't smart enough or brave enough to see it for ourselves. Sometimes you just need to have a little faith."

I nodded subtly and offered a small, uncertain smile before I left without another word. I drove to the airport where I parked my car in the long-term parking garage and boarded a jet to Bozeman, Montana. Once there, I transferred to a smaller plane that flew straight into Big Timber Airport. I had learned that there were a lot of fly fishing, whitewater rafting, and dude ranch adventures in the vicinity which made the airport a great thing for their local commerce.

The first thing that stood out in my mind when I walked out of the small airport was how crisp and fresh the fall air was in the mountains. I noticed the resplendent shades of yellow, orange, and red leaves on the trees as we descended. In Ohio, things were still green. The second thing I noticed was the breathtaking views of the mountains. What must it be like to look at that view every single day? Did people take it for granted after seeing it their entire lives? I didn't think I could ever get tired of seeing the majestic mountains. The final thing I noticed was the tall, imposing figure waiting for me by his big SUV with the sheriff's logo emblazoned on the side. It was quite telling about my current state of mind that I noticed the air, trees, and mountains before I noticed a sexy man wearing tight blue jeans, a pressed beige shirt with a star-shaped badge pinned to his chest, a Stetson hat, and aviator glasses. Hollywood couldn't have cast a sexier sheriff if they'd tried,

Friends my ass.

"Are you Emory?" he asked as I approached his SUV.

"In the flesh," I replied. "You must be Sheriff Rossi."

The man removed his aviator glasses, and his icy-blue eyes assessed me from head to toe. Was he wondering what my relationship was to Jon? I'd asked myself that several times on the trip west. I half convinced myself that I was doing it for justice, which would at least be a noble reason. My conscience told me it was my guilt that propelled me to google the case and the sheriff's number not thirty minutes after Jon left my house. My heart told me it was something more—something that I didn't want to consider.

"Call me Beau," he said with a smile. He extended his hand to me courteously, and I accepted it. "So, you and Jon…"

"No," I said firmly. "There's no me and Jon. I'm here to see if I can help you solve a missing persons case. I have to be back home on Friday for a wedding."

"Jon told me about Josh and Gabe's wedding this weekend." Beau chuckled then added, "I think it might be the first wedding he's attended."

"Really?" Jon eluded to the fact that the majority of his past was filled with harrowing experiences, but I was surprised someone in his inner circle wasn't married.

"Not many are brave enough to take on a portador de la muerte," Beau replied sardonically. *Death bringer?* I knew Jon had blood on his hands, but I didn't expect them to give themselves nicknames. Yet, Beau didn't sound boastful; it was more like lonely acceptance. "Are you ready to head to your B&B?"

"Sure." I'd booked myself into a bed and breakfast that promised the best biscuits and gravy in the US. I'd just have to see about that because Emma at the diner in Blissville made the best I'd ever had the privilege to cram in my mouth.

We were both quiet once we got inside the SUV, but at least it wasn't an awkward silence. I had many questions on my mind, and I figured he did too. I also suspected that both of us questioned the other's role in Jon's life, but I didn't pick up a jealous vibe from him. I still found it hard to believe, but maybe they were only friends.

It didn't take us long to reach Miss Martha's Bed and Breakfast. I looked up at the charming two-story Victorian home, complete with turrets. I had expected something a bit more rustic, but I guess it wasn't that uncommon for city folk to have different style homes than their rural counterparts.

"This house was built two hundred years ago by a big timber ty-coon as a hush payment for his mistress. She turned it into a bed and breakfast so she could be independent of men," Beau told me. "His original ranch is still operated by a younger version of him."

"Did the bed and breakfast stay in the mistress's family also?"

"Yes, sir." He tipped his head toward the wide porch where a young man exited the front of the house in haste. An older woman was hot on his heels giving him a piece of her mind. "The apple didn't fall far from the great, great granddaddy tree. It seems Miss Martha doesn't want Chase Kissander coming around her granddaughter."

"I guess by the way he tucked his tail and ran that he won't be back for quite some time."

"Wrong," the sheriff said. I turned to look at him when I heard the humor in his voice. "This happens at least once a damn day."

"Miss Martha's website didn't tell me that daily entertainment was included with my room and meals."

"That boy isn't going to give up," Beau told me. "I'll give Chase credit because he doesn't act like an entitled asshole like the rest of his kin." He smiled and shook his head. "You've been traveling a while so why don't you get checked in and have a bite to eat. I'll come around and pick you up in a few hours. We'll go over what little information I have and go from there."

"Sounds good."

A beautiful young lady with long, dark hair with an unhappy pout stood behind the check-in desk looking down at her phone. I instantly knew that she was the one who captured young Chase's at-tention with her cornflower-blue eyes and heart-shaped face with the cutest little chin dimple. I also could tell that she wasn't very happy with her grandmother. She squared her shoulders, put her phone in her pocket, and pasted a smile on her face when she saw I had arrived.

"Welcome to Big Timber, Mr. Jackson."

Hearing her addressing me by name caught me by surprise, but then I remembered the online express check-in process required me to provide a photo of my driver's license. "Thank you."

"My name is Caroline, and I work the front desk each day until three. Give me a buzz or stop by if you need anything."

"It's nice to meet you, Caroline. I'll try not to be a pest during my short stay, but I could really use something hot and tasty to eat to tide me over until dinner. If the kitchen isn't open, can you point me to—"

"Nonsense," Martha said when she swept into the room. "I'd never send one of my guests in search of food after traveling all day to get here. How does grilled cheese and a bowl of my homemade vegetable beef soup sound?"

"Divine," I said just barely loud enough to be heard over my growling stomach.

"Caroline, please give Mr. Jackson his room key so he can go upstairs and get settled." Martha turned to me and said, "I'll bring up a tray in fifteen minutes."

"Oh, please don't go to any trouble."

"Nonsense," she said again. "There's a tray stand outside each door for occasions like this. I'll knock on the door to let you know the food is waiting for you."

"That's impressive," I said genuinely. "I think I'm going to like it here."

"It is my hope that you enjoy it so much that you return many times and recommend us to your friends. I'll be up as soon as your food is ready." I didn't have many friends, but I would be sure to tell them about the hospitality. If the food was as good as promised, I was sure Josh would want to fly west and swap recipes.

"Here you go, Mr. Jackson." Caroline handed me an ornate-looking skeleton key on a keychain with the B&B logo on it. Maybe most guys my age wouldn't like to be addressed so formally, but hearing the name I shared with River warmed my heart.

"Thank you, Caroline." I started to walk away but then stopped and leaned a little closer. "Does that scene I witnessed outside happen every day?"

She blushed prettily and nodded her head. "Grandmother thinks Chase is bad news, but I love him."

"She runs him off, and he keeps coming back?"

"Yes, sir." Caroline giggled then covered her mouth so Martha couldn't hear her. She lowered her voice and said, "He's loved me since we were five years old." I guessed them to be in their early twenties, so that was almost their entire lives.

"And have you loved him that long, as well?"

"Yes, sir," she replied proudly.

"Don't give up, Caroline. Fight for love, and you'll never regret it." I gave her a conspiring wink. Some might say I was giving bad advice because look at the heartache I continued to endure after losing River, but I could never regret the eight years, five months, three weeks, two days, and twelve hours we had together.

Once I got upstairs, I unpacked my small bag and kicked off my shoes so I could lounge on the bed while I waited for the highly anticipated knock. The room wasn't as frilly and fussy as I expected as some of the B&Bs that River and I stayed in over the years. The furniture was antique, but sturdy and modernized with neutral fabrics with small pops of color from the current era rather than a reproduction of materials from yesteryear.

I suddenly remembered that I needed to turn my phone back on after the flight. I had promised Memphis I would call when I arrived. It seemed to take an inordinately long time for my phone to turn on, so I set it aside when "the knock" came on the door. I whipped the door open and stepped into the hallway before Martha made it back to the top of the stairs.

She smiled and shook her head at my eagerness. I hoisted the tray off the stand and took it to the small table inside my room. I lifted the lid and inhaled the delicious aroma of bread, butter, melted cheese, and slow-cooked soup into my nose. I paused for a second to appreciate my bounty then devoured it in minutes. I stopped just shy of trying to lick the bowl clean.

My phone vibrated on the bedside table where I left it when it started to come to life. I could tell I had several messages waiting for me. I expected them to all be from Memphis and all of them were but one. I stared down at his message on my phone and told myself not to read it. I didn't do this for him. *Liar.*

Curiosity was the only reason I clicked on his message. *Thank you, Emory.* I spent the rest of my time trying to figure out why those three little words made my heart race while I waited for Beau to arrive.

FOURTEEN

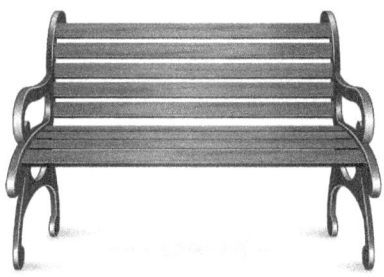

Jon

"H E'S CUTE."

"Who?" I asked Beau, feigning dumb. My friend's warm chuckle let me know he wasn't buying my act.

"He landed safely and is currently at the bed and breakfast getting settled and grabbing a bite to eat before I go over the case with him," Beau said. "He seems nice."

"I wouldn't know." Even I heard the slight bite of bitterness in my voice.

"Well, you must mean something to Emory for him to drop what he was doing and fly to Montana to help me," Beau countered.

"It probably has more to do with a dislike of injustice." *Or perhaps guilt.* "Regardless of his reasons, I'm glad he showed up to help you. When I talked to Emory about your situation, he asked me a question that I couldn't answer."

"What?" Beau hesitantly asked.

"Emory asked me what had changed to cause the sense of urgency and frustration I'd detected in your voice on Sunday. I felt like you were keeping something from me."

"I've been completely honest with you from the beginning," Beau calmly said. "Once his family found out there was a new sheriff they pressed me to look into the cold case. That's all."

"All of that makes perfect sense to me, but you sounded despondent on the phone Sunday morning in a way I haven't heard in a long time. It gives me the impression that this case is more personal to you than you're letting on."

"I was just exhausted and frustrated that I haven't gotten any further in the investigation. I'd hoped that enough time passed that people started loosening up their lips a bit," Beau said dejectedly. Yeah, I bought that excuse too, but I knew there was more he wasn't telling me. I was pissed because we didn't keep secrets from each other, but I respected him enough not to push. He'd tell me when he was ready. "So, there's nothing you want to tell me either?" he asked.

I shook my head no then realized he couldn't see me through the phone. "No," I finally answered. "I still haven't figured out who stole money or hooch from my club and the person must've been scared straight because nothing hinky has happened since we had our staff meeting."

"Could be a glitch in the software program, you know," Beau suggested. "It's not like computers, gadgets, and programs are one hundred percent accurate all the time."

"I've considered that too." And I had. I was cynical by nature, but I truly liked and respected everyone on my staff. None of them gave off shady vibes so I was truly in a conundrum and there was nothing I could do unless the thief struck again. "Time will tell."

"So, there's nothing going on between you and Emory?" Beau

asked. I had a sick feeling in the pit of my stomach that Beau would pursue him if I said no. Yes, there was something going on between Emory and me, but I couldn't claim him. I didn't have the right to after what I'd done.

"Nope. Nothing."

Beau's laughter rumbled through the phone connection. "How about everything else? Did that Broadman guy's confession bring you the closure you were looking for?"

"Yes and no," I replied. "Yes, I feel better knowing that Nate's killer is off the street, but it won't bring my brother back." I still felt the sting of heartache every day, which was why I understood why Emory fought the idea of us. He wasn't ready to move on. "I'm still fucking angry that Rylan Broadman valued farmland over my brother and his other victims' lives." I was especially resentful on behalf of Rick Spizer's widow. Making her think her husband took his own life for even a second was the cruelest act of them all.

"We made a living engaging in battles on behalf of our grateful nation over land disputes, but you never expect that bullshit to happen in your backyard."

"So fucking senseless," I replied.

"Besides New Orleans, this is the longest you've stayed in one spot as long as we've known each other. You haven't met someone special in all this time?" Beau questioned, changing the subject to one that wasn't as sad. Of course, lately my love life—or lack thereof—was pretty pitiful.

"Have you?" I countered.

"I have a *friend*." His answer made me laugh out loud. "What's so funny, asshole?"

"Emory thought that you and I were *friends*," I replied.

"And he didn't like the idea because there is *something* between the two of you, even though neither of you will admit it."

"Shut the fuck up, Dr. Phil," I groused. "When the fuck did we start talking about our feelings?"

Beau laughed hard at my temper. "Maybe now that we're not constantly running for our lives or shooting our way out of trouble we can all find someone that makes our lives a little more pleasant." My response was a grunt. "Then you won't mind if I ask Emory to be my *friend*?"

"I will slit your throat while you sleep," I answered between gritted teeth. The thought of anyone's hands on Emory's body besides mine made me physically ill. Would he feel the same way when I told him what I'd done with Alexander?

Beau laughed until he was out of breath while I gripped my phone hard enough to break it. "I... won't... touch your... man," he told me in between gasps for air. "You're both a couple of idiots."

"Well, this has been fun, but I have things to do."

"Like what?" It was apparent that Beau was enjoying my discomfort.

"Things." I wished that it was true so I could have an excuse to hang up the phone.

"I gotta run anyway. I need to head back over to Miss Martha's and pick up Emory. Or, I can just hang out with him in his room to review the case."

"Beau." I put as much warning into that one word as I could muster. My friend laughed and hung up the phone without saying goodbye.

I looked down at my phone in disbelief. That was the closest thing I'd ever had to a heart-to-heart talk with either of my friends. Sure, we asked what was going on in our lives, but none of us ever hinted around to being lonely or wanting relationships. Fuck, maybe we're just getting old.

Before I could talk myself out of it, I sent a text to Emory's phone. *Thank you, Emory.* That was all I said because nothing else was needed. I set my phone on my desk and turned my attention to my laptop. I was reviewing figures when Beau called me to let me know Emory had arrived safely. I knew he wasn't going to respond to my text and

I was surprisingly okay with it. He knew I was grateful and that was what I hoped to accomplish.

A column of figures caught my attention, and I enlarged the screen so I could look at the column a little closer. I double-clicked at the top, and it brought up more detailed information such as charts and graphs of liquor sales and the times they were made. In addition to the sales, it showed when inventory was checked in from our vendors. Either there was a glaring anomaly in the software, or I had discovered where the new thefts were taking place.

I opened the last inventory order and compared it to the uploaded delivery details. There were two cases of liquor missing, and not just any liquor either. The value of the top-shelf liquor exceeded $2,000 in value. Not only did I find the discrepancy, but I also had the employee code of the person who entered the inventory into the system. I clicked on the number and was shocked when the name came up.

"Michelle?" I asked out loud as I stared at my laptop. "I can't believe it." Or I just didn't want it to be true. She was more than my manager; she had been a rock I could count on during the most difficult time in my life.

I heard my cell phone buzz with an incoming message, but I ignored it in favor of focusing on my problem. I swallowed hard, rose from my desk, and headed out to the bar area of the club. Michelle was there laughing with Stella and Antonio as they got everything ready to open. Her smile was so happy and genuine that I wanted to discredit the evidence. Fuck, I'd gone soft since leaving ops. I blew out a frustrated breath loud enough that the trio heard me over their laughter.

Michelle read my mood immediately, and her smiling lips turned into a frown. "What's wrong, boss?"

"Can you come into my office?"

Michelle dropped the towel in her hand onto the bar and walked toward me. "Sure." Concern and curiosity were the only two emotions

I picked up from her as she followed me into my office. I would have expected to see or feel her fear or guilt if she were the one pilfering booze or money.

"Have a seat," I said, gesturing to the chair in front of my desk.

"What's going on?"

"Was there anything missing in the shipment last week?" I asked, getting right to the point.

"No," she said shaking her head. My heart sank because I knew she was lying to me. "Wait," Michelle said suddenly. "I got a call from my niece's school that she was sick and needed to be picked up. My sister was out of town on business and Tiana was staying with me. I had just started logging the inventory into the system when they called me."

I was a good judge of character and knew damn well she was telling the truth. In fact, now that she mentioned it, I recalled seeing her shorter hours for that day. "The entire inventory was entered with your employee number. Who finished the task for you?" I asked her. Michelle's eyes widened in alarm as she realized something was wrong.

"Alexander," she said quietly. "I didn't log off, and he must've continued logging them in under my number." She swallowed hard before she asked, "Is there liquor missing?"

"More than two thousand dollars' worth."

"Oh my God!" Michelle covered her mouth and closed her eyes. "You think Alexander stole the liquor and used my employee number so that I would take the fall?"

"There's only one way to find out," I replied.

"He's off tonight," Michelle told me.

"That gives us time to formulate a plan and set a trap then, doesn't it? Will you be able to act like nothing happened until the next shipment arrives in a month?"

"That little fucker! I'm going to kick his puny ass!" Michelle rose from her chair and placed her hands on her hips and blew out a harsh breath. "There, I got it out of my system for now. I'm good to go."

"Are you sure?"

"Positive, boss. I won't let you down. I'm sorry that you doubted me for even a second." I could hear the hurt in her voice and knew I needed to act fast.

"I'm the kind of man who's had to rely on gut instinct more than physical evidence for the majority of my life. Even though the computer program was telling me that you misplaced or stole the liquor, in my heart, I believed there had to be another explanation. I'm pretty sure you know which reality I wanted to believe. I've always been able to count on you no matter what happened here or in my personal life."

"That means a lot to me, Jon," she said softly. It wasn't often that she addressed me by anything other than sir or boss, but it seemed like the right time to let the formality drop just a bit. "You took a chance when you promoted me to manager over people who'd been here longer, including Alexander." She shook her head like she still couldn't believe it. "What will you do about him?"

That question required zero deliberation from me. "Alexander can pay me for the loss of liquor, or I'll have him arrested." I lifted a brow in question. "Is that a problem for you?"

"No, sir. Tell me what your plan is."

"Next month, you're going to get another emergency phone call and have to leave after you've started inputting the inventory into the system. You're going to stay logged in and ask Alex to fill in for you again. I don't think he'll be able to resist the temptation to steal again."

"Then what?"

"Then I'll record him in the act on the hidden cameras I'll have placed in the stockroom." It was one of the few areas that we didn't have a camera. That was going to change.

"Do you plan on leaving the cameras in place after you catch Alexander red-handed?" She chewed on her lip nervously.

"Yes, but I'll make an announcement, so employees quit screwing in there during their breaks."

"Of course, you knew about that." Michelle broke eye contact by looking down at her feet. I could tell that something was on her mind, but she was afraid to bring it up. I suspect I knew what made her so uncomfortable.

"Has Alexander been talking?" She raised her head, and I knew I didn't need to expand on my question. "You don't have to answer me; the truth is written all over your face."

"It wasn't anything he said; it was the way he acted."

"Fair enough," I told her. I didn't owe my manager an explanation or an apology because I didn't break company rules, just my personal ones. "It won't happen again," I said anyway.

Michelle held her hands up in the air. "Not my place to judge. I just wanted to let you know in case he tries to threaten you."

"His threats won't faze me one bit."

"Good to know." She hooked her thumb to point at the door. "I'm going to get back out there unless you need something else."

"I'm good if you are," I told her.

"Then we're both good. I'll see you later tonight."

Once I was alone again, I blew out a frustrated breath. No matter what I'd just told Michelle, I had a feeling that things were about to get fucking ugly. I hadn't moved to replace Rick as my attorney since his death because I hadn't needed one but realized that could change quickly. I hadn't made any real friends since I moved to the Queen City besides Rick and I couldn't very well ask him for a fucking referral for a good lawyer.

There was someone I could call, but I didn't want to hear his voice. Marlon Bandowe was a self-loathing gay man who led my brother around by his short and curlies for more than a decade or longer. He was the kind of guy who spoke out about homosexuality ruining family values right after soliciting a blow job in an airport bathroom. I had no use for bastards like him. I got that not everyone could live openly—hell, that had been my life for the majority of my career in the military and black ops. The difference was that I had never led someone on. I never told a man that I loved him in one breath while denying him in the next.

"Fuck!" I decided to bite the bullet and call him. I picked up my phone and saw that the text I missed earlier was from Emory.

Happy to help your *friend* out.

Just like that, I forgot all about calling Marlon.

FIFTEEN

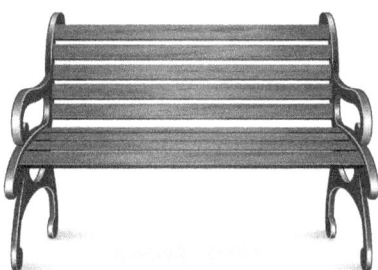

Emory

I HADN'T PLANNED ON RESPONDING TO JON'S TEXT MESSAGE, LET alone act playful. *Jon? When did I start thinking about him as Jon again?* Somehow, I just didn't have it in me to ignore his text after the way things ended between us at my house. I was finally ready to admit that I'd flown to Montana because of him, and it would be my farewell gesture. I sent my reply text to him in the same spirit. I didn't want there to be animosity between us any longer. I didn't want there to be *anything* between us. *Do this thing and make a clean break, Emory. Delete his number from your phone and purge him from your mind. If only it were that easy.*

I texted Memphis to let him know that I had arrived safely, had a bite to eat, and was getting ready to meet with the sheriff to review the case. I had promised to call him later that night, figuring that would be enough to tide him over, but I should've known better. Memphis fired a reply before I could put my phone away.

Is he hot?

Smoking! I replied because it was true. Why lie about it? He just wasn't for me. *He's just your type too. Piercing blue eyes, light brown hair with a touch of gray at the temples, and a hard body that came from working rather than a gym membership.*

As usual, Memphis always did the opposite of what I expected. I thought he'd reply to my teasing right away, but he didn't. His reply came five minutes later at the same time there was a confident knock at my door. Funny how a knock could reveal the character of your visitor, or at least their present mood.

Pictures or it didn't happen, Memphis wrote.

Have to go. Talk later.

"Sheriff," I said by way of greeting when I opened the door.

"What's it going to take for you to call me Beau?"

"I just like to keep things very professional with the law enforcement agents I'm working with on a case," I said in an apologetic tone. "Tell you what, I'll call you Beau when we find out what happened to Kent Jessup."

"Deal," he said, "but I'm going to call you Emory."

"Fair enough."

When we got downstairs, I noticed that Caroline was no longer behind the desk. A dour-faced man stood in her place, and I noticed the atmosphere wasn't nearly as welcoming.

"We don't run *that* kind of establishment, Sheriff," the man said. "Maybe your out-of-town *guest* would be more comfortable at one of the hotel chains out by the highway."

Did that grouchy bastard wearing the Mr. Roger's sweater in a putrid shade of green just imply that I was the sheriff's whore or something? I wanted to confront him, but Beau's swift and strong grip on my elbow stopped me from turning around.

"He's here consulting on a case, not to suck my dick, Virgil," Beau tossed over his shoulder as we walked out the door. "Old homophobic prick. He better be glad I'll never be the one answering a nine-one-one call should he ever dial that number." He mumbled the last part under his breath but loud enough that I heard it.

"I guess hatred exists everywhere, but I'll never get used to it."

"Me either, and if he were smart, he'd keep his fucking mouth shut since both the fire chief and sheriff are gay men. Chances are he's going to need our fucking help someday, and I'm going to try to be a better man when that time comes," Beau bit out angrily.

The mood in the SUV was somber with neither of us saying anything until we reached the sheriff's office, which was the typical nondescript brick building with a satellite and antennas on the roof. The inside was as standard and basic as all the other law enforcement agencies I'd visited over the years. Everything was beige and boring, but that stopped once we entered Beau's office. Oh, it was beige too, but he personalized his space with pictures of him with two other men in various places in the world. I recognized Jon and assumed the other was the Corbin guy that Jon had mentioned.

The photos looked like they dated back twenty years or so. In fact, one of them looked like it was taken during boot camp. I was inexplicably drawn to the pictures and found myself studying each one to catalog the changes in Jon throughout the years. He'd changed from a fresh-faced young man to a world-weary one full of cynicism. I couldn't begin to imagine the things he'd done and saw to make the bright-eyed boy so jaded. Well, maybe I could imagine it, but I didn't want to.

"I'm sure you recognize Jon in those pictures. The other guy is Corbin, who I grew up with in New Orleans. We joined the service together and met Jon at boot camp. The three of us became inseparable for the two decades that followed. Corbin is back in NOLA with his family, I'm here in Big Timber, and Jon is in Cincinnati. It's the longest we've been apart since we met." I heard the pride and love he had for his friends. I suddenly understood why they chatted every Sunday morning. It was their way of staying connected.

"You must miss them."

"Every day, but our lives took paths that none of us anticipated," Beau said somewhat cryptically. His words and actions convinced me that Kent Jessup's disappearance was more personal than he let on. He hadn't told Jon, so I knew that he wouldn't confide in me. It was also possible that Jon just didn't tell me the full story. "There's never been anything between us except amazing friendship, Emory."

I pinned him with a heated look. "Why would you say that to me?" I asked, even though I knew the answer. "That must've been some phone call the two of you had this afternoon."

Beau put his hands up peacefully. "I simply called Jon to thank him. I might've mentioned that you were cute because I thought that maybe you and he—"

"No."

"Yes, he made that clear." Hearing that Jon denied the connection we shared pissed me off. It was hypocritical and irrational, but true all the same. "Jon also mentioned that you thought he and I might've been *friends* instead of friends."

"I'm sure I don't know what he's talking about," I said while wishing the ground would open and swallow me. "He's of no concern to me."

"Yeah, he tried that same song and dance with me too. Neither one of you is very convincing though." Beau smiled wryly then said, "I talked to Jon on the phone instead of using Skype so I can't be sure of his facial expression when he denied he has feelings for you, but I imagine it would look just like that." He pointed to my face. "You two idiots are fighting the wrong battle. Stop being stupid, because life is too damn short." *As if I hadn't learned that the hard way.*

"Thanks for the pep talk, Dr. Phil. Can we get down to business now?"

Beau threw his head back and laughed hard for several minutes.

"Oh boy," he said, wiping his eyes. "Jon said pretty much the same thing, but I think he was slightly more colorful."

"Well, I'm starting to think saltier language is called for in this situation," I said wryly.

"Have a seat, and I'll get the file for you to look through." Beau went to a storage locker in the corner of his office and began turning the lock. "I wouldn't really say there has been a new development, but what I did discover reaffirms my belief that Kent Jessup never left this county alive." The lock audibly clicked when it unlocked, and the door swung open. Beau pulled out a worn, leather duffel bag from the locker. "This bag belonged to Kent. There's no way in hell he would've left it behind."

The look of devastation on his face and the anguish in his voice confirmed my suspicion that this was no ordinary cold case to Beau Rossi. He had a vested interest, but why? Then I realized it didn't matter. What mattered was whether I could touch Kent's things and get a psychic connection to him. I walked to the table Beau had set it on and reached for the bag. An image didn't immediately come to mind, but a feeling of sorrow and fear washed over me.

I blew out a shaky breath and unzipped the bag so I could touch his possessions. "Have you gone through this bag?" I asked.

"I have," Beau confirmed.

"Are you confident that all the items are his?"

"A ranch hand from Kent's last known residence gave the bag to me recently, claiming it was Kent's. His mother also described the bag he'd left home with in great detail, so I'm confident it belonged to him. I can't say for sure whether all the items inside are his though."

"Fair enough," I said. I pulled each item out separately to see if I could pick up any vibes from them. Mostly the bag consisted of clothes and a grooming kit. Odd that he would've left them behind, but not necessarily an indicator that foul play was afoot. None of the items gave me anything to work with. The second to last item I removed from the bag was a half-empty box of condoms. I got my strongest psychic hit from them, but that didn't surprise me at all. Lust and love are two of the strongest emotions that people experience. It wouldn't be odd to feel the connection if that bag had been hidden and preserved well the last ten years. The residual vibes of lust and the joy of discovery were still strong when I ran my hand over the box.

As intense as the emotions were, I had to believe that Kent's sexual experiences were new to him. "He was intimately involved with someone here," I told the sheriff. "The relationship was brand new and thrilling to him." I closed my eyes and embraced the residual psychic echoes Kent left behind. My heart raced with the excitement that he had felt. "The man was older and more experienced. Their relationship was a secret, which added to the thrill for him." I kept my eyes closed while I waited to see if Kent gave me more information from that item but there was nothing else.

"You're certain he was involved with another man?" Beau asked once I set the box on the table next to the clothes.

"Yes, an older man, but it feels like maybe a ten to twelve-year age difference."

"Most likely one of the other ranch hands and not the ranch owner then," Beau said, but it felt more like he was thinking out loud rather than speaking to me.

"That is the impression I got." A wallet was the final item in the bag and the biggest indicator that Kent left in a hurry or not at all. A guy doesn't go very far without his wallet. A sharp knife of fear stabbed me when I held the worn leather in my hands. "Did you look inside?"

"Yes," Beau said tersely. "His ID, credit card, and a few hundred dollars in cash are still inside."

"He was terrified when he threw his wallet inside the bag. It was probably the last thing put in the bag before he zipped it up. It wouldn't take much for the wallet to fall to the bottom of the bag." An image of a young guy with shiny black hair and vibrant blue eyes came to me. He was inside rustic-looking rooms with bunk beds. He had packed his belongings as fast as he could and saw his wallet on the nightstand. Instead of tucking it into his pocket, he tossed it inside his open duffel bag because he needed to make a fast escape. "He was trying to flee for his life."

"I fucking knew it. What else do you see?"

I slowly opened my eyes and looked into blue ones that were eerily similar to Kent Jessup's. I opened the wallet and removed the driver license, and a younger version of Beau Rossi stared back at me. The only differences were their hair color, age, and last name. I had read that Kent was twenty-two when he went missing, so Beau wasn't old enough to be his father. I was curious to know their real connection, but I didn't want my visions compromised by asking too many questions.

I shared with Beau the few details I saw in my vision. I could tell by the fierce look in his eyes that he knew the location I described. "I'm sorry that I couldn't tell you anything else. Sometimes things will come to me days later, so don't give up hope."

"I wish I could take you out to that ranch, but I can't do that without a warrant. I have talked to the owner a few times, and he threatened me with a harassment lawsuit if I showed up without a signed warrant from a judge." Beau pinched the bridge of his nose. "I'll just hope that something more comes to you—something that leads to a solid piece of evidence so I can get that warrant. I know that my… Kent didn't just disappear without a trace. He had help. At this point, I just want to return his body to his family."

"I hope that I can help you with that," I told him. "Do you know any of Kent's favorite places around Big Timber? I can see if I pick up any details."

"I can tell you what I've learned from interviewing people around town that knew him," he replied.

"Okay, that's a good start."

Beau rattled off a few locations including a diner and the library while he drove me back to the B&B. "Do you want me to come with you?"

"If it's okay with you, I'd rather go by myself so that I'm not confusing your energy with anything that Kent might've left behind."

"Sounds fair," he said amicably. "Just give me a call if you need my assistance."

The B&B was in an uproar when I went inside. Two couples that looked to be in their mid to late forties stood inside bickering back and forth.

"This is your son's fault," a raven-haired woman said. She had the same cornflower-blue eyes as Caroline, and I started to get a sick feeling in the pit of my stomach. "He seduced her into leaving town with him."

The other woman narrowed her eyes and said, "That little trollop is the one using her—"

"Finish that sentence, and I'll kick your pretentious ass up and down this fucking street," the first woman said.

"See, Steven. This is what our son tied himself to when he ran off with *that* girl."

"Everyone, calm down!" Martha yelled. "Maybe we can have the marriage annulled."

"Yeah, right," a man I assumed to be Chase's father said. "She'll do her damnedest to get pregnant so she can sink her claws into him for the rest of her life."

"That's it!" Caroline's mom said, lunging toward Chase's father. Her fingers bent to resemble claws, and I was pretty sure she would've scratched his eyes out had her husband not grabbed her around the waist.

"Don't give them more fodder to use against us, Betsy."

I skirted around the feud and headed up to my room. I flopped on my bed without taking off my shoes. I had a sick feeling that the kids took my advice and literally ran with it. Holy hell, I should've just kept my damn mouth shut. I was hungry again, and even though dinner time was fast approaching, I was pretty sure the kitchen wouldn't be serving food that night. I told myself to get up and go to the diner that Beau told me about, but my eyes suddenly felt heavy with exhaustion.

I fell into a deep, hard sleep like I do when a vision reveals itself to me. Instead of dreaming of the fate that befell Kent, I dreamed of Jon. My heart raced with excitement when I felt his presence right before the vision unfurled, but it skidded to a stop when I saw Jon having sex with someone else. I recognized the guy too; it was the bartender from Vibe.

I woke up drenched in sweat and shivering from head to toe, gasping for air as if I'd been holding it for several minutes. My lungs burned when I sucked precious oxygen into them. I felt tears streaming down my face, but couldn't figure out why I was crying. Didn't he tell me he was going to try and forget that I existed? Maybe that was his way of doing just that. It was no more than I deserved, but why then did I feel so fucking betrayed? Jon and his fuck boy didn't matter to me. I told myself that at least a hundred times while I took a quick shower to warm the chill that had pervaded my body.

I sat in the bathtub when I couldn't stand any longer and let the water beat down on me. I could try to convince myself I wasn't crying over Jon all I wanted, but I tasted the salt of my tears when I licked my lips.

Damn you, Jon. You weren't supposed to matter.

SIXTEEN

Jon

KNEW THAT EMORY WAS BACK IN OHIO AFTER TALKING TO BEAU on the phone. He told me that Emory hadn't led him to any new evidence, but the psychic energy that Emory detected seemed to confirm Beau's theory that something bad had happened to Kent Jessup. I was tempted to do some research of my own to figure out Beau's connection to the missing man but chose to wait until my friend felt comfortable confiding in me. I owed him time and patience.

I was relieved that Emory made it back to Ohio safely, but I dreaded looking into his eyes. I'd learned how to mask my emotions long ago, but I knew that Emory would take one look at me and see right through my charade. I shouldn't have felt a moment's guilt for having sex with Alexander, but I did anyway. I thought about skipping Josh and Gabe's wedding to avoid him, but I wasn't the kind of man who backed down. I'd own my actions and accept the consequences. Besides, what the fuck was he going to do? Stop talking to me? Deny that he wanted me as bad as I wanted him? He'd already done those things, so I had nothing to lose.

Josh and Gabe's wedding was a first for me though. People in my line of work didn't settle down with spouses, kids, and dogs, not that I gave marriages and happily ever after much thought back then—or now for that matter. An image of Emory laughing at someone's joke at one of the Sunday gatherings popped into my mind. *Liar.* I was getting sick and fucking tired of that little voice calling me out every time I turned around. What was it anyway? A newly developed subconscious? He could go back to my fiery-pit-of-hell soul and burn.

Josh and Gabe's back yard looked stunning; even a knuckle dragger like me recognized beauty when presented with it. There were two groups of chairs separated by an aisle. I had no idea which groom was standing where so I just picked the right side since it was the direction my dick hung. I felt the moment Emory arrived. The hair on the back of my neck stood up, and I felt my pulse pounding in my neck. I swallowed hard and turned to look for him and wasn't surprised to find him staring back at me. It was like we couldn't help it.

Emory looked the same, yet different. The designer beard was gone, but his hairstyle still looked the same. Yeah, I still mourned the loss of his beautiful hair. The dark circles under his eyes from lack of sleep weren't new, and that same disapproving frown graced his beautiful face. Nothing changed about his outward appearance, but something was off about him. I couldn't quite place it until his light green eyes ensnared me and held me captive. I saw anger and hurt in his gaze, but why? I hadn't talked to him since our text exchange, so why... My eyes widened when I realized that he knew about Alexander. If he saw that, what else could he see? I didn't want Emory to know some of the things I'd done on behalf of Uncle Sam.

My prediction that Emory would belong to me—at least physically—would never happen if he knew the kind of man I was—am. I was trying to be a better person, but I wasn't stupid enough to think that a few good deeds would erase the bad ones. In the pit of my soul lived a monster undeserving of love and it was best if I kept reminding myself of that instead of hanging on to false hope that some shiny love was out there waiting for me. Some people were destined to walk this world alone; I was one of them.

What right did he have to be hurt or angry? I turned my head, breaking our connection, and focused on the altar. I tamped down the urge to get up and leave before I did something stupid or said something I couldn't take back. I was a grown-ass man who was capable of making decisions for myself. I allowed no one to lead me around by my ball sac and that wasn't going to change just because I wanted to fuck a man who was too damn busy denying what he felt for me.

I bit the inside of my cheek hard enough to draw blood because the physical pain was so much easier for me to accept than the tangled emotions Emory brought out in me. I was so conflicted about Emory that I barely registered the wedding. I snapped out of my funk long enough to watch the grooms exchange vows. The tenderness and love Josh and Gabe shared as they committed their lives to one another only made me feel more miserable. After the ceremony, the guests retreated to the large, fancy white tent in their yard that was set up for the reception dinner. The meal was one sure thing I could count on that night because Josh was hardcore about his food. I doubted he did the cooking, but I knew he wouldn't just pick any ole caterer without seriously vetting them either.

The food was incredible and lived up to Josh's high standards. I wondered how long I had to stick around before I could leave. I didn't want to be rude by doing an eat and run. Could I amble on over to the grooms after their first dance and congratulate them? Make up a fake emergency at the club as a valid reason I burned rubber getting out of Blissville? I knew this: I had no intention of returning to the town ever again.

The grooms took the floor and slow danced while staring into each other's eyes. Their expressions and smiles told me that they were in a place that only the two of them existed. The song ended just as I thought I could sneak off. Instead of leaving the dance floor, a fast song started playing, and they performed a dance for us that they'd obviously choreographed for the occasion. I couldn't help smiling as they busted their moves in time to the music. Some people sang along, some recorded the moment on their phone, and others clapped along with the beat. Once that was over, I stood to make my move, but the mothers of the grooms were asked to take to the floor.

Instead of just dancing with their moms, they had a large projector screen showing a video of them with their families as they grew up. I got a little choked up when I saw the pictures of Gabe with his older brother. Eventually, the pictures were of the two men as they started dating and falling in love. It was honestly a beautiful moment—one that I never expected to experience for myself. Happily ever after wasn't in the cards for someone like me.

Throughout the night, I'd felt *his* eyes on me. During the times in between, I checked to see if he was still sitting there like me watching the world move around us. There were a few instances where one of us didn't look away quick enough and our eyes connected. That same yearning to hold him in my arms and kiss him washed over me each time. I thought it would've faded by then, but it didn't; it just kept getting stronger until it felt like I was suffocating.

I tore my eyes away one last time and rose to my feet. I'd had as much socializing as I could take for the night—especially in an atmosphere like that one. I tapped Gabe on the shoulder, and he stopped spinning his husband around the dance floor.

"I'm going to head south," I told them. "I want to congratulate you both and wish you the very best."

"That sounds like goodbye, Jon," Josh said, narrowing his eyes.

"Not at all," I replied. I was no longer willing to give up my friends because Emory was stubborn. "I hope you have an amazing time in Hawaii. I'll see you when you return."

"Drive safely," Gabe said to me as I walked away, making me smile. I didn't know that I was suffocating on my longing for Emory until I left the wedding. I breathed easier with every step that took me away from the venue. I had nearly reached my sleek, black sedan when I felt Emory's presence. The strong breeze that suddenly kicked up out of nowhere felt like an omen. The trees that lined the street began to sway; their drying leaves rasping and scraping against each other like my frayed nerves. I had to get away before I snapped and said—or did—something I couldn't take back.

"Jon." Emory said my name so softly that it almost felt like a caress.

I stopped at the hood of my car and turned back to face him. The street lamp shone down on me, bathing me in a bright glow, which made the gaps between lamp posts look darker. It had taken several heartbeats before I detected Emory's movement in the shadows as he got closer to me. Finally, he stepped into the circle of light with me. He looked up into my eyes, and I saw acceptance. Unfortunately, it was a grim acknowledgment, not joyful.

"I didn't think I had a heart left until I met you, Emory. Watching you struggle to deny what's happening between us tears me up inside." I closed the small distance between us and pressed my lips to his forehead. Emory gasped and gripped my shirt at my waist with both hands. I couldn't tell if he wanted to pull me closer or push me away; I didn't think he knew either. "I'm not sure I can stay away from you, but I'm going to try. I can't keep hurting you like this."

Emory stepped even closer. "Don't go," he whispered brokenly. "Not yet." He raised his head and looked up at me. His eyes glistened with unshed tears, and there was no way I could deny him anything. "I don't have the right to ask—"

"Yes, you do."

Emory swallowed hard and shook his head. Then he closed his eyes but not before tears escaped and slid down his cheeks. I had never been a tender person—never wanted to be either—but Emory changed that. I brushed his tears away with my thumbs and pulled him tight against me, rocking us back and forth. I knew it was probably the closest thing to a slow dance that I'd ever get with Emory.

"I'm so sorry, Em," I whispered into his hair.

"For what?" Emory asked, his words muffled by my chest. "You're not responsible for the hand that fate dealt me. Or are you apologizing for the bartender?"

I slid my hand beneath his chin and tipped his head back so that he looked into my eyes. "If my actions hurt you, then yes, I apologize for them. I was angry and tried to force you out of my mind."

"Did it work?"

"Not even close, and I regret it more than you'll ever know." My answer seemed to mollify him a little bit.

"What am I going to do with you, Jon?"

"I have some suggestions, but you're not ready to hear them." I wanted to add *yet*, but the reality was that Emory might never be ready.

Emory snorted. "Probably not."

I ran my thumb over his bottom lip, and it was just as soft as I imagined. Emory's tongue darted out to dampen the flesh I just touched, and it broke the little control I had. "I'm going to kiss you, Emory." I lowered my head slowly, so he had time to react. Nothing with him needed to be fast or hard—yet.

He swallowed nervously but didn't pull away or tell me no. I paused just before our lips touched to give him one last chance to reject me. He didn't, so I pressed my lips against his. We both gasped and pulled back in surprise at the electrical current that ran between us. Emory reached up and touched his lips in disbelief. Then he surprised me by putting his hand on the back of my neck and pulling me to him for a deeper kiss.

My body demanded that I take, but I knew I would ruin everything if I pushed him too far, too fast. I traced his lips with the tip of my tongue learning the shape and taste of them. Emory parted his lips invitingly and sighed softly. I took my sweet time drawing out his pleasure before I eased my tongue into his mouth. My God, I wanted to ravage and devour that sweet mouth, but I loved learning the texture of his tongue as it rubbed and twirled around mine. I tasted the sweetness of the wedding cake he ate and the champagne he drank to toast the new grooms. I wanted so badly to strip him bare and learn every single texture of his slim body, but it wasn't the right time.

Emory wasn't immune to me either. I felt his erection pressing against mine as he aligned his body fully against me. The only way for him to get closer was to crawl inside my body. I kept my hands in safe zones; one was on the side of his neck and the other cupped the back of his head. Emory wasn't as shy and ran his hands up and down my ribcage before he moved them to my lower back. He dug his fingers into the flesh above my waistband when I sucked his tongue into my mouth like I planned to do with his cock someday.

Emory broke our kiss and looked into my eyes. "Jon," he whispered brokenly. I saw the invitation in his gaze in place of the grim acceptance I saw just a few minutes prior. "Come home with me." I knew it took a lot for him to speak those words out loud.

"I can't, Emory. You're not ready, and I don't want to be someone you regret. We both deserve better than that." It killed me to deny him, but for once in my life, I wanted to do the right thing.

Emory jerked out of my arms and walked a few feet from me. "This is just incredible. I finally am ready to give you what you want and—"

"No, Emory," I said, interrupting him. "You're just horny."

"You didn't seem to mind helping Alexander out when he was horny," he fired back. "Why is he different?"

"I'm not in love with him!" I roared. Both of us jerked at my confession. *Was I out of my fucking mind?*

"No," Emory said, shaking his head. "You can't love me."

"It's fucking crazy, it makes zero sense, yet it's true. I'm not just attracted to you, Emory. I don't just want to fuck you. I'm in love with you. I want all the pieces of you, including the ones you think are too shattered to repair. I'm not afraid of your jagged edges, baby."

"I don't want you to love me." Emory's words cut me deep, testing the commitment I had just made. "I don't want to love you." He said he didn't want to, not that he didn't. I would hold on to that for as long as it took for him to embrace the idea that we belonged together.

I reached for Emory, but he took another step back. I dropped my hands and took a patient breath. The last thing I wanted to do was push him further away. That kiss would just have to be enough to tide me over until the next time. I promised myself that when it arrived, we would be horizontal and wearing a lot less clothes. I glanced around the neighborhood and saw that an elderly woman was watching us through her big picture window. She wore a large, shapeless nightgown and curlers in her hair. Okay, I also wanted to do it without an audience.

"If it makes you feel better, I don't want to love you either." I could tell by his scowl that my words only made things worse. As heartfelt confessions go, mine was pretty lame. I yelled my feelings at him then told him I wished they weren't there. I had a long way to go for improvement.

"Jon, I'm not trying to be cruel to you; I'm trying to be as honest as I can. The only thing I might ever give you is my body."

"I call bullshit, but if that's the case, I refuse to settle, Emory," I said, walking toward my car. "Call me when you reach that point too."

Driving away from him that night was the hardest thing I'd ever done. My body begged me to reconsider, but I knew I had made the right call. I just hoped he didn't make me wait long.

SEVENTEEN

Emory

PRESSED MY FINGERS TO MY TINGLING LIPS AS I WATCHED JON drive away. *He's in love with me.* I didn't want him to love me, and I didn't want to feel anything for him either. I might never love him the way he deserved, but my God I wanted him so bad. The way he expressed his feelings was nothing like the first vision I had of us together. His confession was raw and loud, like it was ripped right from his soul. And I don't mean that because he practically yelled it at me in frustration. It almost sounded rusty, like he'd never spoken the words to someone before me. My heart raced over that possibility. In my premonition, the words were smooth and flowed from him as natural as breathing. I found myself looking forward to experiencing the progression of his confessions from the new and untried to the polished and effortless.

Damn it, Emory. Stop being an idiot and go after him! I closed my eyes as a broken sob slipped from my lips. *River!* How long had I waited to hear his voice again? And when he showed up, he tells me to chase after another man? Sweet Jesus, I had finally lost my mind. I'd probably been slowly slipping for quite some time, but I had apparently hit rock bottom. No man would urge his husband into the arms of another man.

He would if he loved him more than he loved himself. Go to him, Emory. He's the reason you're in Blissville.

"No!" I shook my head then realized how crazy I looked. If I kept it up, the guys with straight jackets would show up and haul me off to the behavioral science floor at the nearest hospital.

Go to him, Emory!

No. That time I just thought my refusal instead of voicing it out loud. I didn't want to go to Jon after he confessed his feelings for me. Having sex with him knowing that he was emotionally engaged when I wasn't would be cruel. I lived with enough guilt already.

Live, damn you! You did not die with me, Emory. Stop being a coward and fucking live.

I angrily wiped the tears off my face as I walked to my car. I had no intention of driving to Cincinnati to chase after Jon, but I was probably only five minutes behind him when I hit the interstate. I knew I could catch him if the traffic was light and I didn't get pulled over for speeding. I had no clue where the man lived, so I either caught up to him and followed him home like a creep, or I called him and asked for directions. I thought option number one was my best bet and pressed down harder on the gas pedal.

My heart raced faster than my car as I scanned the highway the best I could without being reckless. I spotted his car up ahead and fell in behind him. "What the fuck am I doing?"

Living!

"Shut up, River." I could almost hear his laughter at my irritation.

I expected Jon to live in a downtown high-rise, but he drove to a neighborhood in Hyde Park that looked like old money. I could see Jon's head turn to look in his rearview mirror every time we pulled up to a red light or stop sign. Did he know it was me? How could he miss those silver racing stripes on my Mini Cooper? Was he going to reject me again or accept what I was willing to give? *Did I even know what I was willing or even capable of giving?*

He paused for a few seconds at a four-way stop, and I wondered if his hesitation was because we were getting closer to his house. The driver behind me didn't seem to care about Jon's need to weigh his options because he laid on his horn until Jon began to move. I continued to follow him up roads that led higher and higher up a steep hill. Finally, Jon turned into a gated driveway. It was his chance to send me away, but he didn't. He must've pushed a button inside his car because the gates slowly swung open.

Jon drove his car through the gates as soon as they were open wide enough for him to fit, and I followed closely on his bumper. Lamp posts lit the curving drive up to a modern, two-story brick and stone home that I thought must look amazing in the daylight. At night, it looked regal and proud nestled in the trees with landscape lighting strategically aimed at the house, bathing it in a soft glow. As gorgeous as it was, it didn't feel like Jon to me.

I wasn't sure why I thought that, and I didn't have much time to dwell on it because Jon pulled to a stop in the circular driveway in front of the house rather than continue to the garage that was attached to the side. He shut his car off and got out; so did I. Jon walked toward me, but I stayed by my car in case he asked me to leave, which was no more than I deserved.

"What are you doing here, Emory?"

"I think you know."

"I have a pretty good idea, but what has changed since I left Blissville forty minutes ago?"

"Nothing," I answered honestly. "I don't love you, Jon."

"Yet," he corrected. "You don't love me yet." He reached for my hand and slid his fingers in between mine. "If you walk across that threshold with me, I'm going to push you up against the nearest surface and fuck you. Probably more than once. Can you live with that?"

His words sent an electrical current racing through my body. My dick hardened fast and almost painfully beneath my tight briefs. No one had ever talked dirty to me or tried to dominate me, but it ignited something inside me like he was holding a lit match near gasoline fumes. In Jon's eyes, I saw the raw need that burned through him just as strong as it did me.

"Take me inside."

Jon didn't ask me if I was sure; he gripped my hand tightly and pulled me up the broad, stone steps to the front porch. I expected him to drop my hand to unlock the front door, but he hit a few numbers on a keypad with his left hand before twisting the knob to let us inside.

I had caught a brief glimpse of the living room beyond the foyer before Jon turned to me. He didn't even bother shutting the door before he backed me up against the foyer table. Jon's hands immediately went to my neck to loosen my tie while he swooped down and captured my lips in a hard, demanding kiss. He released a torrent of emotions he'd repressed since we met, and I tasted each one on his tongue.

I wasn't sure where to put my hands first because I wanted to touch him everywhere at the same time. I started with removing his tie as he'd done for me then yanked on his shirt hard enough to send buttons scattering onto the marble floor. Jon growled sexily into my mouth and ripped my shirt open too. I hungrily gasped when he touched my bare skin for the first time.

Jon placed his palms flush against my chest then slowly slid them down until he reached the waistband of my pants. Instead of releasing my belt, he slid his hands even lower to stroke my straining erection through the fabric of my slacks and briefs. Years ago, I would've wondered if I was wearing good underwear, but not with Jon. I didn't care as long as he yanked them down, spread my legs, and fucked me like he'd promised.

I didn't dwell on my inexperience at handling a man like him; I acted on instinct. I placed my hands between Jon's shoulder blades and let my fingers bump along his vertebrae until I reached his fine ass. I cupped and squeezed a firm cheek with each hand then released him so I could touch his chest and stomach. I teased his hard nipples then ghosted my fingers over scars on his abdomen as I made my way south. I was relieved that Jon's scars didn't reveal to me how he got them, because that was a closeness and a connection I wasn't ready to experience. Still, my heart pinched painfully in my chest when I felt the old energy radiating from them. Jon hadn't been exaggerating when he said he'd experienced some close calls, and it shook me harder than I was comfortable with.

In fact, the feelings of fear and pain rose up so swiftly that it nearly ruined the sexy vibes that had consumed me earlier. I pushed those unwelcome emotions away to focus on what I did want. I didn't tease his cock like he did mine, I released that beast and stroked it with my bare hands.

Jon tore his lips away from mine then tipped his head back and closed his eyes while I worked his dick with long, sure strokes. Suddenly, as if it was too much, he placed his hands over mine and stilled me. "I've waited too long for it to be over so soon. I promised you a fucking, and you're going to get one."

Jon spun me around, and I was shocked by my reflection in the mirror that hung above the table. My eyes looked huge with only a tiny ring of my green irises showing around my blown pupils. My mouth hung open as I sucked air into my lungs and a dark pink blush spread across my cheeks. I looked up and caught Jon's eyes in the mirror as he cataloged my features too.

He finally opened my pants so he could slide his hand beneath the waistband of my underwear to stroke my bare flesh. It felt so fucking good that I couldn't help but grind my ass against Jon's erection while fucking the fist he had wrapped around my cock.

"Easy, baby. I got you." Jon pressed his nose behind my ear and inhaled deeply. "I can smell how badly you want me." He nipped the sensitive skin with his teeth, sending lightning straight to my balls. "I can taste it too." Jon rolled his thumb over the head of my leaking cock, using my pre-cum as lube to tease that ultra-sensitive spot beneath the crown.

Too lost in the sensations he created inside me to take it easy, I braced my arms on the table and pushed my ass against him, feeling the hard length of his cock nestle between my cheeks through the layers of fabric that separated our flesh. Knowing he would soon be inside me had my dick drooling like crazy over his fingers. I needed more and kept grinding myself against his erection hoping to push him over the edge.

Jon yanked my pants down to my ankles and spread my legs as far apart as he could, then parted my cheeks. "Look at that greedy hole twitching to be filled." Then he slid his cock between them and began sliding up and down the crack. My pucker twitched with need every time the head of his dick rasped against it.

"Is this what you wanted?" Jon pushed my cheeks together so that they hugged his cock as he pleasured himself. His pre-cum acted as lube to help him glide smoothly up and down until I thought I would combust. "Do you want to feel my big cock stretching you wide open, baby? Are you ready for me to slide in and out of your tight hole, raking over those nerve endings that will have you begging me for more? You're going to plead for harder, faster, and deeper. Are you prepared for me to own this sexy ass?" Jon slapped my right cheek sharply for emphasis. I'd never had any kind of spankings before—not for punishment or pleasure. Instead of scaring me, I pushed my ass tighter against him seeking more of everything he promised me with his words and the look in his eyes.

His expression was virile and dominant and more beautiful than

I ever imagined because I saw the truth of his words in the depths of his blue eyes. He was in love with me and the moment meant something entirely different for him than it did me. Lust had its wicked grip on my body, and I was too far gone to ask him to stop. Guilt and shame clawed at my insides, and I couldn't look at him anymore. I let my head fall forward until it hung between my shoulders.

"Answer me, Emory. I need to know that you're with me." Jon reached beneath my chin and tilted my head up until I looked into his eyes through the reflection once more.

Fuck, I wanted it so bad I couldn't answer him right away. "Yes! Damn you, Jon. I need to feel your cock inside me."

He grinned triumphantly at me, and I expected him to suit up and mount me, but instead, he dropped to his knees behind me.

Jon spread my cheeks apart wide and used his thumbs to tease my hole. "I know you expected to be on your way after a quick fuck, but that's not the way we're going to do it. This might be my only chance, and I'm going to experience it all." His hot breath ghosted across my tender flesh and made me even hornier. Surely, he wasn't…

Jon placed the flat of his tongue against my taint and licked a path up my ass crack until he reached the dimple above my ass.

It was my turn to say "fuuuuuuck." It was the most erotic thing I'd ever felt in my life, and I wanted more. "Please, Jon," I begged.

I could tell by the dark chuckle that vibrated against my ass that he loved to hear me plead for more. "Greedy, baby," he whispered. The tip of his tongue circled the nerve-laden crinkles surrounding my hole until it softened and relaxed. Jon sucked and licked me until I was a quivering mess and had to support my full weight on his foyer table. "You taste so fucking good, Em."

Just when I thought my torment was over, Jon kicked it into high gear by speering my hole with his skillful tongue, making me cry out for more. Every forward motion of his tongue fucking drove my dick against the edge of his table giving me the delicious friction I needed. I felt my orgasm building hard and fast.

"I'm going to come, Jon." Was I warning him? Did I want him to stop? Fuck no! It felt too damn good that I didn't want it to end. Every muscle tightened in my body as I tried to fight off my orgasm, but the sensations were too much. "Oh, Jon!" I arched my back and pressed tighter against his face to feel his tongue deeper inside me. My balls drew up tight against my body then I came loud and hard, spurting my cum all over the table. "Don't stop, Jon. Please don't stop," I cried brokenly. I had never had pleasure so intense that it hurt.

Jon remained on his knees after he pulled his tongue from my ass. He turned me around, and I leaned my ass against the table for support. I looked down into eyes so intensely blue that they appeared to glow in the semi-darkness. Instead of rising to his feet, Jon leaned forward and licked the cum off the tip of my cock then sucked my length into the back of his mouth. I hissed between my teeth because my cock was painfully sensitive, but yet, I couldn't pull away from his seductive mouth.

Jon reached around and slid a finger inside me. He continued to work my semi-erect cock with his mouth as he crooked his finger up and rubbed my prostate gland. I fisted my hands in his dark hair and panted for air while my dick began to harden beneath his ministrations. Once I was fully erect, Jon let my cock slide from his mouth and licked his wet lips as he rose to his full height. He never took his eyes off of mine when he reached into his back pocket and pulled out his wallet. I didn't need to look down to know what he was doing.

I heard the familiar sound of a foil wrapper when he pulled a condom free of his wallet. Jon ripped the package open with his teeth. I only eye broke contact to watch him roll the condom down his long, hard dick. He pushed his pants down to his mid-thigh and said, "It's my turn."

I stood up straight, turned my back toward him, and presented my ass. It's shameful to admit it, but I didn't want to look into his eyes when he slid inside my body. It was too intimate and something I'd only given to one other person.

"I don't think so, baby." Jon slid his big hand around my neck to cup my chin. He lifted my head up so that his eyes locked on mine again. "There will be no hiding from what you want and who you're doing it with."

EIGHTEEN

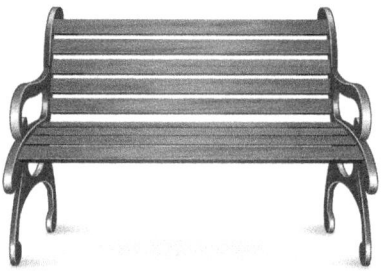

Jon

FUCK ME; I DON'T KNOW HOW THE HELL I KEPT FROM BUSTING A nut all over the floor when Emory came with my tongue in his ass. He was so fucking sensitive and responsive that I wanted to rim him daily and hear the jagged way he said my name when he shot his load. My dick throbbed painfully, and my body demanded that I fuck that eager ass of his, but I held back. I'd felt how tight his hole was when I worked my tongue or a single finger inside him. It was obvious to me that Emory had gone a long time without sex, and I wanted to make it so fucking good for him.

The boneless way he rested against the foyer table while I licked and sucked his cock back to full mast told me I was well on my way to completing my mission. I might've been a screwup in many areas in my life, but I always finished what I started. I stared into Emory's eyes through his reflection in the mirror. I saw how badly he wanted to look away, but I wouldn't let him. There was no way I would let Emory deny what was happening between us for another second. I knew he'd run home once I was through with him, but I was also just as certain that he would return to me—where I knew he belonged.

"Can I trust you to stay here while I go get the lube or should I take you with me?" I asked, not recognizing the gravelly voice as my own.

"I don't need lube; use spit."

"I won't hurt you, Em."

"Don't coddle me, Jon. Fuck me like you mean it. Right now." He sounded both desperate and sure.

Then, as if he couldn't bear to look at me any longer, Emory closed his eyes. Was he embarrassed by his need or his crass words? He had nothing to be ashamed of, and I refused to let him withdraw from me. There would be no pretending that it was his dead husband fucking him.

"Eyes on me, Emory, or go home."

I gently squeezed his neck, but not enough to hurt him or cut off his air. Emory's eyes flew open in shock. I eased the pressure and caressed his racing pulse on the right side of his neck with my thumb. I held up two fingers on my left hand to his mouth. Emory's eyes widened when he realized what I wanted from him. If he wanted it rough, then he was going to own it. I expected him to back off and ask for lube, but instead he sucked my fingers into his mouth and worked them like he would a cock, coating them with saliva. I removed my fingers from Emory's mouth, reached between his round ass cheeks, and fingered his ass again until he began grinding himself against me. I pulled out and slickened my cock with more spit before pressing it against his eager hole. Then I broke eye contact so I could watch the moment he became mine, even if he didn't realize it yet.

I pushed in slowly and watched as his pucker greedily sucked the head of my cock into his vise-like grip. Emory cried out my name, and I jerked my gaze back up to his to be sure I wasn't hurting him. All I saw was raw desire and need. I inched inside him ever-so-slowly, allowing Emory time to adjust to my size. My eyes darted back up to the mirror a few times to make sure he was still with me. Oh, he was with me all right and none too patient as I took my time penetrating him until my pelvis pressed flush against his round cheeks. I leaned over him and pressed my lips to his ear.

"This is just the beginning, Emory. I'm going to imprint myself on every sexy inch of your body."

I glanced at his reflection again and saw how badly he fought his emotions. Panic is the word I would use to describe his wide-eyed expression. He even shook his head to argue at the same time he pushed back against my pelvis, urging me to fuck him. It was like denying you wanted chocolate as you devoured a huge piece of triple chocolate fudge cake. I ate my baby's cake and icing and was already craving more.

My need to fuck was too strong to debate what was happening between the two of us. I stayed lowered over Emory's back and pulled my hips until only the tip remained inside his tight ring. I snapped my hips forward hard and fast, driving him up on his tiptoes.

"Jon!"

"That's right, baby. Yell my name."

I pulled back and slammed forward again to hear my name roll off his beautiful lips once more. Out, in; out, in. I rocked back and forth until I thought I was going to lose my fucking mind from the pleasure. Emory's ass hugged my cock tight, and nothing had ever felt as good. I couldn't wait until there was nothing between us and I could fill his ass and truly mark him as mine. The thought caused my rhythm to falter because I had never wanted to have bare sex with anyone. Once the thought came, I couldn't push it out of my mind. I immediately imagined sliding my finger in and out of his cum-slickened hole after I filled him, or jacking off on his tight pucker then pushing it inside him with my cock. I wanted to paint every part of him with my cum and rub it into his skin.

"Fuck you if you think I'm done with you after tonight, Emory," I suddenly snarled as I gripped his hair.

In and out; in and out. I felt my balls draw tight against my body as that familiar tingle started in my spine then spread to my balls. I rose up behind Emory and grabbed his waist with both hands and began hammering his tight ass like I might never get another chance. His hot chute had a strangle hold on my cock, sensually massaging me until I thought I'd lose my fucking mind.

"Jon… oh p-p-lease, make me come. Please." As if I could deny him.

"Stroke your cock, baby."

Emory braced his weight with his left arm while he reached beneath him with his right. I pegged his prostate hard until his eyes rolled up in his head and he shot his load for the second time. His ass spasmed tightly during his climax, pulling me over the edge with him.

I grunted as I rutted inside Emory. "Mine," I roared when I filled the condom. I lay over him as he rested and panted for breath against the table.

"Jesus," Emory said.

I lifted his right hand and licked the remnants of cum left behind on his fingers and palm, loving the salty, tangy taste of him. Emory whimpered as he turned his head and watched me. "I'm not through with you yet."

"Okay," he drowsily conceded.

I eased up and out of him then helped him stand straight. Emory stumbled a bit, and I caught him before he could fall. "You want me to carry you to my bed?"

"No," he said, shaking his head, but he smiled like he thought the notion was charming.

I entwined my fingers with his, tugging gently for Emory to

follow me toward the stairs. "It's a good thing because my legs proba-bly aren't up to the task. Can you carry me?" I teased.

"Not even on a good day."

"Those two orgasms don't equal a good day? Wow, you're a tough one to please."

"Fishing for compliments, Jon?"

"Baby, I tasted how good it was for you."

Emory blushed profusely over my gritty words, and I loved it. I planned to do a lot more dirty talking every chance I got. We stopped at the base of the steps, and Emory looked up at them in a panic. "You expect me to walk up two flights of steps after *that*?"

"I can ravish your ass on the steps if you prefer or we can fall into my comfortable bed."

Emory took a fortifying breath and placed a foot on the bottom step. "Let's give it a shot."

"Which one?" I *had* given him two choices.

"A soft bed would be my first pick," Emory replied. "But if we can't make it to the top, it's going to be your ass sitting on the hard-wood steps, not mine."

I sucked in a sharp breath at an image of me sitting on the pol-ished staircase while Emory rode me. I promised myself that I would make that vision a reality someday. "It would be my pleasure."

"That bed looks like heaven," Emory said when we finally reached my room. "Oh, I bet that view is amazing," he said, gesturing to the wall of windows opposite the bed.

"Stick around and find out."

Emory swallowed hard but didn't respond. I saw the confliction in his eyes. He wanted to stay but was afraid. I reminded myself to be patient and take what he could give me. *For now.*

I released Emory's hand when we reached the bed and pulled back the covers for him to climb in while I discarded the condom in the trash can and wiped my spent cock with tissues. I would've pre-ferred to take a shower, but I could tell every ounce of energy Emory had was depleted by the two orgasms I gave him. I didn't want to risk the chance that he'd sneak out if I showered alone either.

I climbed into the bed beside Emory and was surprised when he turned to me and lay his head on my shoulder after I turned off the lamp on the bedside table. I ran my fingers through his short hair and wished for the hundredth time that he hadn't cut it. One day, I would work up the nerve to ask him to grow it long again for me, but we weren't at that phase yet.

Emory was so quiet that I thought he'd fallen asleep. I closed my eyes and let my fatigue move in so I could get some shut-eye. Just before I fell asleep, Emory moved his hand and placed it over my beating heart.

"Maybe someday," Emory whispered sleepily.

My eyes popped open in the darkness, and my mind immediately began processing the possibilities of his words. Did Emory think he could love me someday? Damn, I was desperate to cling to that hope but too scared to chance it. For all I knew, he could've been talking in his sleep. My eyes grew heavy, and I gave up trying to sort out what he meant.

Just ask him in the morning.

I knew I was alone in the house when I opened my eyes the next morning. Years of training made it possible for me to analyze my surroundings immediately, even seconds after waking up out of dead sleep. I couldn't remember the last time I'd slept so hard. "Or so long," I said looking at the angle of the sunbeams shining through the window. "Fuck, it must be ten o'clock or later."

I threw back the covers and headed into the shower to wash the dried cum off my cock and balls. I had wanted to start my day showering with Emory, but it looked like he returned to Blissville without waking me. The hopefulness I had felt the previous night washed down the drain with the soap I rinsed off my body.

How long had he stayed? An hour? Five? Or did he bolt as soon as I fell asleep? I swallowed hard and ignored the pity party for one I wanted to throw in the marble and glass shower. I knew what the hell I got myself into and had no one to blame but myself. I stood beneath the spray, hoping the hot water would soothe the tension in my body, but it didn't.

A flash of movement out of the corner of my eye got my attention. I used my hand to wipe a circle of condensation off the inside glass door and saw Emory sitting on the vanity buck-ass naked sipping a cup of coffee. *Maybe my skills are a little rusty.* Emory set the coffee cup down then raised his legs and propped his heels on the edge of the vanity. He slowly spread his legs then reached between them to tease his hole with the middle finger from his left hand while he lazily stroked his cock with the right.

I opened the door and said, "Get in here."

Emory smiled and shook his head before he pushed his finger inside his pucker. Damn it, that was *my* job. I exited the shower with it still running and dropped to my knees in front of the vanity, not caring about the water I dripped all over the floor. Emory smiled wickedly as if that was what he wanted all along.

Am I still dreaming? Did I die and go to heaven?

It didn't matter because everything I wanted was right in front of me. I pushed Emory's hands out of the way and took over by sliding my middle finger deep inside him and swallowed his cock to the back of my throat. Emory braced his hands on top of the black marble vanity and pushed up on his heels so that his ass lifted a few inches in the air.

I could tell that he wanted to take control so he could fuck my mouth, and I wanted to let him. I tightened my lips, relaxed my throat, and let Emory have his way with me. He gripped my hair at the front of my head and thrust his hips forward fast and hard, grunting as he chased his orgasm. My mouth and throat ached from the pounding they took, but tears of pure pleasure burned my eyes.

Emory's cock drooled profusely, his pre-cum telling me how much he liked taking control of me. My dick begged and ached for relief, so I reached down and stroked myself in rhythm with the pace Emory set.

"Fuck yes," Emory moaned. "So fucking good, Jon. Are you going to swallow me down? I saw the greedy way you licked your fingers last night. You want more?"

I nodded the best I could with a mouthful of cock. Emory pumped his hips harder, gripped my hair tighter, as he gave into his body's release. He pulled out at the last minute, and his salty essence splashed on my tongue, nose, lips, and chin. Emory lowered his legs back down and watched me jack myself. The triumphant look on his face had the same effect on me as if he'd squeezed my ball sac. I blew my load all over the marble floor then collapsed my head against Emory's thigh while I tried to catch my breath.

The room felt like it was spinning; I wondered once again if I was dreaming. If so, I didn't want to wake up.

"Can you stand?" Was that arrogant pride I detected? "I could use a shower and some more sleep before I head home."

I didn't want Emory to leave but decided to accept the little victory I'd won when he not only stayed the night with me but initiated oral sex. "Where were you when I woke up? I couldn't sense you."

"Sense me?" he asked.

I rose from the floor, and Emory slid off the vanity. "I usually have stellar senses and can tell when I'm alone in a building or detect the presence of someone else." It came in handy when engaging in battle, including the battle of wills waging between us.

"Maybe your skills are getting rusty from misuse," Emory teased.

"Maybe you weren't inside the house," I countered.

"I went onto the back porch to watch the sunrise then just sat there thinking for a few hours. I decided to wake you up, but you were already in here pouting because you thought I'd left."

"I wasn't pouting." *I totally was.*

Emory's smug smile called me a liar. I just rolled my eyes and finished washing before I passed the soap and washcloth to Emory. At the last moment, I jerked them back and washed his body myself. It was the most intimate moment I had ever shared with another person. To be honest, I wasn't sure that kind of tenderness existed inside me until I met Emory.

Emory closed his eyes and breathed deeply through his nose like he was trying to calm the panic that wanted to rise inside him. I recognized the signs from that time in the kitchen, and it killed me I brought out that reaction in him. Emory placed his hand over his heart where the infinity tattoo containing his husband's name in the upper left curve was permanently inked in his flesh. I'd seen him do that before too and understood why he did it. He was comforting himself because the tenderness and intimacy of the shower had pushed him too far.

Emory may never love me. It was a bitter pill to swallow, but I accepted it even if I was disoriented and confused how things could go from so good to so bad in a heartbeat. I could accept what Emory offered or try to move on with my life. I wasn't ready to make the decision, so I shut off the water like nothing was wrong and handed Emory a towel before grabbing one for myself.

We got back in my bed once we were dry, but Emory didn't curl into me like he had the night before. He lay stiffly with his back to me. In my heart, I knew it could be the last time I ever had a chance to hold him. I spooned myself around him and slid my arm under his to cross it over his chest. I placed my hand over his heart, not caring that it bared the name of another man. I knew Emory had enough love for both of us, but Emory needed to believe it too.

I kissed the back of his neck then rubbed my nose through his hair. This was it, maybe my only chance to tell Emory how I felt in a way that I could be proud of. "I love you, Em."

He stiffened in my embrace but didn't pull away. I regretted not kissing him in the shower before everything went wrong because I worried I might never get a chance to taste his lips again. It took a long time for either one of us to fall asleep. When I woke again, it was mid-afternoon, and Emory was gone.

NINETEEN

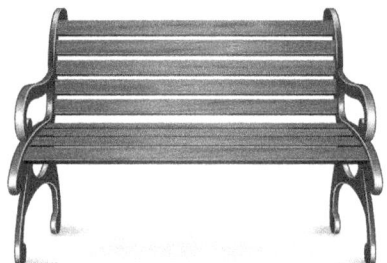

Jon

M Y EXISTENCE WAS BLEAK ON MORE OCCASIONS THAN I could count, but none were as dark as the days that followed Emory's departure from my life. He refused to answer my calls, return my messages, reply to my texts, or even answer the door the one time I worked up the nerve to drive to his home. I accepted that the one, magical night was all I was going to have with him.

I found it ironic that I was so certain Emory would accept he was destined to belong to me, but I was the one who had to accept that he wouldn't. I put up a good fight for a few weeks before I decided to let him go and hope that he'd come back to me when he was ready. *If, not when.* The only bright side, if you could call it that, was setting the trap to catch Alexander in the act of stealing from me.

I'd had plenty of experience with subterfuge while doing Uncle Sam's dirty undercover work, but Michelle was new to lying through her teeth to people who trusted her. She performed remarkably well under the circumstances, and I made sure I expressed my pride in her abilities.

"You're proud that I'm an effective liar?" she had asked in confusion.

"I'm proud that you can put aside your justified anger at Alexander for the time being to focus on our plan to bust his manipulative ass," I clarified. "You are grace under fire, and that's not easy."

"Thanks, Jon." She released a long sigh. "I will be glad when it's over, but I have a feeling that it won't be for quite some time."

"Why would you say that?"

"Alexander's attitude has changed a lot since you've put him back in the hands-off zone. He's not going to like getting fired or arrested, whichever you decide, and I worry that he's going to make a lot of noise."

"Let him."

I didn't know if it was my anger and frustration over Emory's absence or having to wait so long to address Alexander's theft, but I grew angrier as timed passed. I decided I wasn't giving him a chance to pay me back. I set up the hidden camera and had an undercover cop posing as a new bartender. I'd gotten to know a few detectives on the CPD during the investigation into my brother's death. I wanted to think they agreed to help because they liked me and not as an attempt to keep me from suing the police department. One of the undercover cops who frequented my club as a patron had a pending trial for his role in Broadman's string of crimes, but I didn't paint them all with the same broad stroke. I did want five minutes alone with Broadman to meet out my brand of justice, but Nate's memory deserved better from me.

The plan was simple: Michelle would begin entering and stocking the inventory until she would get interrupted by an emergency call. She would specifically ask Alexander to take over for her since he did such a great job the last time and wouldn't sign out. We'd record Alexander's activities in the stockroom, and the undercover cop would arrest him as soon as he made his move. It sounded easy in theory, but when was life ever easy?

I watched it all unfold in the monitors and had a sinking feeling in the pit of my stomach when Alexander didn't jump all over the chance to steal the liquor. That should've been my first clue that something was off about the entire thing. Michelle kept pleading with him, and he kept refusing to help. Finally, Michelle came into the office looking dejected and a little bit fearful.

"I'm sorry, Jon. I tried everything I could think of to get him to do the inventory for me again. He just kept refusing."

"What was the reason he gave?" I asked.

"He said he wasn't doing anything extra around here because it wasn't *appreciated*."

So it was about me and the lack of attention I showed him. "This asshole is something else, or he thinks his asshole is something else," I amended. I regretted my words when Michelle blushed either from embarrassment or discomfort. I should've quit while I was ahead, but I was on a roll. I blamed Emory for my sleepless nights, sexual frustration, and bone-deep wounds I worried might never heal. "He steals from me then has the nerve to get pissed when I don't fuck him." Something wasn't adding up.

"What do you want me to do?" Michelle nervously asked.

"I want you to play along and leave like you planned to do." I handed her my credit card. "Go get a manicure and pedicure on my dime and time. You deserve it. I'll take care of the rest. Just leave your employee number logged in."

"Are you sure?"

"I'm positive."

If Alexander was my thief, he should've jumped at the opportunity to steal from me again, if for no other reason than to get even with me. So why didn't he? There was only one way to find out.

I waited for Michelle to leave as planned and headed into the club area where Alexander was working behind the bar. He looked up when I walked up to him but didn't say anything.

"Michelle had to leave for a little bit, and I have an offsite meeting in thirty minutes that I can't miss. Can you step up and help out?"

"Step up and help out?" Alexander repeated incredulously then laughed. "I do plenty around here, but you never notice. Well, you used to notice." The last part was said suggestively and loud enough for everyone around us to hear since the music wasn't thumping yet.

"There are other clubs for you to work as a bartender if you're unhappy working for me, Alexander. Finish stocking the shelves as Michelle asked you to do, or you can start applying for those jobs in person today." I felt the tension build around us, but I wouldn't back down to the manipulative little shit. Somebody wasn't getting his ass plowed and wanted to take his misery out on everyone around him.

Alexander threw down his towel on the bar and walked away. I wasn't sure what the answer was until I returned to my office. I was fine with whatever choice he made because I was the winner in either scenario. Apparently, Alexander liked his job more than he let on, or I had pushed him enough to risk stealing from me again.

I watched on the monitor in my office as Alexander pulled his phone out of his pocket and made a call. I could tell he was angry, but my hidden camera was video only. He only spoke to the person for a few minutes before he hung up and began logging boxes of liquor before setting them on the shelf. He didn't start acting funny until he got to the boxes with the good stuff. He stocked some of the bottles on the shelves while the rest of the expensive liquor was put in a box he set off to the side.

I watched in shock as he moved the metal rack that had the bar napkins, plastic cups, straws, and other miscellaneous bar items away from the wall to reveal a hidden door that I didn't know existed. The building wasn't old enough to be used during prohibition, so I had no idea why it was there, but I knew where Alexander had stashed the booze until he could cart it out of there.

"Well, now you know for sure," Grant, the undercover cop, said. He'd followed me to my office once Alexander stomped off. "We just need to catch him taking it out of the building. Who knows how long that will be."

"He's expecting me to leave for a while, so I bet he makes his move then." I held up my cell phone and wiggled it a bit. "I'll watch him remotely through my phone app. Can you stick around?"

"I'm yours for the day," he said then blushed. "Well, not like that…"

"I knew what you meant," I assured him. "I'll be in touch if I see something."

I drove a few blocks and parked my car in a coffee shop parking lot. I wanted to be out of sight, but not so far that I would miss the takedown.

I had a feeling that Alexander would wait until the club started to fill up so that he could sneak out the hooch during his break with a smaller risk of getting caught since most of the staff was preoccupied. On my phone, I had a split screen showing hidden cameras in the stockroom and the one hidden in the awning over the back door so that I had a clear view of the employee parking lot behind the building, but the camera remained hidden.

Sure enough, Alexander entered the stockroom about an hour after the club opened. He checked his phone then quickly accessed the hiding spot and pulled out the hooch. He peeked around the door of the stockroom to make sure the coast was clear then disappeared off camera until he stepped out the back door. I watched in shock as a familiar silver car pulled up behind the club.

The trunk of the car popped up, and Alexander lowered the box of stolen liquor into the car then approached the driver's door. Alexander smiled down at the driver then leaned in for a kiss before he said something and stepped back. Grant came out the door with his gun before the car could drive off and I grinned to myself when I realized I had killed two birds with one stone.

Grant told the driver to park the car then escorted both of them to my office where they waited until I showed up. "Hello again, Marlon."

The man nervously twitched when he heard the dead calm in my voice. "I can explain."

"I don't want to hear your explanation, Marlon. Save it for court." Marlon was a wealthy guy, so it made no sense that he would steal from me, unless it was to get even because I refused to take my brother's place in his bed.

"Court?" He sounded astounded that I would consider such a thing. "Surely, you'll just let me pay you—"

"Oh, this is payback for the way you treated my brother, Marlon."

"I..."

"Not another word from you," I warned him. I didn't so much as look at Alexander. I knew I'd acted foolishly when it came to him. I was just grateful I hadn't tipped Marlon off by asking him for an attorney referral. Sure, Alexander could still make allegations about me or go to the press with his sordid story, but people weren't as likely to believe him once they saw the evidence of his thievery. They'd assume he was trying to get even with me. Still, I'd be ready for whatever he threw my way. "You can take them away."

"Let's go, boys," Grant said. "There should be a squad car waiting for you out front."

"Out front?" Marlon asked. "Please, don't do this to me. My family—"

"Probably already knows you like to suck cock."

He gasped and sputtered, but I ignored both of them and returned my attention back to my work. For the most part, ignoring emotions was easy for me. The only chink in my armor was Emory. I tried my hardest not to think about him, but memories of our night together kept popping up in my head until I thought I was losing my fucking mind. I had the strongest urge to get drunk, but that wouldn't solve anything.

As much as I just wanted to go home, I knew the staff would have too many questions about what happened. Yeah, it was a dick move to have them hauled out through the crowd and out the front door, but I was feeling exceptionally dickish lately.

I waited until the club closed and had an impromptu staff meeting where I laid everything out for them. My staff was shocked and disappointed about what happened, and I was grateful that not a single one of them appeared to be an Alexander sympathizer. If so, I'd weed them out and send them packing.

I went straight home after the meeting and went right up to bed. I was too fucking old for that three o'clock in the morning bullshit anymore. I had just closed my eyes and drifted to sleep when my ringing phone woke me. I don't know why, but I thought it was Emory calling me.

"Em, are you okay?" I sleepily asked.

"Soooo, he's nothing to you, buuuut you expect his phone call in the early morning h-h-hours." I hadn't heard Beau sound so drunk since we lost half of our platoon early in the war with Iraq.

I sat up fast; my drowsiness immediately disappeared. "Beau, what's wrong?"

"Emmmmory," he slurred.

"Emory? Is he hurt? I don't understand."

"Heeee had another v-vision."

I closed my eyes as understanding dawned. "Were you able to recover Kent's body?" I softly asked.

"Y-yes." That time his voice broke from emotion instead of booze. "He was j-j-just a kid, Jon. Had his whole life ahead of h-h-him. Why?"

"I don't know, Beau, but I know you'll find those answers." I cleared my throat to dislodge the emotional lump lodged there. "Are you ready to tell me who Kent was to you?"

"C-c-can't. I might've located his b-body, but I don't know who put h-h-him there. I c-can't risk the truth getting out."

I wanted to know so badly but understood his reasoning. If people realized Beau had a personal connection they might clam up even more. Innocent people or witnesses could fear he wouldn't give them a fair shake. He was handling it the right way, but I hated to see my friend go through such a difficult time while I was so far away and couldn't help him.

"I'll fly out in the morning," I offered.

"Nooooo," Beau slurred. "I'll be f-fine, Jon. I just needed to talk to someone. It's been crazy ever since I talked to Emory this morning."

Hearing Emory's name cut me to the bone and made me want to rip my hair out. Perhaps I needed to start saying it in the privacy of my own home so that it was easier to take when others sprung it on me.

"Are you one hundred percent certain the body was Kent's?" He'd been missing for ten years so there wouldn't be anything left but bones and clothes.

"There was a personalized g-g-gold bracelet on the l-left wrist of the body we f-f-found. Van is going to compare the d-d-dental records in the morning, but I know it's h-him, Jon." I'd heard Beau speak fondly of the county coroner slash medical examiner. His last name was something odd for a doctor, but I... Carver! Donovan Carver.

"At least you'll get the confirmation soon and can hopefully solve the case. Beau, I will seriously come out..."

"No! P-patch things up w-with Emory."

"I've tried, Beau. It's no use."

"It's not l-like you to give up on s-s-something—or someone—important to you," Beau softly said.

"You can't force things."

"He m-misses you. I can t-t-tell. Don't w-wait until it's t-t-too late."

He sounded like he was talking from experience but, to the best of my knowledge, Beau had never been in love. "You better get some sleep, buddy. You're going to need to be at your best to catch a killer. I have faith in you."

"Thank y-you. Talk soon."

Beau sounded exhausted. I knew it wouldn't be long before he crashed hard. I wished I could say the same about myself. I lay away for another hour thinking about what Beau said about Emory missing me and wondering if it was true. Hell, just thinking his name nearly killed me.

"Emory. Emory. Emory." I repeated his name out loud hoping it got easier to say and hear. It didn't. "Damn it, Emory. What am I going to do about you?"

TWENTY

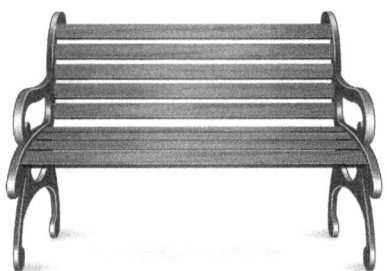

Emory

"**M**R. WHELAN?"

"Hmmm?" My head snapped up, and I looked into Dr. Caitlyn Rosenau's intelligent brown eyes. I had liked her from the moment we met, even though I wished it was under better circumstances.

"I asked if you needed me to repeat any of the information." She smiled softly. "I know it's a lot to process and I want to answer your questions." She tapped the folder on her desk that held my MRI results, my official diagnosis, and the care plan she designed for me. "Everything I've told you is also in this folder, but I'm sure you have questions.

"Mr. Whelan, your MRI results show a tumor in the dura fold that

runs between the left and right sides of your brain. It has the charac-
teristics of a meningioma. These usually start in the membrane lay-
ers called meninges beneath the skull. They grow inward and push on
the brain; the symptoms depend on the part of the brain they appear.
Your tumor is called a parasagittal meningioma, and the symptoms in-
clude headaches, personality changes, vision problems, and arm or leg
weakness."

I'd heard the words tumor and brain in the same sentence and
started to zone out. I still caught bits and pieces of what Dr. Rosenau
said, but I couldn't string them all together to form coherent thoughts
right then.

"Slow-growing tumor…"

"Most likely benign…"

"Surgically remove the tumor to relieve the pressure on your brain
and perform a biopsy to make sure it's benign. You can see the tumor
has smooth, well-defined edges, which normally indicates that cancer is
not present."

"How long do you think I've had this tumor?" I asked her, snapping out of my trance.

"It's hard to say for sure, but I'm going to say at least five years
for it to have reached this size." The tumor on the screen behind her
didn't look that big, but it still scared the fuck out of me.

"Five years is how long I've been having visions," I said absently,
more to myself than anything.

"Visions?"

Here's the part where she decides I'm crazy. "Five years ago, I woke
up from a coma after a nasty accident that claimed my husband's life.
I had a mild brain injury that took a while to heal. When it did, I began having psychic visions. At first they came to me in my sleep, and
I thought they were dreams, but my abilities have grown since then."

Dr. Rosenau placed her elbow on her desk and tilted her head
to the side. I was relieved to see curiosity in her eyes, not disbelief or
derision. "Go on."

And I did. I told the doctor about my work with law enforcement agencies over the years, including most recently assisting Jon's friend, Beau. *Jon.* God, how I missed him. It felt like years—not months—since I left Jon sleeping in his bed. "You think I'm crazy, right?"

"Absolutely not," Dr. Rosenau said, surprising me. "There's been a lot of scientific studies about psychic phenomenon and where it comes from."

"There has?"

Dr. Rosenau nodded and continued. "Psychic ability is associated with changes in function in the frontal and right temporal lobes. One increases and the other decreases. Synesthesia, which is like cross-wiring in the brain, is a legitimate neurological condition. People who refer to themselves as psychic often have synesthesia. They see and hear the world differently. Some people with this condition suffer serious psychiatric breakdowns while others learn to manage their newfound abilities."

"Wow, I could've used you in my life when my mother wanted to have me committed," I said then laughed dryly. "Do you think my head trauma caused both the synesthesia and this tumor?"

"It's entirely possible that your head trauma triggered the cross-wiring in your brain, but your tumor is in the lining of the brain and most likely isn't related at all." Dr. Rosenau folded her hands on her desk. "The brain is a very complicated organ, Mr. Whelan, and there's a lot we don't know about it," she explained, "but I can tell you that your tumor is operable, most likely benign, and I'm confident that you'll live a long, healthy life."

"Brain surgery sounds terrifying," I said honestly. "Can you tell me what it entails?"

"Absolutely." Dr. Rosenau then patiently explained what I could expect if I agreed to surgery.

If? I'd been miserable the last month with unimaginable pain. I couldn't fathom living the rest of my life in that kind of agony. Every day was an endless headache that no over-the-counter medicine could touch. My vision had started to blur and I became dizzy more frequently. I went to the local doctor in Blissville once the tingling started in my arms and legs. I knew that something was really wrong with me. The doctor ordered a series of tests that uncovered my tumor.

"I'll perform a keyhole parietal craniotomy and remove the tumor. My neuropathologist will evaluate the tissue under a microscope to determine if it's benign or malignant so we know what additional treatments you will need. After surgery, we'll prescribe medications to keep the swelling and inflammation down. If I'm unable to remove the entire tumor, we may use radiation to eradicate what remains."

As much as I didn't want to live in pain, the thought of her cutting open my skull and digging things out of my brain was terrifying. "How soon?"

"If it's benign like I suspect, it's a matter of what you can tolerate. The headaches can become debilitating and the tingling you feel in your left arm and leg could worsen or weaken and cause you to collapse."

"I'm going to have the procedure, but there are a few things I'd like to do first."

"Are you talking about days, weeks, or months?" she asked me.

"Weeks." I wanted to spend time with Memphis and my grandfather. I hoped to see Josh and Gabe's babies when they brought them home. I needed to look into Jon's eyes once more and see love and desire instead of resentment and sadness. He'd been absent from Josh and Gabe's since their wedding, except for their surprise baby shower at Kyle and Chaz's house two weeks before Christmas. We spent a few hours in the same house and didn't speak to one another. I had something I needed to tell Jon, just in case things didn't go so well for me.

"Well, Christmas is in a few days and New Year's is the week after. How do you feel about mid-January? Will that be long enough?"

"I'll make it work. Let's get it scheduled."

We went over the pre-op tests that I was required to undergo the week before surgery, so I knew I had to do my traveling and get back to Cincinnati in two weeks instead of three.

"Emory!" Granddad joyfully cried when I entered his study. "Oh, it truly is Christmas. How long are you staying, my boy?"

"I thought I'd stay with you until after Christmas and then I thought I'd ring in the new year with Memphis."

Connor Whelan shoved the quilt that covered his legs to the side and slowly rose to his feet. I would've told him to stay seated, but he wouldn't have listened. "Come give an old man a hug; I don't know how many Christmases we have left together."

"Don't say that, Granddad." My voice thickened with raw emotion. I hugged my granddad as tightly as I dared while being careful not to hurt him. He had always seemed larger than life to me and feeling his frailty rocked me to the core. He had always been my champion in the world; my hero. There was no way I'd risk not seeing him one more time.

"Don't be sad for me, Emory. I've lived a long, happy life." I pulled back and smiled into his eyes. I wasn't about to correct his notion that it could be *his* last Christmas. "Have you talked to your mother lately?"

"No," I admitted. "I attempted a few months back," more like eight, not that I was counting, "but Audrey couldn't be bothered with returning my call. You and Memphis's family have always been enough for me though."

"Now that you're here, I'll have Juanita make all your favorite foods for the holiday meal. How does that sound?" His excitement was contagious, and I stopped worrying about my upcoming surgery and the phone call I still had to make. I sent an expensive bottle of Whelan Whiskey to Jon for Christmas, but he didn't call or text to acknowledge that he received it. I knew it would take more than a bottle of fine liquor to apologize for my behavior, but I thought it was a good start.

The five days I spent at my granddad's house was the most peaceful I'd had since River died. We spent most of our time in the cozy library reading books by a crackling fire or watching his favorite black-and-white movies. Alcohol was prohibited with the medications I started taking, so I enjoyed hot teas, coffee, and hot chocolates. When it was time for me to leave, Granddad took my hand and looked up at me through watery, green eyes.

"I can tell that you're going through a difficult time, Emory. You're a very strong man, and I'd like to think you get that from me. Even the strongest men need to unburden their souls and lean on someone from time to time." Granddad squeezed my hands and added, "You're not alone."

"I'm in a good place, Granddad."

He quirked a brow like he didn't believe me, but didn't call me on it. "Don't wait another year to visit, okay?"

"Okay," I said around the lump in my throat. "I love you."

I needed to say those three little words to a few people over my remaining days before surgery. Memphis was next on my list. I expected him to take one look at me and demand answers. Instead, he hugged me tightly. He probably assumed my mood was more of the same he'd witnessed in the five years after losing River. I had hoped to wait until the last minute to come clean and ask him to stay with me and act as my medical power of attorney. Unfortunately, I'd left my prescription bottles on the bathroom sink for him to see.

Memphis walked into the living room with my pill bottles in one hand and his cell phone in the other. Tears streaked down his face, and he struggled to speak. I knew that he'd looked up information about my drugs online and had jumped to the worst conclusions.

"It's not as bad as you think." At least I hoped that was the case. I sat Memphis down and told him everything I knew up to that point.

"Were you even going to tell me?" Memphis asked once he

calmed down.

"Of course," I said casually. "I also planned on asking you to be my medical power of attorney in case I'm not able to make decisions regarding my care." He was also the executor of my estate, but I didn't tell him that after I saw the fear on his face when I mentioned the medical POA.

"Of course, I'll do it." Memphis took a shaky breath and released it slowly.

Neither of us was up to a wild time to ring in the new year, so we settled for delicious pizza and some rousing board games. I kicked Memphis's ass at Clue, and he whipped me good at Monopoly. "You have a knack for business, Memphis. Maybe it's time you did something with it."

"The only thing I love is comic books and memorabilia. I can't see myself making a living off of either of those things."

I let the subject drop because the last thing I wanted to do was make Memphis feel bad about himself. I just wanted him to be happy, and I also wanted to live long enough to see it happen. I pushed the maudlin thoughts aside and looked back at the television where they ball was starting to drop in the Big Apple. I picked up my cell phone just as the hosts started the countdown to the new year.

I pulled up Jon's contact info and sent a quick message to him before I could change my mind. *Happy New Year, Jon.* I didn't expect him to fire back a message right away, but I expected him to respond within a day or two. When that didn't happen, I realized that I had hurt him far worse than I imagined. *Well, it looks like I can cross that conversation off my list.*

Three days before my surgery, Josh and Gabe came home with their babies, Dylan and Destiny. I went to their home for a celebration with our friends and was shocked when Jon showed up. I had hoped that his lack of response was from him not getting my message, but I could tell by the distant look in his eyes that he got it and chose to ignore it. I told myself not to be sad, but my heart didn't listen.

I fussed over the babies and breathed in the happiness, love, and joy I felt in the room. I laughed along with everyone else when Josh had a little meltdown when he learned that Kyle and Chaz got married in Vegas. I was truly happy for the newlyweds and hoped that I would be around to celebrate the reception that they planned for their friends and family.

I was too nervous to eat the pizza we'd ordered before Josh and Gabe arrived. The tension was making my low-grade headache worse. I decided to say goodbye to the happy new dads and head on home for a hot bath and a quiet evening. Memphis was due to arrive in two days, and I just needed to stay busy until then. I caught Josh and Gabe outside the kitchen as they headed in to get a bite to eat.

"Can I talk to you guys for a minute?"

"Is something wrong?" Gabe asked me. Both he and Josh wore matching looks of concern on their faces. I guessed my voice wasn't as calm as I had hoped.

"No," I said, hoping that I sounded convincing. "I just wanted to let you know that I'm leaving town for a little bit to take care of some personal things. I don't like to just drop out of sight without telling you." My voice cracked, and I broke eye contact to look down at my shoes. *Damn, this is harder than I thought.* I knew I was going to lose it and decided to say what I needed to and leave.

Josh stepped up to me and placed his hands on my shoulders. "Emory, there's something obviously wrong. Won't you tell us?"

I only shook my head. I wouldn't burden them with my troubles. I just couldn't leave without saying goodbye.

"Is this like the last time when you left before our wedding?" Josh asked. "You're coming back, right?"

"I hope so," I replied softly. "But if not, I want you to know that your friendship has come to mean the world to me. The two of you have restored my faith in humanity."

"Emory, is there anything we can do to help you?" Gabe asked.

"I appreciate that so much, Gabe, but, unfortunately, this is something that I'll have to do alone." I hugged Josh first then Gabe. "I love you both. I'm sorry that I ruined your first night home with the babies. I'll be leaving soon, and I couldn't go without saying goodbye."

"So long for now. You'll be back, Emory," Josh said confidently. He added a wink and said, "I know things." I smiled at Josh's attempt at a joke, but I couldn't give him the response he wanted.

"There will always be a place for you at our table, no matter how long it takes you to find your way back to us," Gabe told me.

Tears slid down my face unchecked, and I turned and left without another word. I had almost made it to my car when I heard Jon calling my name. I stopped and let him catch up to me. His strong hands landed on my shoulders then turned me. Just the weight of his hands on my body made me feel better. I looked up into his worried blue eyes and fell apart even more.

"Hey now." Jon pulled me into his arms and held me tight against his chest. "It can't be that bad, Em."

I pulled back and looked into his eyes once more. My heart thundered in my chest when I noticed that the icy distance from earlier was replaced with the same tenderness I saw in his eyes when we'd made love. Yeah, I realized that it was love even when I tried to make it all about the physical release.

"Come home with me, Jon. I need you."

He didn't ask questions nor did he hesitate. Jon simply drove to my house and followed me inside. We didn't stop in the kitchen or living room. I didn't offer him something to drink. I led him up to my bedroom and took my time stripping him down. Jon did the same for me then our mouths eagerly met at the same time our hands reached for one another.

We'd only had one night and morning together, but my body knew Jon like he'd been a part of me for my entire life. Jon's groans spurred mine, his sure hands emboldened me to explore him, and I felt complete for the first time in ages when he slid deep inside me. I didn't try to look away; I kept my eyes open and focused on his while he rocked in and out of me. I kissed his lips, his chin, and his jaw. I dug my fingers into Jon's muscular ass while gripping him tighter with my thighs. I was terrified that I would never know his love again and desperate to commit every second to memory so I could relive it over and over the next few days.

Once the loving was over, Jon pulled me to him and held me tight. I wanted to think he would still be there in the morning, but I wasn't willing to take the chance. I placed my head over his heart and took comfort in the steady thumping in his chest.

"I love you, Jon."

A soft snore escaped his lips as soon as the words left mine. I wasn't even sure if he heard my confession, but his arms tightened around me, so I figured his soul at least recognized them.

PART 3

Embrace

TWENTY-ONE

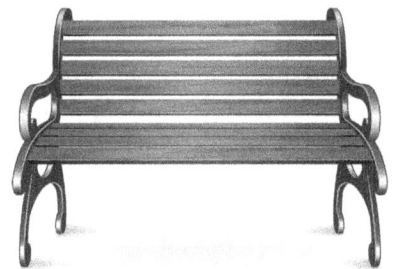

Emory

I COULD TELL BY THE DIP IN THE MATTRESS THAT JON WAS STILL beside me in bed, but he wasn't nearly as close as I would've liked. I hadn't even opened my eyes yet, and I already craved the feel of his bare skin against mine, so I scooted closer toward him. I expected him to turn into me and pull me close because I'd seen it in my dreams and visions at least two dozen times since I met him. Instead, my leg bumped up against a thigh that was hard and unyielding. My brain registered tight, bunched muscles as if he were angry, but what...

My eyes flew open, and I sat up in bed so suddenly that I got dizzy. My stomach pitched and rolled, and I got out of bed and went to the bathroom as quickly as I could because I knew I was going to be sick. Even though it happened quickly, I still saw the folder of information that Jon held in his hands.

"Emory?" Jon asked in alarm. I heard him get out of bed and follow me.

"Don't come in here," I said firmly. "I don't want you to see me like this, Jon." Of course, he didn't listen.

There wasn't much for my stomach to reject, but it wasn't satisfied with only purging my food. I dry-heaved for what seemed like thirty minutes as tears of anguish and humiliation ran down my face. When I finished, Jon was there with a cold washcloth and broad shoulders to rest my head on.

"You have some serious explaining to do, baby, but it can wait until you feel better." Jon released a stuttering breath as he held me tightly against him. It was the first time since my diagnosis that I knew everything was going to be okay. It had to be. "What am I going to do with you, Emory?" I heard the fear in his voice and realized that he'd read at least part of the information in the folder.

"Just love me, Jon."

"I'm going to love you as you've never been loved before, and that's a guarantee."

A few months ago, his words would've made me angry, but right then my tears of pain turned to tears of joy and contentment. I was at peace for the first time in so long that I fell into an exhausted sleep right there in his arms on the cold bathroom floor. The next time I opened my eyes, I was in bed again, and the daylight coming through the windows told me it was almost noon.

"First time the sun has been out in weeks." I slowly turned my head and saw that Jon was lying beside me. His elbow and forearm supported the weight of his upper body as he looked down at me, giving the impression that he had watched over me while I slept. "I'm going to try this a bit slower to see if I have better results than last time." I had to piss something fierce, and I wanted to scrub my teeth so I could spend the day kissing the man I loved. Then I owed him an explanation.

"Do you want me to come with you?"

A thought occurred to me then. Jon had lovingly washed my body once before, but I'd never experienced the pleasure of running my hands all over his wet body. "Shower with me?" I asked.

I started the shower to let the water heat up, which took a while in the old house I rented. I pulled a new toothbrush out of the vanity drawer and handed it to Jon then brushed my teeth, cheeks, tongue, and roof of my mouth to get rid of the nasty taste. In fact, I went back in a second time after rinsing my toothbrush and applying fresh paste then chased it with a few rounds of mouthwash.

"You have stellar oral hygiene habits," Jon remarked with a raised brow when I finished and turned to face him.

"I have a lot of ass kissing to do today, and I want minty fresh breath while doing it." That wasn't all that I planned to kiss, but I wanted to get the apologies and explanations over with first. "The water should be hot enough by now." I reached around the curtain and stuck my hand in the spray. It was the exact temperature of the first shower we shared—hot as it could get without scalding us. "Perfect."

I got in the shower first, and Jon got in after me. My shower could've fit inside his four or five times, but it was hard to be upset about it when there was only enough room for us to hold on to one another while the water cascaded over us.

"You're going to be okay, Em." Jon's voice was thick, husky, and filled with so much tenderness that tears threatened once more.

My headache eased considerably during my morning nap, but it hadn't disappeared fully. "I do feel better."

"Not just today, baby; I meant everything. Surgery, recovery, and us." *Us.* I loved the deep timbre in his voice when he linked our lives together. "You don't have to be afraid anymore."

I'd been afraid for so long, and of so many things, that I wasn't sure I could just turn it off like a switch, but I sure as hell wanted to try. I stared into his eyes, hoping he saw the truth in my words. I needed him to know that I wasn't just saying these things because I had a tumor. I spoke from my heart. "I do love you, Jon. I denied it for months, gradually accepted it for a few more, and now I'm ready to embrace the love you bring into my life. I'm sorry it took me this long."

"I'm sorry I didn't respond to your Christmas gift or text message on New Year's Eve. I was in a bad place and…" Jon's words trailed off. I wasn't sure I wanted to know what he was doing, and my expression must've belied the direction my mind had gone. "No! I wasn't with another guy. Mentally, I wasn't in a good place. I got shitfaced drunk on the booze you sent me and having myself a pity party for one. Another new year but nothing had changed. Then I got your text."

I wanted to believe that it made him feel better, but he would've responded to me sooner if it had. In the grand scheme of things, it didn't matter that it took him two weeks to respond to my text after the hell I had put him through. I didn't realize it at the time, but his appearance at Josh and Gabe's the night before was his response. He was letting me know he was still there, but in person and not through a message.

"I can't change what has happened between us, Jon. I can tell you that I'm sorry until I'm blue in the face, but it would be a lie." That got his attention. "I am not proud of the way I reacted to you, or sometimes treated you, but I'm not sorry for loving my late-husband with my whole heart until I was ready to acknowledge I could love you just as much." Understanding dawned in his blue eyes then he gently traced the tattoo inked over my heart. "This moment right here with you makes me want to fight in ways I never have in my life. Five years ago, I wanted to die too when I found out that River was taken from me. Today, I want to live a long life filled with… what is it you like to do?"

We both laughed at my question, realizing we didn't know much about each other beyond our tragedies. I was a broken widower, and he was the mysterious man who'd witnessed the worst in humanity too many times to count. We were broken men with jagged edges that could cut a person deep if they were foolish enough to venture too close, but, somehow, we aligned perfectly to form something whole and beautiful.

I realized that it didn't matter how much time I had left—hours, days, or a lifetime; I was going to discover everything there was to know about Jon Silver.

"Honestly, Emory, I don't know what I like to do." He grimaced when he heard how odd that sounded. "I didn't have much time to discover anything about myself. The boy I used to be entered boot camp and stayed there. I emerged as a man, and my life experiences that followed made it harder and harder to remember who that boy was or what he liked."

I admit that Jon's tough, rugged side turned me on, but the more vulnerable parts of him owned me. I was pretty sure that very few people saw the real man and that made me feel even more special. I placed both my hands at his temples and narrowed my eyes like I was reading his mind.

"Careful," he playfully admonished and lightly swatted my ass, "there's top secret intel stored in there."

"Yeah, I'm not getting anything that I could leak to a conspiracy theorist," I said, playing along. "I see round, firm balls."

"Yeah?" Jon waggled his brows because he liked where the conversation was going.

I closed my eyes and played up my abilities. "Hmmmmm. I see white balls with red stitching." I reopened my eyes dramatically. "You love baseball!" Jon looked at me suspiciously like he was debating whether I pulled that out of his head or made a lucky guess. "Neither," I said after a good chuckle. "I remembered you talking about the Reds game from the bachelor party weekend. I heard the excitement in your voice when you talked about it going into extra innings and the one time you saw a perfect game as a kid."

"That was a magical night for a twelve-year-old boy," Jon told me. "I'd won those tickets for making the honor roll all year long.

They were up in the nosebleed section, but I didn't care. The atmosphere was amazing, and, for once, my mom seemed carefree and happy. We ate hotdogs, popcorn, cotton candy, and drank way too many sodas." Jon closed his eyes briefly and swallowed hard. "You could feel the crowd's excitement build as the innings passed without the opposing team reaching base. Pure magic." Jon smiled and said, "I remember my mom covering her eyes when the last batter hit a line drive toward the gap between second and third base. She yelled for the shortstop to catch the ball." He laughed at the memory then added wryly, "He made a diving catch that still makes highlight reels nearly thirty years later."

"That does sound like an amazing time," I told him. "So, let's plan to see a lot of baseball games this year."

"I thought you didn't like baseball."

"Who said that?"

"I just assumed since you didn't go to the Reds game that…" Jon's voice trailed off. "Ah, you didn't go because of me."

"Yep." Why bother denying it? "My hot water tank isn't nearly as generous as yours, so we better get to washing up."

"I'm only in here because you asked me. I have no problem smelling like you."

"Well, I guess I'll have to rub my scent all over you again." I hardly recognized the husky voice that came from my lips.

We had so many things to discuss, but neither of us wanted to talk right then. I had other ways I wanted to communicate with Jon first. Washing my body was difficult to do in the small shower. Instead of getting frustrated, I used it as an excuse to brush my leg against his erection. Jon jerked the washcloth out of my hands and shut the water off.

"You're clean enough."

He wasn't nearly as forceful when he toweled me off though. I looked forward to the day that he would feel safe enough to toss me down and fuck me like an animal, but I was willing to settle for slow and sweet until then. Jon lay me down and lovingly kissed, licked, or nibbled on every part of my body until I couldn't take it anymore.

"Please, Jon," I pleaded.

He stopped tormenting me and reached for the drawer where I kept the supplies. I wrapped my hand around his wrist, halting him. He looked at me with a concerned gaze.

"Nothing between us ever again."

"Are you sure, Emory? I mean, I get tested regularly and—"

"I'm sure." I took the lubricant and slicked his bare cock with it. "I want to be yours."

Jon dropped the condom wrapper and positioned himself between my legs. As much as I wanted him to take me hard and fast, I could feel the amount of pressure building in my skull and knew it wasn't what I needed. Jon lowered his body over mine, supporting his weight on his forearm beside my head. He reached between our bodies to grip his dick and slowly pushed into me.

I whimpered at how good it felt having him inside me after that final barrier was removed. I wanted to close my eyes but didn't want to miss a single expression that crossed his face as he loved me. I caught each of his gasps with my mouth, just as he did for me. I ghosted my hands all over his hard-muscled body and felt goose bumps pop up beneath my touch as Jon loved me thoroughly. He built my pleasure up slowly, turning me into a bundle of raw need by the time I reached the peak. I teetered back and forth—almost there, but not quite—until Jon said the magic words that pushed me over the edge.

"I love you, Emory."

I soundlessly came apart in his arms, unaware that I was holding my breath as I came all over my stomach until my lungs started to burn. I sucked precious air into my lungs as I watched Jon join me in nirvana. He kept his eyes open, and I could see the pleasure of his orgasm slowly wash over his beautiful body.

"I love you too, Jon."

Jon collapsed on top of me after he was fully spent. I wrapped my arms around him and held him tight, even though it made it harder to breathe. I didn't care that his dick was still in my ass and he didn't care that he was lying in my cum. Hell, if it were up to me, I would stay in bed naked with him all day. Jon had a different idea though.

"Do you think your water heater has anything left in the tank?" The pillow muffled his words.

"Why?" I asked suspiciously. "I thought you liked smelling like me."

"I do, but I'm not sure how Gabe and Josh would like it." Jon raised up and looked into my eyes. "They're worried sick about you. They love you. Let them be here for you right now."

"Okay."

I showered again, dressed, and took my medication with the soup and sandwiches Jon made us for lunch. While we ate, I told Jon about the symptoms I'd experienced that prompted me to seek medical attention, and I repeated everything my surgeon had told me. I could tell he was still going to read every single word in that folder later that night. After lunch, Jon drove us to the Roman-Wyatt's house so I could tell them what was going on.

"What time is your surgery?" Josh quietly asked. I could tell how much it hurt him that I had planned to go through the procedure without telling them. They'd been so generous and kind to me already. I just didn't want to be a burden to them while they had their hands full with the twins.

"I have to check in at seven and surgery is at ten."

"We'll be there," Gabe said.

"You guys don't…" I let my words trail off when I saw Josh's Don't Fuck With Me expression.

"The grandmas will have everything under control here, and we can be there for Jon while he waits and for *you* while you recover." Josh wasn't asking; he was telling us how it was going to be.

"I'm sure Jon and Memphis will be glad to have company."

"Memphis?" they all asked at once.

"He's my cousin and best friend." I told them about some of our less colorful shenanigans growing up. "You guys are going to love him."

Two tiny cries split the air, and we laughed as Josh and Gabe hauled ass over to the bassinettes to pick up their babies.

"What do you think? Hungry or stinky?" Gabe asked.

"I don't think I care for the new nicknames you've assigned to our angels," Josh said, earning a glare from Gabe. "Hmmmm. Dylan has his poop face rocking, and Destiny is trying to eat her fist."

"One of each," Gabe said, nodding.

"We're going to take off so you guys can enjoy time with the twins," I told the new dads.

"You don't have to go," Josh said. "We'll just go change their diapers, and you guys can help us feed them."

"We don't have the right equipment," Jon teased.

"And we do?" Gabe countered then rolled his eyes.

"What if we drop one?" Jon asked, getting to the crux of his wariness.

"Try your best not to do that," Josh quipped as they headed upstairs to change the babies.

Fifteen minutes later, Jon and I sat on the couch feeding Destiny and Dylan. Josh had tucked a pillow beneath my arm when I told him about the potential for sudden weakness. I glanced over at Jon, and he smiled at me. *Dear Lord, those big strong hands were meant to cradle babies.* He squinted his eyes like he could read my mind and wanted to discourage me from getting big ideas. Too late! *Maybe someday,* I said to myself.

TWENTY-TWO

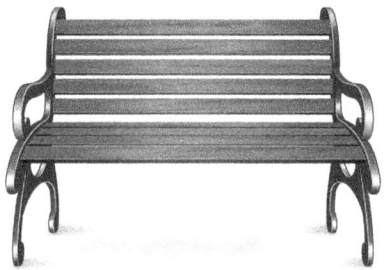

Jon

BARELY SLEPT THE NIGHT BEFORE EMORY'S SURGERY BECAUSE too many wild thoughts jockeyed for attention and I couldn't shut my brain down. The predominant emotions were joy and happiness that Emory was finally in my arms and admitting he loved me too. Unfortunately, I was afraid of what drove him to that point. I wanted to believe it was an epiphany that we belonged together, but I figured it had more to do with the tumor they discovered.

We'd spent every private moment talking and getting to know one another, and I came right out and asked him some tough questions while he was tucked up against me in the privacy of his bedroom. "Em, do you think we would've arrived at this moment if you hadn't found out about the tumor?" As much as I tried, I couldn't push all the doubt out of my mind to focus on the positive. A person didn't shake their lifelong habits overnight.

Emory propped himself on his elbow and looked down at me. "I do." He sounded so certain and resolute, but how? Before I could ask, he answered my unspoken question. "It was fated to happen. I could cut my hair and fight it all I wanted, but it was going to happen."

"So, you just settled for a future you didn't want?"

"Oh, I wanted you, Jon. The strength of my connection to you is what I resisted. Loving someone as much as I love you is a huge risk. I know how it feels when…" Emory's voice broke off and he shook his head. "At first, I felt disloyal to River's memory for wanting you, then I resented you when I couldn't banish you from my mind. Once I finally realized that you were the key to my happiness, I worried that I had pushed you too far and lost my chance at something amazing."

"What would you have done had I not shown up at Josh and Gabe's the other night?"

Emory ran his hand over my chest and smiled. "I would've shown up at your fancy iron gate."

"Nate's fancy iron gate," I corrected. I thought the home was beautiful, but it never felt like mine.

"I know this seems like a sudden reversal of feelings, and I get it, but in time you'll accept that my love is real. We're real, and we belong together. Loving you doesn't take anything away from the way I loved River. I know that now."

I tugged Emory down for a long, lingering kiss that turned into another round of lovemaking. I'd never connected to someone the way I did him and the thought of losing him terrified me. I couldn't be angry anymore about his previous determination to remain loyal to his deceased husband. I finally understood how he felt the night before his surgery as I tamped down terrifying thoughts of what if.

What if Emory doesn't survive the surgery? What if he wakes up a different person and the new guy doesn't want me? What if I gave my heart to a man who only thinks he wants it?

I closed my eyes and willed happier thoughts to replace the worrisome ones. *Emory is going to come out of surgery with flying colors, and I will be by his side every step of his recovery. Trust that Emory knows his heart and quit looking for excuses to build walls around yours.* I was the tough-ass man who had faced down many enemies and survived. There was no room for doubt in war nor was there room in the battle for happiness. Winning Emory had been an epic battle, and I would celebrate my spoils instead of worrying about how long they would last.

We had finally drifted asleep a few hours before his alarm went off. The mood could've been somber, but I refused to allow it. Emory wasn't allowed to eat or drink anything, so I didn't either. "When you feel up to it, I'll make you my famous Spanish omelet."

"Do you cook often?"

"Nothing like Josh so don't get excited, but I do the basics pretty damn well," I replied proudly.

"I can't wait to sample your cooking. There are so many things I'm looking forward to doing with you, Jon." I thought Emory's voice was thick with sleep, but I realized it was something more when he said, "I want to go into that hospital smelling like you."

Who was I to refuse him? Besides, the scent of him on my skin could comfort me when I was ready to lose my mind during the long procedure. Em was right about Memphis; he was a lovable guy who kept the drive to the hospital interesting. I admired the way he openly showed love to Emory inside his pre-op suite without worrying that it made him look less manly or some shit. He patted me on my shoulder and left the two of us alone so we could have some privacy in the last minutes before surgery. I took a page from Memphis's book and ran my hand over Emory's smooth, bald head. He had decided at the last minute to have Josh shave off his hair instead of a stranger.

"It's not surprising that your head is a perfect shape," I whispered against his lips. "It matches the rest of you."

Emory's smile warmed the cold, sterile hospital room. "I'm

going to grow it back out. I miss the long hair, and you never had the chance to run your fingers through it."

"I'll take you any way I can have you." I pressed my mouth to his ear because my words were only for him. "There are so many ways that I'm going to have you, baby." It might not have been the best time to whisper dirty words to my man, but then again, one should never waste an opportunity to tell someone how they feel. What I wouldn't give to tell my brother that I loved him. Even though I'm pretty sure Nate knew what our time together meant to me, I wished I had been less concerned about my masculinity and said the words out loud to him. I cleared my throat because I wanted my voice to sound confident and sure. "I love you, Emory. I'll be right there waiting for you when you open your eyes."

"I'm counting on it. I love you too, Jon."

I gave him one more kiss before I left his pre-op room. I headed out into the waiting room area with the little buzzer thing that would go off when I was permitted to see him again. There was a large television in the waiting room that alerted me to Emory's progress as he went through the various phases of surgery. It reminded me of how the airports display flight information. Each patient was assigned a personal number rather than putting their names up there for people to see.

I expected to find Memphis there but was surprised to see Josh and Gabe had arrived already. They didn't come alone either. Mere, Harley, Chaz, Kyle, the Dorchesters, and the Goodes were sitting in the waiting room with Memphis when I walked in. Their smiles were confident and compassionate as I settled in for the long haul.

The mood in the room was upbeat and positive, which I appreciated. I also liked the fact that they didn't try to talk me out of staring at the monitor. They included me in their conversation while giving me space at the same time. I wasn't sure how a person accomplished that balance, let alone eleven people, but they did. Deanna brought me a piping hot coffee and a warm blueberry muffin after an hour passed.

"I know you don't want to leave the waiting area in case there's news, but you need to keep your strength up," she said softly.

"Did you make this yourself?" I teased. Josh was known for his homemade goodies while Deanna had a reputation for buying things in the freezer section and passing them off as homemade to her husband.

"Picked the berries before we arrived," she replied sassily before returning to her husband's side.

I bit into the warm muffin and was grateful for her thoughtfulness. I liked it even more that it irritated her husband. John Dorchester was a wisecracking smartass. I liked him a lot.

"You didn't bring me one?" John asked in a pouty voice.

"You should've been the one to get up and treat me to a blueberry muffin after this morning."

"What?" Gabe asked in a shocked voice. "Did John finally get lucky after a three-year dry spell?"

I nearly choked on my bite of muffin due to the oversharing going on, but then I recalled John tormenting Gabe and Josh about the lack of sex parents have when they brought the twins home earlier in the week.

"He's good for another three now," Deanna said proudly. John hooked his arm around his wife's neck and pulled her close so he could kiss her temple.

The longer I waited, the harder it became to sit still. "Em's doing great," Memphis softly said. "I promise you that he's much stronger than we realize."

"Thanks, Memphis."

Around one o'clock most of the group decided to head to the cafeteria to grab some lunch. They offered to bring me something back, but I wasn't hungry. I heard Gabe warn Josh about being on the lookout for loser ex-boyfriends before his husband left. Memphis had chosen to stay with Gabe and me.

"I appreciate you guys being here for Emory," I told Gabe. "It's going to mean the world to him."

"We're here for you too, Jon."

I nodded because I was too choked up with emotion to say anything without making an ass of myself. I hadn't given them many reasons to want to be my friend, yet there they were supporting me. I vowed to become a better friend to each them. Emory wasn't the only one who built a fortress around him to protect himself from unwanted emotions. Corbin and Beau had always been with me, but it was time I opened the gate and let others get to know the real me. I would do it as soon as I figured out who the real me was.

Emory's surgery took six hours and forty-five minutes. I relaxed a little when I saw his patient number move from the operating room to recovery. I wasn't aware of how tensely I sat in the chair until my muscles ached after I relaxed the tension in them.

"It won't be long now," Memphis said in relief.

It had taken another forty minutes before the pager went off signaling that it was time to meet with Dr. Rosenau. "Here," I said, handing it to Memphis since he was Emory's medical power of attorney, "you'll need this."

"Hang on to it because you're coming with me."

Memphis and I approached the desk and handed the buzzer to the guy who had checked Emory in when we arrived that morning. He thoroughly matched the buzzer to his computer and a written patient roster in front of him. He placed some stickers with a barcode on the roster and then gestured for us to follow him back to the room where Dr. Rosenau would speak with us.

My legs bounced nervously while we waited for her, but luckily, she entered the room not long after we sat down. She introduced herself to Memphis first, who identified himself as Emory's cousin and POA, and then she turned to me.

"Jon Silver," I said, shaking her hand. "I'm Emory's boyfriend."

"It's good to meet you both," she said cheerfully. "I have good news and great news. Which would you prefer to hear first?"

"Great news!" Memphis and I both said at once.

"Okay, the great news is that Emory's tumor tested benign. The good news is… Hell, who am I kidding? It's all great news today. The other great news is that I was able to remove all of the tumor so he will not have to undergo additional treatments to remove tentacles that might've attached to inoperable parts of the brain. We also discovered that his tumor wasn't compressing the brain as severely as we first thought. Emory should make a full recovery without any side effects. However, it might take him a while to get there. He could be tired and weak for several weeks, possibly months. His speech and motor skills might also be impacted. We'll provide any kind of therapy he needs while he stays in our Neuroscience Critical Care Unit. He'll be taking medication for at least the next six months or longer to minimize swelling and inflammation. He may require additional physical therapy for an extended period. We won't know that until we examine him. We're also going to restrict driving until we're sure he isn't having seizures."

Relief washed over me, and I slumped back in the chair. "That is great news," I said. "How long before we can see Emory?"

"He's sleeping off some pretty serious sedation, so it might be a little bit longer still. I promise you that we'll call you back as soon as possible.

"He has quite a few people waiting to see him," I told her.

"We have to limit them to two visitors at a time for the first twenty-four hours, but tomorrow he can have as many as he'd like. We'll take you back to see him in recovery before he's moved to his room in the NCCU," she told us.

"Okay, but you need to know something very important, Dr. Rosenau. I'll sleep in the waiting room if I must, but I'm not leaving this hospital without Emory."

"That won't be necessary," she assured me. "I'll make sure a cot is brought into Emory's private room for you. I'm sure that knowing you're close by would make him feel better and rest easier." She glanced at the clock on the wall. "Do either of you have any more questions for me right now? I will be by Emory's room to check on him after I make my rounds."

Memphis looked at me, and I shook my head. "I guess we're good for now, Dr. Rosenau." We both shook her hand again before she headed off to check on her patients.

Our friends rose to their feet when we returned to the waiting room. The smiles on our faces must've told them that we had great news because they were hugging us in relief before we even told them anything.

"He can only see you guys two at a time, but I know he'll be so happy to see you when he wakes up."

"I'll have my phone ready in case he says something funny," Adrian said, but we could tell he was joking.

I was a lot more talkative once I knew Emory was out of the woods. I took the first steps at making a real connection with the people who cared enough about us to give up their day to hang out at the hospital. I opened the gate and welcomed them in.

I jumped out of my chair when the buzzer went off because I was minutes away from seeing Emory again. "We'll let you know when we learn his room number so you guys can come see him."

I handed the device to the nurse who met us at the door to escort us back to Emory. She double-checked the buzzer number against her patient roster and smiled. "I'm sure he's going to be thrilled to see you guys. He's mumbling quite a bit as he comes out of anesthesia. Which one of you is River?"

Her words were like a knife to my heart, and I jerked to a stop. I might've left the hospital had Memphis not placed his hand on my shoulder. "It doesn't mean anything," he assured me. "Who knows where his mind went during anesthesia. Maybe he's saying goodbye."

I swallowed hard, wanting to believe him. I plastered a smile on my face and nodded. I opened the door to Emory's suite, and

Memphis went inside first. I stayed back for a second as I tried to bolster my courage. *Please let this be real. Let Emory be the one I finally call my own.*

"Hey, Em," I heard Memphis softly say. "How are you feeling?"

"High," he slurred. "Where's Jon? Did I dream him?"

Tears of relief burned the back of my eyes as I stepped into the room. "I'm right here, Em."

TWENTY-THREE

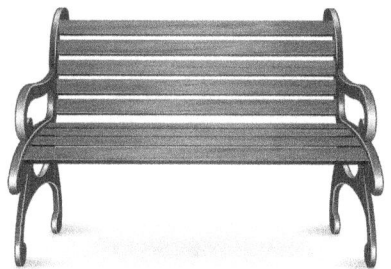

Emory

W HEN MEMPHIS FIRST CAME INTO MY ROOM, IT FELT LIKE déjà vu. For a few heartbeats, I was back in that hospital room five years ago expecting to see River walk through the door. Memphis's blinding smile was what snapped me back to the present day. It was nothing like the expression he wore the last time. Once again, I looked over Memphis's shoulder in search of the man I loved.

"Hey, Em," Memphis said. "How are you feeling?"

I looked at my cousin as I struggled to process my thoughts. "High," I slurred. "Where's Jon? Did I dream him?" Had I dreamed up everything that happened since the accident?

"I'm right here, Em."

Tears of relief and joy slid down my face as I raised my hand off the bed and reached for him. "You're real. I didn't dream you."

Jon came to my side in quick strides and lowered himself into the chair by my bed. He took my hand in his then kissed it before holding it to his cheek. "Some people might call me a nightmare," he said.

"Huh-uh," I said. "Not me."

"Give it time," Jon replied softly then kissed my hand again. "Did they tell you the great news?"

"The basics," I said. My voice wasn't quite as sluggish, but I sounded anything but alert. "I think they're waiting for me to be fully awake. My nurse said that Dr. Rosenau would stop by later." I shifted my eyes between Memphis and Jon. "According to your dopey smiles, it went okay."

"Better than okay, Em." Jon leaned over and kissed my forehead just beneath the bandages they had wrapped around my head.

"I'm really tired still."

"Well, damn. I thought we'd leave here and go clubbing tonight," Memphis remarked.

"Let me take a nap first," I replied. My eyes felt so heavy that I could barely keep them open. "On second thought, we better make it tomorrow."

"Rest, Em," Jon said tenderly. "I'll be here when you wake up. You have some amazing friends who showed up and waited with us all day. They want to say a quick hello once you get moved to your room. Is that okay?"

"I'll always have time for Josh and Gabe."

"They didn't come alone, baby. They brought half of Blissville with them."

"They did?"

"Yep," he replied. "John, Deanna, Adrian, Sally Ann, Kyle, Chaz, Mere, and Harley have been hanging out with us all day."

"I love your friends," Memphis said. "You have an amazing life here."

I kept my eyes locked on Jon's when I replied. "I'm very lucky."

"You're also very tired," Memphis told me. "Do you want them to come back tomorrow when you're feeling a little more alert."

"No!" My reply sounded loud in my brain, but it was a hoarse whisper when the word passed through my lips.

"How about you take a little nap first then," Memphis said.

"It'll probably be another hour before we move him to his regular room," the nurse informed us. "He might feel a little more alert then."

"Close your eyes and rest, baby." Jon leaned over and pressed his lips to my ears. "I'll be here when you wake up."

"Promise? I don't want this to be a dream."

"I promise, Em. I love you."

"Love you too."

His assurance spoken in a dark, velvety voice eased my mind, and I stopped fighting sleep.

The next time I opened my eyes, I did feel a little more alert. As promised, Jon's face was the first thing I saw. Jon raised my hand that he still held to his mouth for another kiss. I looked around the room and noticed that at some point while I was sleeping off my anesthesia high they had moved me to my hospital room. The television was playing a college basketball game, but I was still too groggy to follow the action on the screen.

"Are you ready for your visitors?" Jon asked. I nodded slightly. "You can only see two at a time, so I'm going to step outside and let them say hello to you."

"Okay, but don't go far." I would've rolled my eyes at the neediness I heard in my voice, but I saw how much Jon liked it.

"I'll be right outside the door."

Memphis was right. My friends were awesome, and I had an

amazing life in Blissville. I sent up a silent thank you to River for sending me there and pushing me into Jon's arms. That thought sparked a memory of something—a conversation I had with River while I was under sedation. As happy as I was to visit with my friends and accept their gentle hugs and warm wishes, I needed to tell Jon something very important.

"Hey, baby," Jon said when he and Memphis entered the room after the final two visitors left. "How are you feeling?"

"Tired, but okay. I think these meds are strong enough to keep the worst of the pain at bay." I waved him over. "I need to tell you something."

"What is it, Em?"

My eyelids felt weighted down again, and I knew sleep was just around the corner. I wanted to tell Jon before I forgot. "River kept me company while I was in surgery and he…" I felt Jon's hand stiffen in mine and I paused. I reopened my eyes and turned my head slowly to look at him. "He sent me to you, Jon. There's no need for you to be afraid. I love you. He told me something important; a few things, actually. One of them is a message for you."

I felt Jon relax before he asked, "What did River have to say, Em?"

"Well, it was strange because we were sitting on a bench in a lovely park that overlooked a river. I'm not sure where it was because I didn't recognize it. He joked and said he chose it because of its name, River's Edge. Anyway, it was a lovely place, and we had a nice chat." Jon's grip tightened on my hand, but it relaxed just as quickly. "River took my hands and said, 'Atta boy, Emory. I knew you still had a lot of love to give some lucky guy. You just needed to come to terms with the fact that you were the love of my lifetime, but I wasn't meant to be yours. I want you to smile and be happy when you look back on our life together, but I need you to always keep your focus on what's in front of you and the future you're building with Jon. He's a good man, even if he doesn't know it.' Then he got a crooked smile on his face then said, 'Tell Jon that Nate is okay and he's happy that Jon found you. Nate said to start with Yankee Stadium.' I tried asking him what he meant, but he said that Nate was waiting for him." I smiled at Jon. "I got the idea that they've become quite friendly. That makes me really happy."

Jon was quiet for so long that I worried I had upset him. He closed his eyes and tears slid silently down his face. "Me too."

"What did Nate mean when he said we should start with Yankee Stadium?" I asked.

"Nate and I planned to visit every MLB stadium because we both loved baseball so much," Jon said. "You probably think it sounds silly."

"I think it sounds wonderful," I said on a drowsy sigh.

"Sleep now, baby. We'll talk about it later."

The rest of my stay at the hospital followed a pretty consistent pattern. Sleep, wake up and rejoice that I didn't conjure Jon up in a dream, eat a little, try to chat with my visitors, do my physical therapy exercises, then sleep again. I felt stronger each day and looked forward to going home. Dr. Rosenau's enthusiasm about the success of my surgery made me hopeful that this would just be another speed bump in the road of life. I had some amazing plans to carry out with my guy.

Jon. True to his word, I don't think I opened my eyes one time when he wasn't right there by my side. That cot had to be miserable to sleep on, but he wouldn't listen when I suggested that he go home and get some sleep at night in his comfortable bed.

"I'll return to my comfortable bed once you're able to sleep beside me," he had replied. "Or, we can go straight to your house."

Jon's house was closer to the hospital where I would need to return for therapy, scans, and other tests over the next few weeks, so I chose to go there with him rather than have him drive me back and forth to Blissville. It didn't surprise me when Jon invited Memphis to stay with us, but Memphis accepting the offer did take me by surprise.

Memphis simply shrugged and said, "I like your people. Maybe Blisstucky would be a great place for me to make a fresh start too."

"I'd love to have you here with me," I said excitedly. "You can stay with me until you can find a place to rent."

Memphis smiled sheepishly and said, "I found a place already. Chaz told me that his aunt Sandra's house on Maple Lane is available to rent at a low cost. He warned me that I would be surrounded by overbearing, meddling women who would only want what's best for me. Sounds like a great place to live.

"I've done some research, and independent stores do well in that tiny little town. Somehow, someway they're not gobbled up by the chain stores. There's an open retail space, and I'm thinking about accepting someone's very generous offer to help me start my own business."

"Memphis, that is so exciting. I will love having you so close by."

Later that night, I worried that my excitement over returning to Blissville would hurt Jon's feelings. I loved the weeks we spent at his house in Hyde Park during my recovery, especially watching the sun rise through the amazing wall of windows while he slowly made love to me, but the house wasn't his home.

"It doesn't feel like home to me either," Jon said when I brought it up to him that night. "I feel more at home in Blissville than Hyde Park too."

"My house doesn't afford an amazing view though," I told him.

"Oh yes, it does." Jon dropped a sweet kiss on my nose and added, "I'll be happy as long as you are the first thing I see each morning. Your sexy body and tender heart are my home, Em. Where you go, I go."

"What about your job?" I asked him. Vibe was a thriving club that would need his attention.

"Michelle has done an amazing job of running things while I've been home with you. I have every confidence she can run the club with very little input from me. I'll still pop in there a few days a week during the day to conduct staff meetings and make sure everything is running smoothly, but I don't need to be there in person every single night. Vibe was Nate's dream, and it's time that I find my own."

By the time mid-March rolled around, I was strong enough to go back to my home and start living again. Each scan and test showed that I was healing beautifully. I had very few side effects, and they became less and less noticeable as time passed. Memphis had already settled into his new place on Maple Lane the week before, and I was eager to see it and talk about his plans for his comic book and vinyl record store. I wanted Jon to move with me, but I was afraid it was too bold of a move or too soon. I searched for ways to bring it up the night before I planned to return home but kept chickening out.

Jon pulled a suitcase out of his closet and started packing it with his clothes. I perked up when I noticed he was taking a lot of things, not just a few pairs of pants for a weekend stay. "Do you mind if we keep this house? Maybe use it like a vacation home or something? Especially when we come to the city for ballgames and *theater*." I didn't miss the change in pitch at the end. I smiled because he was answering the questions I was afraid to ask. Jon looked up from packing when I didn't answer right away. How could I with that joker grin spread across my face?

"I think that's a great idea."

The next morning, we loaded his trunk with the things he wanted to take to my... our house. He didn't take the exit for the interstate like I thought he would but drove to an empty park instead. Spring was on the horizon, but it was still a bit nippy to hang out in the park. I looked at him with a raised brow, and he pointed over to an ornate park sign that read: *River's Edge*.

My mouth fell open in shock, and I got out of his car. I walked straight to the bench that I sat on when I last talked to River. I sat down and rubbed my hand over the smooth wooden planks. What did it mean? Were my psychic abilities still intact? It wasn't abnormal that I'd gone a few months without a vision, so I wasn't sure what to think. I heard Jon walk up behind me. He came around the other side of the bench and sat down.

"This park was my first revitalization project to honor my brother." He ran his hand over the golden plate that read: *In Loving Memory of Nathan Thomas Turner.* "Nate loved this city and thought she had potential to be the finest one in the Midwest. Since his death, I've had two goals: honor him by revitalizing his city and make sure he got justice. Gabe and his team took care of one of them, and I'm still working on the other."

"It's beautiful, Jon. He must love it too, and that's why River brought me here for our final chat."

"You think it's the final one?"

"I do," I said nodding slowly. "There was a finality in his voice that was never present before our chat here on this bench. You know what? I didn't feel sad. I felt happiness and fondness for the memories we shared, but I sat here for a long time after he left, and all I could think about was the new memories I couldn't wait to make with you."

Jon pulled me to him for a long, tender kiss as the nippy breeze whipped around us. I stopped feeling the chill the second his warm mouth pressed against mine. His teased my lips apart and slipped his tongue between them to learn my mouth like it was the first time.

"Mmmm, you taste like caramel, coffee, and cum," Jon said when he finally pulled back. God, his dirty talk never failed to turn me inside out, leaving me horny and breathless. He rubbed his nose against mine. "You ready to start making those memories together?"

"Here?" I asked, looking around the park. "It's a bit chilly, isn't it?"

"I'd never let anyone watch us together," Jon said with a growl. "I meant other, non-sexual things."

"Yes, as long as the sexual things can be tossed in on occasion."

"Oh, baby, there'll be plenty of that," Jon said hoarsely. He put his mouth against my ear and told me the naughtiest, dirtiest things he planned to do to me in the months to come.

I held out my hand, and Jon entwined his fingers with mine. "I'm ready," I said eagerly.

TWENTY-FOUR

Jon

'LL BE HONEST; I WASN'T SURE HOW I WOULD REACT TO LIFE IN Blissville, and not just because of the size of the town or Emory's house. I had lived in various-sized towns and cities throughout the US, and some of my humble abodes I would classify as squalor. I madly loved Emory, and I wanted to be with him, but I'd never attempted a relationship of any kind before, let alone moved in with someone. I had always been more than a little selfish because my downtime was minimal, and I wanted to spend it doing things that made me happy or at least made me feel good.

A month into my new life, and I couldn't imagine living anywhere else. There I was, happily strolling down the street holding hands with the man I loved as we made our way to the newly expanded coffee shop in the center of Blissville. The Brew had become Books and Brew with the addition of a bookstore inside the space.

"I'm so happy for Maegan and Milo," Emory said. "They're such lovely people."

"Who are they again?"

Emory looked at me and rolled his eyes. "The people who own Books and Brew." Emory had missed their grand reopening and was eager to check out the revamped space. He'd explained that their coffee shop was one of four window fronts in their building. The other three had been empty and "sad-looking" for quite some time. "Maegan and Milo knocked down a wall on one side to add a bookstore then renovated the space directly to the right for Maegan's new venture called Curious Things."

"How curious?" I asked. *Are we talking sex toys kind of curious?*

Emory playfully jabbed me with his elbow. "Antiques, knick-knacks, china, and other things she finds at estate auctions. She's had an online store through eBay for a few years and decided to turn her passion for antiques and oddities into a brick and mortar retail space," Emory said. "No whips, shackles, floggers, or cuffs."

"Huh."

Emory stopped walking and looked at me. "Is that a good 'huh' or a disappointed one? Something tells me it's the latter."

I hadn't told Emory about my past membership at Voodoo and wasn't sure when, or if, I would. Did it matter? Would it change how he saw me? I had just found him and was afraid to find out. Besides, that part of my past felt like a different lifetime. As cheesy as it sounded, I fell in love with Emory and became a changed man. Sure, I was more than willing to get kinky with Emory if he was up to that sort of thing, but other past activities were off limits. There was no fucking way in hell I'd ever have sex with Emory in the middle of a room with people watching, cheering us on, or masturbating in rhythm to my thrusts inside him. Nor would I share him with anyone else. No.

Fucking. Way. I'd snap the neck of anyone who even attempted to put their hands on my man.

"Where'd you go just now?" Emory asked hesitantly.

"I dragged my knuckles back to my cave," I replied. I knew that answer made zero sense to him. Emory narrowed his eyes like he was trying to peer inside my brain. I gathered him close and kissed him as a distraction. It wasn't a little peck on the lips either; I'm talking a full-on passionate kiss in broad daylight in the middle of the sidewalk. I didn't give a damn what anyone thought, and I dared them to flap their gums in my direction. I'd never get my fill of Emory, but it was enough to tide me over. I rested my forehead against his and said, "You don't want to look inside my brain, baby. There are dark places that I'd never want you to witness."

"Huh?" The confusion on his face was adorable. He'd forgotten what we were discussing before our kiss. I wasn't about to remind him that my brain had taken a trip back in time.

"What about the fourth window front?" I asked, trying to steer our conversation back to safer topics.

"Um…" Emory blinked a few seconds before he could answer. "Memphis is going to rent it for his comic book store. I've never seen him as excited about anything as he is now, Jon."

"It's a wonderful thing you're doing for him," I said. I also thought it was cool that Memphis could shove male pride out of the way and accept Emory's help.

"I probably owe my life to Memphis," Emory said soberly. "If not for him, I might not be standing here with you right now."

"You're much stronger than you give yourself credit for, Em." It wouldn't matter how much someone else wanted Emory to live if he'd truly given up. It was easier to give credit to Memphis or even visions of River than it was to accept that, even during his darkest hours, he wanted to live. That was something Emory would need to learn for himself though. Our mood had turned heavy suddenly, and I was eager to get it back to the lighthearted tone we'd had before my brain took a detour and distracted us both. I tugged on Emory's hand to get us moving forward again. "When will Memphis open his store?"

"I believe Beefcake Andy is starting renovations today so hopefully soon." *Beefcake Andy?* Emory laughed when he saw the brooding scowl on my face. "That's what Kyle calls him. Apparently, Andy hit on Chaz a time or two and Kyle isn't a fan." Emory squeezed my hand reassuringly then added, "Memphis is working part time for Maegan and Milo, either at Books and Brew or Curious Things, so we could see him there if he's not at his store going over renovations with Andy."

It amazed me how quickly Memphis fit in with everyone in our new social circle. He seemed like a completely different person than the one who showed up a few days before Emory's surgery. He smiled more and laughed often. My lips quirked up in a half-smile when I realized I had also described myself. I wasn't dumb enough to think that my scars would all miraculously heal because I'd found Em, but he made it easier to accept the things that I couldn't change and focus on the gifts in front of me—life and the promise of an amazing love. *Jesus! Maybe I could start writing cards for Hallmark on the side.*

"You'll have to tell me what's making you smile like that." Emory grinned from ear to ear like perhaps he already knew.

"I was just laughing at how sappy I've become."

"You aren't sappy," Emory said. "That's sappy!" He pointed to where John Dorchester was obviously wooing his wife outside the coffee shop. Deanna waited beneath the black and tan striped awning for John to reach her. It looked like they had driven separately and were meeting for coffee and a pastry. John whipped a bouquet of flowers from behind his back and presented them to Deanna, who smiled happily at her husband.

"You don't think that's sweet?" I asked. Hell, even I thought it was fucking adorable.

"It's precious," Emory admitted. "I wonder what he did."

"What do you mean?"

"Most guys buy flowers when they're in the doghouse." Emory sounded like it was a matter of fact, not his opinion.

"Is that right?"

"Just my personal observation," he said. I thought it sounded more like personal experience than a mere observation. If so, I would have to change his opinion over time.

"Hey, guys," Deanna said when we walked up to them. "How's it going?"

"We're doing great," Emory said. Then an ornery grin split his face. "What did John do this time?"

Deanna threw her head back and laughed throatily at Emory's question.

"It's our anniversary, asshole," John said. He wasn't one to tiptoe around anyone, and I liked that about him.

"Ohhh, so it's your annual apology then," Emory commented, nodding as if he understood.

"You've been hanging around Gabe too long," John told him with mock indignation. "I'm a fabulous husband."

"Yeah, and men who brag about their sexual prowess usually don't have any," Deanna remarked.

John glared at his wife. "What exactly are you implying here, darling?"

"Oh! I didn't mean it to sound like that. I just meant that people aren't always the best judges when it comes to themselves. You *are* a fabulous husband." She stood up on her tiptoes to kiss him, but he placed his hand on her lips to block her.

"Your sweet lips won't get you out of this one," John said huffily. His twitching lip was making it hard to believe his act.

"You say that now, but I can convince you otherwise when we're alone," Deanna smugly said before she turned and walked into the coffee shop by herself.

"I'm going to play hard to get when we get home," John announced. "That woman takes me for granted." Emory and I both burst into laughter at the same time because we knew better. "You're a couple of assholes," John mumbled then followed his wife inside.

"I think I'm going to play hard to get too," I told Emory. Instead of laughing, he smiled mischievously.

"Oh, please do, Jon." That sounded a lot like a challenge.

I opened my mouth to respond, but my ringing phone interrupted me. We both expected it to be club business, but Corbin's name popped up on the caller ID. I instantly knew something was up because Corbin didn't usually get out of bed until two in the afternoon. He enjoyed staying up all hours of the night at his club where I preferred to be home with my guy.

"I'll order our drinks and grab a table while you talk to Corbin." Emory kissed my cheek and went inside.

"Hey, Cor. What's up?"

"Hey, Romeo. If I had to guess, I'd say it's your dick," Corbin replied. His funny remark couldn't disguise the tension in his voice. He cleared his throat nervously when I didn't take the bait. "I'm going dark for a little while."

The hair stood up on the back of my neck. "Are you in trouble?"

"No, it's not me," Corbin replied quickly. "It's someone else, and he's… um… important to me. I need to make things right."

"Do you need help? I can be there in—"

"No, Jon," Corbin said, swiftly cutting me off. "I can never express how much it means to me that you'd drop everything to help me, but you have an amazing life with a wonderful man. I'd never ask you to put that on hold to help me with something that might not get resolved very fast."

"Corbin, I owe you and Beau everything."

"You can repay us by living the happy life you deserve. Whether Beau wants to admit it or not, I'm pretty sure he's on the same path to happily ever after."

"What about you, Cor?" I asked him. "Will this mission ensure you find your happily ever after too?" Happily ever after? *Who the fuck was talking? We weren't some motherfucking Disney princes.*

"I think it might, Jon."

"Then do what you must. If you get in a bind, you only have to call me. Anytime..."

"... or anyplace," he finished for me. It had been our motto for two decades. "I appreciate it, brother."

"Have you called Beau?"

"I'm calling him next. I'm sure his nosy ass will ask more questions than you did."

"Well, he's a lawman now, so asking questions is what he does," I reminded him. "Take care of yourself, Cor."

"I'd tell you the same, but you have someone doing that for you. I'm looking forward to meeting Emory," Corbin said. I heard the genuine smile in his voice. "I've enjoyed talking to him on the phone, but I have to meet the man who won Jon Silver's heart."

"We're looking forward to it also. Make sure it's sooner rather than later."

"I'll check in when I can."

"Do that," I said firmly.

I stood outside for a minute after we said our goodbyes. I couldn't help worrying about my friend, but I knew he was more than capable of handling whatever he'd gotten himself involved in. I couldn't help but wonder about the identity of the man who he classified as important to him. Of the three of us, Corbin was the most allergic to the idea of relationships and love. He said his southern mafia roots soured him on the idea that people entered the bonds of matrimony for any reasons other than money, manipulation, or politics.

I looked up from my phone, and my eyes met Emory's through the large window front. Memphis sat beside him talking a mile a minute, but he wasn't paying a bit of attention to what his cousin said. I shoved all my thoughts of Corbin aside and smiled at the man who fucking owned my heart. It wasn't that I suddenly stopped worrying about my friend; I accepted that he knew what he was doing and would call me if he needed me.

I opened the coffee shop door and took a deep breath so I could savor the delicious aroma of pastries and coffee. "Hey, Em and Mem," I said when I sat at the table.

"No!" Emory and Memphis said at the same time.

"We don't do cutesy shit anymore," Memphis said.

"It's not fair that we have shortened versions of our names, but you don't, Memphis," I told him. "How about Phis?"

"How about you choke on that cranberry orange muffin," he replied in a singsong voice. "Oh! There's Andy." Memphis bolted from his seat like his ass was on fire.

I looked over and saw that Andy was indeed quite a beefcake. Could his fucking gray flannel shirt get any tighter? I glanced over to make sure Emory wasn't checking the guy out. He was looking at me and grinning like a fool.

"Memphis seems quite smitten with Beefcake Andy," I told him.

"He has to get in line though," Emory said, hooking his thumb over in the direction of the coffee counter.

I saw that Milo was watching Andy flirt with Memphis and his clenched jaw made it obvious that he didn't like it. I was shocked that he openly lusted after a guy with his wife standing right there. Even odder, Maegan appeared to encourage him when she handed Milo a cup of coffee that was obviously for Andy because she kept tipping her head in the carpenter's direction. Milo kept shaking his head no.

"They must have a really open marriage," I said to Emory.

"Who?" He looked around the room as if trying to figure out what I saw. He turned back around and took a sip of his coffee.

"Maegan and Milo."

Emory practically spat his coffee at me. "That's so gross," he sputtered. "They're brother and sister. Twins, to be exact."

What? They looked nothing alike. Maegan had curly blonde hair that she had wrestled into a messy bun on top of her head, fair skin, and light eyes. I thought they were green. Milo was taller, had a darker skin tone, medium brown hair, and blue eyes. The only thing similar about them was the scowls they aimed at one another while they silently argued over Beefcake Andy.

"Twins?"

"They're paternal twins instead of identical," Emory explained. "Maegan is clearly trying to encourage Milo to go over and talk to Andy. There's definitely some history between the two men, but I don't know their story." Emory had his back to them so how did he know?

"Did you have a vision?"

"No, smartass," Emory quipped. "I can see their reflection in the window. Not only that, I've been observing them for a while now. A person doesn't have to be psychic to know things."

"Smartass, huh?" I asked with a raised brow. My voice had dropped to a lower pitch, and I saw the excited shiver that worked through my guy. For the last few weeks, Emory had hinted that he was ready to be a little more physical with me, but I worried that it was too soon. His green eyes darkened, and he inhaled sharply through his nose. "Grab your muffin and let's go."

I recalled my earlier comment about playing hard to get and Emory's reaction. Instead of snatching up my muffin and cup like I wanted to, I leaned back in my chair casually and pinched off a tiny bite of my baked goodie. I let the flavors explode on my tongue and moaned indecently.

"Oh yeah?" Emory asked. "That's how you want to play it?"

"Baby, I'm not playing."

TWENTY-FIVE

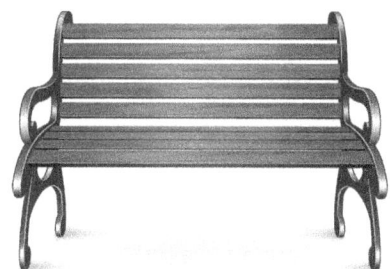

Emory

J ON BROKE OFF ANOTHER TINY CHUNK OF MUFFIN AND POPPED
it in his mouth. He licked the corners of his lips to make sure
no crumbs remained. Not playing, huh? Well, he wasn't the
only one who could play dirty.

"To think I planned to give you a wonderful anniversary gift," I
told him, shaking my head sadly.

"What anniversary?" Jon said in confusion.

I made a big production of looking around the room to assure
that no one was listening. "I really shouldn't say right now. It wouldn't
be proper."

"So we're 'proper' people now? You didn't mind slipping your
tongue into my mouth for the whole town to see fifteen minutes ago."

Jon was a tough customer, but I was only getting started.

"Kissing in public is not the same thing as talking about…" I let my words trail off and sat back in my chair like I didn't have a care in the world. I had many cares, and the primary one was to entice Jon to fuck me without restraint. I saw how hard he struggled to rein himself in these past two months, and I wanted him to be completely free with me. I loved the hard, physical fucking just as much as the tender way he made love to me. It had been too long since he pinned me down and took what he wanted. I rose to my feet and said, "You take your time with your breakfast. I'm going to head on home to do a load of laundry or something mundane since you're not interested in celebrating this special occasion with me."

"What special occasion?"

I left the coffee shop but didn't make it very far before he caught me. Jon grabbed both my shoulders then turned and backed me up against a tree. The heat and possession I saw in his eyes sparked my lust and gave me an instant hard-on.

"What special occasion?" Jon repeated. He lowered his head and brushed his morning scruff against my neck, and it had the same effect as if he reached between my legs and massaged my aching balls. I was no match for him. *Yet.*

"We met a year ago today," I said throatily.

Jon pulled back and tipped his head to the side. "No, we didn't. We met at Gabe and Josh's house on Easter Sunday. That particular anniversary is in a few days."

"That's the day we physically met, but I'd dreamed of you before then," I reminded him. "I didn't see your face, but I heard your voice, and I felt your arms around me as you made love to me slow and deep like you do every morning. Do you know what you said to me afterward that scared me to death?"

"'Thanks for the good time?" he asked smartly. I could tell it was his way of grappling with emotions he wasn't always sure how to process. Jon might've been older and worldlier in some ways, but it was up to me to show him how to love openly.

"You said, 'I love you, Em,' and it scared the fuck out of me."

"Because you weren't ready," Jon replied patiently.

"In part, yes, but also because it felt truer than anything I'd ever experienced in my life. Loving someone is a risk; one I wasn't brave enough to accept at the time."

"You're brave enough now."

"Somedays I still wake up terrified that I'll lose you or that you were a mere dream I created to ease the loneliness I felt in my heart." The burning behind my eyes and in the back of my nose warned of pending tears. "But then you slide up behind me—"

"—and inside you."

"And I'm no longer afraid."

Jon closed his eyes and pressed his forehead to mine. "You're not the only one who worries. There are days I wake up thinking that I'm too dirty and tainted to touch anyone as precious as you."

"Because of your career or your previous club membership?" That got his attention.

Jon looked horrified that I'd had a vision, so I set his mind at ease right away. "It wasn't something that I saw, but overheard. You mentioned Voodoo while talking to Corbin, and I got curious. I looked it up on the internet and saw that it catered to gentlemen with specific needs."

"That was a different lifetime, Emory. I'm not that same man who got off on the things he saw or did there."

"Jon, I'm not bringing this up because I'm trying to shame you or make you feel bad. I wasn't angry about your *past* membership there; I was curious." *Am curious.*

Jon's cocky smile said that he didn't miss the change in tone I used. "I gave up my membership," he confirmed. "Curiosity can be a very dangerous thing, my heart." There was nothing sexier than a badass man saying sugary sweet things or using pet names. I knew it was genuine and came from the heart he'd kept guarded all these years until I came along.

"I simply want you to recreate some of your favorite things in the privacy of our own home. Did you like to tie your man up—"

Jon pressed the palm of his hand over my mouth to quiet me. My tongue darted out to lick his flesh, and I tasted a hint of the muffin he'd held in his hand mixed with his natural saltiness. It made me want other saltier parts of him.

"They were never my men, Emory. That title is yours and yours alone. They were playthings or distractions to keep my mind away from dark places that threatened to consume me. That's a horrible thing to say about living, breathing humans, but I didn't care about them beyond them making me come and doing the same for them. It was the basest kind of sex—hollow and meaningless. Do not compare what I was then to who I am now in the same sentence." He removed his hand slowly from my mouth like he feared how I would react to his words.

"I'm your safe place, Jon. There is nothing you can say or do that would make me love you less. If you're going to be truly happy, then I want to make sure you're not suppressing parts of you. I'm not afraid of your baser needs, in fact, I'm intrigued by them. Ever since I found out about your membership there, I've pictured us doing so many things."

Jon took a sudden step back, grabbed my hand, and tugged me forward to follow him down the sidewalk. "Too bad this town doesn't have a cab service."

"It's only three blocks to our house," I said excitedly. Oh boy! It was all I could do to keep from yanking my hand back so I could rub mine together gleefully. I was finally going to get the fucking I had begged him for the past few weeks.

"Three blocks too fucking many," he groused as he walked faster until I practically had to jog to keep up with his long strides.

His grip on my hand tightened the closer we got to home like he feared I might change my mind and flee. He had nothing to worry

about because there was a higher probability of an asteroid crash-
ing into our house. He didn't let go of me until we reached the front
porch and he needed his hand to unlock the door. He pushed the
door open so hard that it crashed into the wall and rattled the pictures hanging there.

"Oh dear," I said, but it wasn't from fear. I knew I was about to
see Jon take fucking to a whole new level. That first time in his house
was nothing more than an appetizer before the main course.

Jon shut and locked the door before he crooked his finger at me,
and I went to him. He began undressing me immediately, and I stood
before him completely naked while he remained fully dressed. His
dominance was etched in both his expression when he looked at me
and in his rigid posture. Jon placed his hand on my shoulder and
pushed me to my knees in front of him.

"Take out my cock and get it nice and wet, Emory."

"Oh dear." I repeated, sounding like a twittering old lady. Jon's
wicked grin expressed how much he liked his effect on me.

I lowered myself to my knees but didn't take out his hard cock
right away. I teased him through his jeans with my hands and teeth.
Jon's sharp hiss was a reward for my boldness.

"Oh dear," he said. I glanced up to see if he was mocking me, but
he was too far gone to be a smartass.

Jon's hands were firm but gentle when he cupped my head and
pressed his crotch harder against my face while I rolled his firm balls
in my hands. I could smell his arousal, and it made my dick leak all
over the wooden floors. I could tell he wasn't wearing underwear
under his button-fly jeans and it made it so much more exciting to
know only a few buttons separated me from Jon's dick.

I released the top button and licked and sucked his bare skin
just above his trimmed pubic hair, eliciting a deep groan from him.
I worked the next button free and pressed my nose against the short
hairs, breathing in Jon's masculine smell and teasing the base of his
cock with the tip of my tongue. I continued my torture until his

erection was free. I took my time licking a path along the thick vein that ran from root to tip, swirling my tongue around his swollen head and moaning when I captured his salty essence on my tongue. I'd choose his savory taste over something sweet any day of the week.

"Emory," Jon cried out when I opened my mouth wide and sucked him to the back of my throat. I liked that the tables had turned and he was at my mercy. My chuckle vibrated and rippled along the length of his cock, adding to his stimulation. "Feels so good."

I loved giving Jon head because he was so verbal and bossy. He wasn't ashamed of his needs and wants, and it was an insane turn on knowing that I was who he wanted and needed. I worked his cock fast and hard then soft and slow to bring him to the edge then backed him off. I had no issues swallowing his load, but that morning I wanted him to fuck me rough and hard until he spilled inside me.

"Stand up," he demanded.

Jon grabbed my shoulders and nudged me toward the stairs. He swatted my ass playfully once I started up the steps. Instead of continuing up them, I dropped to my knees on the landing halfway up where the staircase turned before it continued its ascent. The carpet runner was soft beneath my knees, and the air felt cool against my bare ass that I presented to Jon.

"Jesus fuck," he snarled as he removed his clothes then dropped to his knees a few steps beneath me.

He pounced and feasted on my ass, working me open with his tongue and making sure I was wet and ready before he gave me what I wanted. Sex—rough, raw, and real. Jon gripped my ass hard with his hands as he worked his dick inside me. My moans had nothing to do with any physical discomfort; they were all about the wicked pleasure he made me feel.

"Damn, you feel so fucking good," he said in a guttural voice. Jon didn't ask if I was sure, he didn't stop to make sure I was okay, he reacted on pure instinct to rut and mate.

Jon gripped my hips hard enough to bruise me, adding to my

excitement, then set out on a fierce pace that expertly pegged my prostate with every hard thrust forward. Jon released my hip to reach around and grip my cock. It didn't take too many pumps before I shot all over the carpet. My orgasm triggered his, and we both yelled each other's names as we rutted against each other as our climaxes worked through us.

"I think you killed me," Jon said when he collapsed onto the carpeted landing beside me. He turned his head and looked at me with concern. "Did I hurt you, Em? I was rough."

"I've never been better." Then I chuckled as a thought occurred to me. "Was that your attempt at playing hard to get?"

Jon snorted then laughed hard at the ridiculous idea that he could somehow resist my charms. "You wore me down," he said, his eyes crinkling at the corner from smiling so wide. It was the most beautiful thing I'd ever seen. "Wait a minute," Jon said as he recalled a different part of our conversation. "I want my anniversary gift now."

"That was it," I said innocently. "I gave you unrestrained access to my hole. Wasn't that enough?" I attempted a playful pout but must've failed because he laughed at me.

"Where's my present?" Jon asked, sounding and looking like an excited little boy. How long had it been since someone gave him an unexpected gift?

"It's up in our bedroom," I said. "Come on."

Jon got to his feet and shoved me lightly so he could run past me to reach our bedroom first. I laughed so hard that I couldn't follow him right away. By the time I got to our room, he'd opened both the drawers in our bedside tables and was heading toward the dresser. I had something hidden in there that I wasn't ready for him to see. It was the only part of my vision that I hadn't told him about yet. I wasn't exactly sure when I would spring that surprise on him.

"Hey," I said, catching his attention. "You can quit ripping and tearing through here looking for your gift. I stashed them so I could whip them out at the right moment." I walked over to the bed, reached inside my pillowcase, and pulled out an envelope. "You sure know how to kill a surprise."

Jon looked worried that I was upset with him.

"I'm kidding, baby," I said. "I love your enthusiasm. Hell, I can't wait to see what you're like on Christmas morning."

Jon pulled me to him and held my nude body against his. "You see my Christmas morning face every day when I open my eyes and see that you're still here."

"Charmer." It worked too because I was ready to melt into a puddle at his feet. Who knew such a gruff man could say such sweet things? "Open it."

Jon took the envelope from me and ripped it open. "Oh, Em!" He looked up from the Yankee tickets he held in his hand. "Are you sure you're ready to travel so soon?"

"Dr. Rosenau gave the okay after my last scan. We're moving forward with our lives, Jon. Someday this," I ran my hand over my stubbly scalp, "will be a distant memory."

Jon chuckled and tucked my head under his chin. "This is an amazing gift."

"We're just getting started, Jon."

EPILOGUE

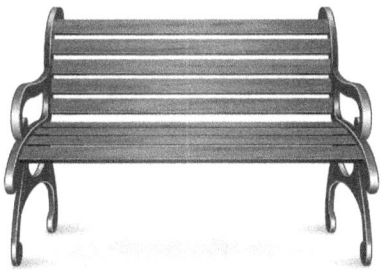

Jon

Six months later…

"T ELL THE TRUTH, EM. DID YOU HAVE TO PERFORM SEXUAL favors to get these seats? This is the World Fucking Series."

"My granddad pulled a few strings, but I doubt he blew anyone," Emory replied after he finished swallowing the bite of hotdog he was quickly mowing through. "We can ask him when we have Thanksgiving dinner with him."

I respected and admired a lot about Connor Whelan, especially the way he loved Emory. "Will your mother be there?" I asked. Over the past few months, Audrey had attempted to repair her relationship with Emory. I'd met her but couldn't say I liked her. I recalled our first interaction vividly.

"Why did no one call me and tell me about Emory's brain tumor? I'm his mother and I had a right to know and be here for him!"

I had looked at her with a deadpan expression and clapped my hands slowly at her performance. Emory had told me all about his mother and her bullshit behavior. Audrey McIntire-Whelan flinched like I had slapped her. I wasn't through though.

I had leaned closer to her and said, "Our government trained me how to kill someone and make it look like an accident. Fix things with Emory or fucking walk away for good. Your hot and cold routine isn't welcome in our lives." So far, she attempted to get on board.

"Yes," Emory said, "but she'll be on her best behavior with granddad around." I didn't want her to *act* like she loved Emory; I wanted her *to* love him.

"Are you hungry or something?" I asked when he scarfed down the rest of his hotdog. "Do you want another one?"

"No," he said around a mouthful of hotdog. He held up his finger for me to wait while he chewed the last bite before washing it down with a long drink of soda. "It's almost the seventh inning." As if that explained a damn thing.

"What? Are you eager to sing 'God Bless America' or something?"

"Um, no."

I narrowed my eyes because he suddenly looked nervous. What the hell was going on?

"I want to be ready in case the Kiss Cam is aimed at us." Emory reached into his pocket and pulled out a tube of lip balm and smeared some on his lips.

"Well, you might want to get rid of that mustard smear," I said, gesturing to his upper lip before I handed him a napkin.

He looked up at the jumbotron and said, "Oh, it's about to start."

"Em, baby, this might be San Francisco, but it's not likely that… Fuck!" I pointed at the giant screen as I stared at my stunned image on display for the entire ballpark, possibly the world, to see. Beside me, Emory grinned like a loon as he reached into his pocket for something. Over our images, it didn't say "Kiss Cam," it said, "Jon, Emory has a question for you."

"Jon?"

I tore my eyes off the screen and looked at Emory. He lowered himself to his knee between the rows of seats while people around us cheered him on.

"Will you marry me?"

I smiled so wide that it felt like my face was about to split in half. "Yes!"

Emory slid the ring on my finger, and I pulled him to me for a kiss. I showed some restraint due to our location, but I was sure he knew that I would express my happiness in more depth when we returned to our hotel room.

We received a lot of congratulations from the fans around us, some funny looks too, but we ignored them. When the game resumed after the seventh inning stretch, I looped my arm around Emory's shoulders and pulled him into my side. I rested my cheek on top of his head and looked up at the sky.

Thank you for sending him to me, River. I promise you that you won't regret it. Be good to my brother. My mouth fell open in shock when a small light shot across the night sky. It was probably a NASA satellite, but I chose to believe it was River answering me. And why the hell not? I never thought I would have someone to call my own either.

"This was a magical night," Emory said happily.

"It's just the beginning, baby."

The End!

OTHER BOOKS BY
AIMEE NICOLE WALKER

Only You

The Fated Hearts Series
Chasing Mr. Wright, Book 1
Rhythm of Us, Book 2
Surrender Your Heart, Book 3
Perfect Fit, Book 4
Return to Me, Book 5
Always You, Book 6
Any Means Necessary, Book 7

Curl Up and Dye Mysteries
Dyeing to be Loved
Something to Dye For
Dyed and Gone to Heaven
I Do, or Dye Trying

Road to Blissville Series
Unscripted Love

Undisputed – coauthored with Nicholas Bella

ACKNOWLEDGMENTS

First, I need to thank my husband and children for their constant support and encouragement. It's not easy living with a writer who often disappears into a fictional world for long periods of time. They do so many things to help me out so that I can realize my dream. I love you guys more than words can ever express.

Many thanks go out to my three best friends, Annabella, Deena, and Kerry. They've stood by me, cheered me on, picked me up, and held my hand through some rough patches. I love you girls so very much. I wish everyone had friends like you because the world would be a much kinder place.

To my creative dream team, thanks seem hardly enough for all that you do. Pam Ebeler of Undivided Editing thank you for your tireless work, feedback, and many laughs while editing. Jay Aheer of Simply Defined art is just an incredible artist, and I love how she brings my words to life. Stacey Blake of Champagne Formats is also an amazing artist who does incredible interior formatting and designing for e-books and paperbacks. Let's not forget Judy Zweifel of Judy's' Proofreading. She does an amazing job of finding the tiniest details that make a book shine.

I would like to thank my beta readers for all the honest feedback they give me on my storyline. I appreciate you guys so much. Aimee's ARC Angels are Racheal, Jodie, Kim, and Laurel. Thank you for all that you do!

ABOUT
AIMEE NICOLE WALKER

I am a wife and mother to three kids, four dogs, and a cat. When I'm not dreaming up stories, I like to lose myself in a good book, cook or bake. I'm a girly tomboy who paints her fingernails while watching sports and yelling at the referees. I will always choose the book over the movie. I believe in happily-ever-after. Love inspires everything that I do. Music keeps me sane.

I'd love to hear from you.
You can reach me at:

Twitter—www.twitter.com/AimeeNWalker

Facebook–www.facebook.com/aimeenicole.walker

Blog–AimeeNicoleWalker.blogspot.com

www.ingramcontent.com/pod-product-compliance
Lightning Source LLC
Chambersburg PA
CBHW071304250626
47159CB00004B/1305